UNLIKELY MATCH

Praise for *Miss Match*

"In this sweet, sensual debut, Riley brings together likable characters, setting them against a colorful supporting cast and exploring their relationship through charming interactions and red-hot erotic scenes…Rich in characterization and emotional appeal, this one is sure to please."—*Publishers Weekly*

"*Miss Match* by Fiona Riley is an adorable romance with a lot of amazing chemistry, steamy sex scenes, and fun dialogue. I can't believe it's the author's first book, even though she assured me on Twitter that it is."—*The Lesbian Review*

"This was a beautiful love story, chock full of love and emotion, and I felt I had a big grin on my face the whole time I was reading it."—*Inked Rainbow Reads*

By the Author

Miss Match

Unlikely Match

Visit us at www.boldstrokesbooks.com

UNLIKELY MATCH

by
Fiona Riley

2017

UNLIKELY MATCH

ISBN 13: 978-1-62639-891-7

This Trade Paperback Original Is Published By
Bold Strokes Books, Inc.
P.O. Box 249
Valley Falls, NY 12185

First Edition: June 2017

CREDITS
EDITOR: RUTH STERNGLANTZ
PRODUCTION DESIGN: STACIA SEAMAN
COVER IMAGE: JB FOLEY
COVER DESIGN BY MELODY POND

Acknowledgments

If we're lucky, there are some people that enter our lives to teach us something, and we learn a lot about ourselves along the way. Those people, those invaluable teachers, help us to uncover a potential in ourselves that otherwise might have gone overlooked. When we find those people, it's important that we recognize their impact on our lives and acknowledge the parts of ourselves that have been improved by their influence.

My good friend Neil is one of those people. This book would not have been possible without his steady, guiding hand and seemingly infinite patience to teach me the ins and outs of computer programming, coding language, and the history of women in science. He brought a new perspective to learning that was refreshing and invigorating for me as both a woman and a writer. It was so empowering to learn about the mothers of science and innovation who had otherwise gone overlooked in my childhood education. Each new discovery felt like an adventure, and I am grateful to be well-versed on the contributions of Hypatia, Ada Lovelace, and Hedy Lamarr, just to name a few.

Neil, I would never have been able to put all of Shelly's quirks, idiosyncrasies, and crazy, fantastic genius on the page if I didn't have you as a model of reference. Thank you for teaching me all the awesome science and math things that only you could teach me. And most of all, thank you for being patient enough to show me the turn-by-turn instructions necessary to conquer the Rubik's Cube. You always took the time to make sure I got the science right, and I am forever grateful. You're the best.

My editor Ruth Sternglantz is another one of those magical, teaching unicorns that enters your life and changes you forever. Ruth, thank you for being kind throughout the entire editing process and never mocking me for my supremely inferior knowledge of words and the way words should play nicely together. Your patience never ceases to amaze me, and you have an incredible ability to empower me while helping me hone my craft. Thank you for guiding me through my mistakes without making me feel small during the process. You are someone who deserves all the praise, all the cupcakes, and all the awards, all the time. I hope you know how much you mean to me, because it's a lot. Like a lot, a lot.

To my colleagues, mentors, and the staff at Bold Strokes Books, thanks for taking a chance on this series and encouraging my shenanigans. I will do the best I can to always keep you on your toes at any social gathering we attend together and represent your brand to the best of my ability. Thank you for the opportunity.

Lastly, to my wife, Jenn, I would be remiss to forget to thank you for the mind-numbing noise you endured during the endless nights I spent spinning and rotating the Rubik's Cube next to your head for "research" while writing this book. I'm sure lots of unpleasant thoughts swirled around your head when I compulsively worked and reworked the cube nearby, but you had the class and dignity to only let me know about it a fraction of the time. You're my favorite sounding board and the best Rubik's jumbler. Never change. :)

For Jenn.

There are many people in this world who spend their whole lives trying to find what I have with you. It's a special type of glitter magic that allows me to live a dream while I'm awake and conquer every obstacle with my best friend and truest confidant by my side. You've been the greatest gift I've ever been given, and still, you have found a way to outdo yourself this time around. Thank you for being the sun, the moon, and the stars. I can't wait to start our next adventure together.

All my *Love*
All that I am.

CHAPTER ONE

S helly White sighed heavily as she stepped out of the cab and walked toward the entrance of Perfect Match, Inc. Usually, seeing Samantha Monteiro was an enjoyable experience—truth be told, this whole process, although entirely out of her comfort zone, had been really great. She had met some wonderful people, learned how to dance, and perhaps most importantly, she'd found out a few things about herself that had surprised her. That's why this meeting with Samantha felt so hopeless. For all the highs she had felt since first walking through the doors of Samantha's matchmaking company thirteen months ago, today was as low as she had ever been.

As she waited for the elevator to take her to the penthouse office space, she reminisced about how much had changed in the last year. When she'd first met Samantha and her business partner, Andrew Stanley, she was an entirely different person. She was nervous, insecure, and convinced she was a hopeless case. Some of that had changed, but then again, some of it was still the same.

"Samantha is just finishing a call, but she said you can head in and take a seat." Samantha's receptionist Sarah smiled encouragingly and motioned toward the slightly ajar door to Samantha's office.

"Thanks, Sarah."

Shelly knocked lightly and waved as Samantha looked up from her desk, a smile on her face as she spoke into the receiver. Shelly sat in the chair opposite her desk and did her best not to pout. This was the moment she had been dreading for the last two weeks.

"Mm-hmm, I have to go. Shelly's here." Samantha pulled the phone away from her mouth. "Lucinda says hi."

"Are we still on for Tuesday?" Shelly asked, already knowing that they were, deliberately prolonging the time until Samantha's entire attention was back on her.

"Tuesday at six thirty," Samantha confirmed and turned slightly, her voice lowering a bit.

Shelly warmed at the genuine expression on Samantha's face as she ended the call. Lucinda Moss was Shelly's private dance instructor and Samantha's fiancée. Somewhere over the course of the thirteen months Shelly and Samantha had been working together, Samantha had found her own perfect match in the beautiful and strong dance teacher she had introduced Shelly to in hopes of helping her find *grace*. That was what Samantha had first said when Shelly had balked at the idea of private dance lessons, but she had been right, sort of.

She looked out the window at the cumulus clouds, so close they almost looked like she could touch them. The view up here was spectacular, heavenly. The thought made her smile as she turned her attention to Samantha, who had walked to the front of her desk and looked at Shelly expectantly.

Heavenly. That was what she had first thought when she had met Samantha so many months ago, all dressed in white with large sunglasses obscuring her face. Samantha Monteiro was so attractive it was distracting. Her initial attraction to Samantha was what had given Shelly the confidence to utilize Samantha's matchmaking services— even the prospect of finding a mate in the periphery of Samantha's scale of beauty was appealing. She often wondered if that was how most of Samantha and Andrew's clients were drawn to them: they were a well-oiled machine of perfectly tailored clothes and charm to match their good looks. But what kept Shelly invested in them and their vision was the amount of heart and sincerity they brought to every potential match. Samantha and Andrew were as effortlessly funny as they were optimistic in the pursuit of matchmaking. Samantha in particular had a way of making the impossible seem possible, and to her credit, she had done a pretty decent job of finding Shelly really compatible dates. Which was why even though Shelly had requested this meeting, she felt like she was in the principal's office at the same time.

"Hey, Shel." When she didn't answer, a soft frown settled around Samantha's perfect lips. "Okay, what's on your mind?"

Shelly was amazed how Samantha defied the logic of physics with how gracefully she moved in that skintight fabric. It was almost superhuman how easily she perched at the edge of her desk, flawlessly graceful, nothing at all like Shelly. The thought made her own frown deepen. "I'm a mess."

"Let's start with *Hello. How are you?*"

"This is no time for pleasantries, Samantha. I'm a hopeless mess and it's a lost cause and I'm sorry."

Samantha stepped away from the desk and turned the neighboring chair toward Shelly. She sat down and reached out, taking Shelly's hands in her own, and gently rubbed her thumbs along Shelly's knuckles. "Let's start at the beginning. What happened with Abby and Sasha?"

The warm contact soothed Shelly and she nodded, looking up from her lap. Four months ago Samantha had thrown a matchmaking mixer at Lucinda's dance studio in hopes of finding Shelly that elusive perfect match. And for the first time in so many months, Shelly had finally felt like things were falling into place. She had truly enjoyed herself, feeling more comfortable in her own skin than she had in years. All the training she had done with Lucinda had made her confident in her ability to lead her dates around the dance floor, and the charm school she had completed with Samantha over the months prior had helped her to present a polished and complete *Shelly* package to the evening. But even with help, Shelly had managed to screw it up.

"Okay, first of all, Abby is great, really, she is. But I just feel like there wasn't any spark there. Like she'd be a really great friend or book club buddy, but that's it."

Samantha nodded. "How many dates did you go on with her?"

Shelly shrugged. "Three?"

"Did you kiss her?"

Shelly felt the blush forming on her cheeks. "No."

Samantha's thumb stopped its gentle caress and she squeezed Shelly's hand once briefly. "Why not?"

Shelly sighed. "I didn't want to."

"Well, that's fair. Did she want to kiss you?"

A wave of guilt washed over Shelly. "Yeah, I think she did."

"All right, well you both need to be on the same page—you weren't. No big deal. How did you end it with her?"

Shelly allowed herself to be relieved by Samantha's encouraging words for a moment before she shamefully admitted the next part. "I, um, texted her and told her I was too busy for another date."

"And?"

"And then I stopped replying to her calls and texts."

"Shelly."

There was the tone she was afraid would make its appearance.

"I just—"

Samantha held up her hand and shook her head. "No. No way. We talked about this. These women are taking just as much of a risk putting themselves out there to try to find a match with you as you are with them. How would you feel if one of these girls just ghosted out of your life like that?"

"Probably like crap." Shelly frowned.

"Right." Samantha cocked her head to the side a little. "Abby is a sweet girl. She deserves better than a brush-off."

"You're right."

Samantha smiled. "I usually am." She shifted in the chair and crossed her legs as she leaned back, releasing Shelly's hand. "Tell me about Sasha."

Shelly let out another long sigh. The Sasha thing had kept her up at night. In fact, that was the primary reason she had asked to meet with Samantha today.

"I like Sasha, really I do. She's flirtatious and attractive and funny."

"Mm-hmm, female firefighters are hot." Samantha looked off in the distance with a dreamy smile. "Go on."

"That's just it, she's great."

The look in Samantha's eyes cleared as she blinked at Shelly. "But?"

"I can't get past the firefighter part. Like, it's too dangerous and time-consuming. Did you know that she has shifts that last up to two or three days at a time? And don't even get me started on the injury risk. Do you have any idea of the statistical variation of life expectancy among firefighters in a city like Boston? The mean age alone is enough to stop you from lighting candles for the rest of your life..."

"Okay, slow down. How many dates did you go on?" Samantha redirected.

"Six."

"That's good. And how did they go?"

"Really well, actually. And before you ask, yes, we kissed."

Samantha leaned forward and rubbed her hands together. "Ah, the good part. Tell me more about the kissing."

Shelly laughed. "It was great, I mean, she's a great kisser. Truly." She paused for a moment before adding, "But she wears cherry lip gloss. And cherry flavor reminds me of Robitussin and being sick as a child. I get a little weird about cherry flavor."

"Not important, Shel. She can swap out her lip gloss flavor."

"What if it's her favorite flavor ever, though?"

"Did you ask her that?"

"No."

"Then it's a moot point. Go on. Let's talk about the kissing some more."

Shelly nodded. "She kissed me at the end of the first date. That's how I knew things with Abby weren't going to work out, because I immediately felt that physical attraction to Sasha that was missing with Abby."

Samantha looked at her expectantly.

"It was really good. Like the kind of kiss that makes you want more kissing, like *all* of the kissing. And we did some more of that on dates two through four. There was a good amount of kissing—you'd be proud of me."

Samantha smiled. "Did you sleep together?"

"No." Shelly knew she looked mortified. Even after all of these months in Samantha's presence, she was still a little shy around her directness.

"Did you want to?" Samantha appeared undeterred by Shelly's reaction.

"Truthfully? Yes. But then something happened between dates four and five that kind of put the brakes on that."

"Feel free to elaborate."

This was what had been bothering Shelly about Sasha. She felt conflicted about what had occurred, but mostly, she was conflicted about her own feelings and how easily she had shut down. "There was a bad fire—a three-story house on Hereford went up like a match and Sasha was injured."

"Jesus." Samantha looked alarmed, "Is she okay? I should call her."

Shelly continued, "It wasn't anything severe—a concussion, some bruising, a slight burn on her arm. But it was scary, Samantha. I was really starting to enjoy her company, really looking forward to it. But that was too much for me to handle. Something changed. I couldn't deal with the idea of getting any closer to her if she would continually be in danger like that. What if something really bad happened?"

Samantha's expression softened. "Shelly, I get that, I do, but we talked about this, too. You need to take risks and be vulnerable to everything life has to offer. Ending a relationship with Sasha because her job was too scary for you isn't a good enough reason. It's her job, not yours."

"I know, I know. But it wasn't just that. We had some other differences, too. Like I was really attracted to Sasha and her personality, but I never really felt entirely comfortable around her. And she's allergic to cats. I can't be with someone who can't be around cats. Cats are the best. But the fire incident sort of solidified my feelings about the whole thing. She's going on a training course out in Washington for a few weeks anyway, so it's not like anything is going to happen romantically."

Samantha seemed to consider this a moment before she stood and strode to the other side of her desk, sitting in her chair and powering up her laptop. She reached forward and grabbed a pen, pointing it at Shelly as she spoke. "All right. Let's start fresh. Tell me what you liked best about Abby. Go."

"What?"

"What was it about Abby that inspired you to ask her out on a formal date?"

"Oh. Well, she's really pretty. And kind. She's funny but not in an obnoxious way. I like the way she wears cardigans."

Samantha looked up from the screen, abandoning her pen in favor of leaning her chin on her palm. "You like the way she wears... cardigans?"

"Is that a weird thing to say or something?" Shelly shifted uncomfortably.

"It's just a very specific thing to say. Like you could have said that you like her outfits, or her style. But you explicitly mentioned the cardigans." She made a note on the page in front of her.

"What are you writing down on that thing?" Shelly leaned forward, only to have her view obstructed by Samantha's hand.

"Don't worry. What are some of the things you didn't like?" Samantha motioned for her to continue.

Shelly thought for a moment. "She didn't ask me anything about what I do. Or she did, but it was very vague and when I tried to explain some of it a little further, she seemed to zone out. Like it was boring. That was a little frustrating. I want to be able to talk about the things that interest me, too. It helps me relax a bit."

Samantha continued to jot down some notes. "How was she with you? Did she seem nervous? Or was she comfortable?"

"She seemed a little nervous. And that made me a little more nervous, I suppose. She was a little indecisive, too. I'm plenty indecisive—I don't need any help in that department."

"Okay. Let's talk about Sasha again. What did you like about her?"

"She's fun. I mean like charming and funny and hot. And bold. Like she was always in control of the situation. No matter where we went on a date, she was so self-assured, it was refreshing. She kissed me first, too. I didn't have to think about it—I just had to react. The kissing was good. I liked that the best."

Samantha underlined the word *kissing* on her notepad. "What didn't vibe with you?"

"We couldn't talk about current events or technology very much. She's not much of a reader. She picked up some workout magazines and fitness stuff once in a while but she didn't love books. She plays some video games with some of the other firefighters at her station, but really prefers to watch or work on her fantasy basketball roster. She was kind of a flirt—which I liked, but we kept running into her exes while we were out. And I really had a hard time with the demands and dangers of her work. We got by okay with all of the physical stuff, but I didn't feel like there was any real growth opportunity there—I'm tired of physical relationships without any semblance of commitment."

This was something that Samantha and Shelly discussed a lot. It wasn't unusual for people to assume that Shelly was this shut-in, virgin type. That was far from the truth. She didn't have any trouble finding a bedroom partner—she had trouble finding a life partner. When her father was diagnosed with Parkinson's a little over a year ago, she realized that she'd been filling her time with short flings and not investing any of herself into the women that entered her life. She had told herself that she was too busy with the growing company and its success, but that had been a lie. She was worried about being vulnerable to another person, so she had closed off that part of herself. Her father's diagnosis left her feeling very alone and wondering if she was destined to be like him someday: cantankerous, paranoid, and cold. When she saw the ad for Perfect Match on a mobile app while in the Uber on the ride home from her father's the day of his diagnosis, she had made an appointment immediately. It had felt serendipitous. She wanted to change her love life, and she knew it had to start with her.

"Okay. Let's compare this list to the wish list in your file."

Samantha turned the laptop to face Shelly and joined her on the other side of the desk. "I paired you with these two women because they both hit the major qualities that you had identified as important: funny, social, friendly, pretty, and centrally located to Boston. I ran them through a few personality tests and compared their results to yours—identifying complements to your fighting style and communication skills. All that got tossed into our Perfect Match algorithm software and a percentage of compatibility was calculated. Abby was more of an intellectual equal to you, whereas Sasha was a clear match to your physical requirements and your desire to be with someone more outgoing. Both women had a decent mix of personal and professional traits that you mentioned were important to you. And if we compare the list of things you just told me, I can conclude only one thing."

Shelly looked at the flowcharts on the screen, skimming the abbreviations and pie charts as Samantha quickly flicked through the pages of her electronic file, opening up to a blank page. Shelly's eyes focused on the blinking cursor and her brow scrunched in confusion. "What can you conclude? This is a blank page."

"Precisely." Samantha pointed to the screen. "These charts, these figures and calculations, they don't mean much. We use them to help narrow down our resource pool. What really matters are the personal connections we make between people. The commonalities help to thin the herd, as it were, but the real successes in this business come from accepting that each match is unique and individual to the persons involved. No amount of data collection can do that—that has to come from you and the lucky lady waiting to meet you."

"Okay. So what's with the blank page?"

"The blank page is a fresh start. You are not the same woman who came through these doors a year ago. You are now able to identify your desires, frustrations, and concerns in an organized and clear manner. What you were looking for when we ran all these calculations is not what you are asking for right now. This Shelly"—Samantha motioned up and down Shelly's form—"this Shelly is no longer the heartbreaker in the rough that Lucinda so keenly first described you as. This Shelly is a full-on confident and legitimate heartbreaker. And what you are looking for is an extrovert with introverted tendencies: playful, friendly, outgoing, flirtatious, attractive, but can turn off the exuberance and settle in with a good book by a fireplace or hang out on your couch and play video games with you, while still looking good in a cardigan."

"There's that cardigan reference again," Shelly noted, laughing.

"I pay attention to details." Samantha smiled.

"Lucinda called me a heartbreaker in the rough?"

"Yep. Totally true." Samantha brushed a few of the hairs off Shelly's forehead and cupped her chin, tilting her head to the side a bit as she examined her closely. "You have the most gorgeous green eyes and naturally clear complexion of anyone I have ever worked with. You are smart and funny and sarcastic, well dressed—which I take full credit for, by the way—and sweet. Any woman would be lucky to have you. That, my friend, is why we are starting from scratch. It is my personal mission in life to find you a perfect match. Let's get back to the drawing board and do just that."

Shelly closed the distance between them and hugged Samantha tightly. Samantha was the first person to ever take the time to help her find the outer beauty that everyone said they saw but she never felt. Samantha had encouraged her to try wearing contacts and overhauled her wardrobe—introducing her to a tailor and a personal shopper, and giving her a crash course in basic makeup application to accent her best features. Growing up without a mother or a sister had left her without much feminine confidence. Samantha had quite literally changed her life. She felt like a different person these days, but it was for the better. She was definitely not the same girl who'd felt inferior to Samantha's beauty on their first meeting. Nor was she the meek woman filling out endless scores of personality tests. She now considered Samantha a close friend, something that she was beyond grateful for. "Thank you."

Samantha hugged her back and smiled. "Let me see what I can come up with—how about I swing by your dance lesson with Lucy on Tuesday and we brainstorm a bit?"

"Sounds great." As Shelly said her good-byes and headed to the elevator, she felt like that dark cloud around her was finally starting to dissolve. If anyone could solve the puzzle that was her romantic life, she was confident Samantha Monteiro was that person.

CHAPTER TWO

Jamie?" Claire Moseley called up the stairs of the home she grew up in, trying to track down her youngest older brother. She had to swing by the office before their softball game later, and he was going to make her late.

"Coming!" Jamie flew around the corner and skipped the second landing with the skill of a gymnast, landing squarely on his feet before thrusting his arms into the air in victory. "And the judges award his finish with a...?"

"Six at best. No points for originality. Tardiness deductions all across the board." Claire folded her arms in mock annoyance.

"This is why they never let you pitch first string, 'cuz you cranky," Jamie teased and jogged into the kitchen to grab an apple off the counter. "Race you to the car?"

He took off before she had a chance to reply, her annoyed huff unheard or ignored. She grabbed her keys off the table by the front door and gave a quick glance to the last portrait that contained her entire family. The stern look on her father's face was in complete contrast to the gap-toothed grin she was sporting as she sat on his lap in her favorite frilly dress. She was only six years old at the time. Her mother looked weary, forcing a smile with her hand on her father's shoulder, while her four brothers were very clearly barely keeping it together for the photo. Her oldest brother Craig was in his early twenties at the time and appeared to be pinching Austin, who was scowling and must have been about seventeen if that earring in his ear was any indication. The twins were next to her and her father, eleven-year-old Jerry's braces shining like a disco ball and his untucked shirt peeking out below the matching sweater he and James wore. James, who everyone just called

Jamie, had obviously just finished crying, his eyes wet with tears and a pout on his face, his glasses slightly askew. The only person who looked truly happy to be there was Claire. She vividly remembered her father scolding the boys afterward, her mother shaking her head in frustration as she scooped up Claire and took her and Jamie to the front of the ice-cream line while her brothers complained behind them. She often thought that had they all known that would be the last time they would all be together in a photo they might have been on better behavior. She certainly would have shared her strawberry shortcake with Craig that night when Austin knocked his ice cream to the ground while they wrestled by the barn attached to the ice-cream shop. He had playfully asked her to share since it was his favorite too but she had put up a fit. That's why she always made him strawberry shortcake for dessert when he came to the holiday dinners, perhaps trying to make up for that night.

"Claire! We are going to be late," Jamie called from the driveway, leaning on the horn and jarring Claire from her reverie.

She sighed and closed the front door, locking it before she trudged down the steps, feeling like the wind had been knocked out of her. This was why she had moved out as soon as she was old enough. Sometimes the ghosts of her past were too much for her here.

❖

"Drinks on you, little sis!" Jamie cheered as he pushed open the door to Connelly's, their favorite watering hole.

Claire laughed and nodded—it was only fair. She'd been sure that his last wild swing would result in a foul. In fact, she was still unconvinced black magic hadn't assisted with a little extra wind to sail it into home run territory. Jamie was on a streak—he had one home run for every game of this season so far, and tonight, he very nearly missed out.

"I still can't believe that last hit actually counted. I think the official was intoxicated."

"And just for that, ye of little faith, we are starting with tequila shots." Jamie grinned and plunked down on the corner barstool at the far end of the bar, waving over the bartender.

"Jamie, I have to work tomorrow." Claire halfheartedly resisted, her attention drawn to the pretty redhead by the dartboard. Nikki was a regular here. She was edgy, with long hair tied up into a sloppy topknot, the left side of her head shaved short, her left ear pierced over a dozen times, and there was always some accent of leather somewhere. They had shared a heated, albeit drunken, kiss after the softball championship last year ended with Claire's team finishing just short of the title. So it wasn't a total loss—they had maintained a light flirting relationship whenever fate brought the two of them to Trivia Tuesdays, although she had not been able to consistently attend since her promotion last month.

"Ahem." Jamie was staring at her with an amused expression when she realized the bartender had put two shot glasses in front of them.

"Those don't look like tequila." She looked at the red-tinted liquid with skepticism.

"Well, Sherlock, had you not drifted into that weird little lust haze, you would have heard me order a Red Headed Slut shot instead…you know, since that seems to be your poison of choice at the moment." He nodded toward Nikki as she high-fived her darts partner and rewarded the brunette with a long-drawn-out open-mouthed kiss and a slap on the ass.

"Shut up." Claire pouted and took the shot with a wince. "She's nice."

"I bet." Jamie pushed his now empty glass to the front of the bar. "I bet she's nice to *all* the girls."

Claire glared at him while she sipped on her glass of water. "Anyway, James, tell me all the things."

"Ooh, *James*, huh?" He teased, "When was the last time you got laid?"

"C'mon, Jamie," she whined. It had been way too long and he was probably right—it was about time for her to scratch that itch, but she had been so focused on work, dating wasn't even a blip on her radar.

"All right, all right. Things are good. It's been busy at work. Jerry just bought a new frozen yogurt machine for the Cambridge location. We've been trying out some new flavors. You should swing by sometime and check them out—we'd appreciate the input. I think my taste buds are revolting. Everything is starting to taste the same."

"Well, that's a job I don't mind helping with." The twins had opened a café shortly after high school; Jerry took on the culinary tasks while Jamie ran the administrative and accounting side of the business. Two years ago they had expanded and set up two little storefront locations that sold small meals for commuters on the go. They had been toying with the idea of starting a specialty dessert line for a while, and this froyo thing was the first step.

"Speaking of jobs, I feel like I never see you anymore. How's the promotion going?" Jamie ordered their usual post-softball feast of burgers and sweet potato fries as the bartender poured them each a beer.

"It's good. It's a lot all at once, but I think I'm finally getting into a groove." Claire had been putting in long hours trying to get everything in order after the shake-up at work. A little over four months ago, her boss at Clear View Enterprises, Lucinda Moss, fired senior executive Richard Thomas. After a week of absolute insanity, Lucinda had called her into her office and informed her that she and the board had decided to promote Claire into the head executive position. It was a fast-track dream come true. She had a new office all to herself, a higher salary, and more responsibility. But ironing out the details proved a difficult task. This was the first week she felt like she was actually ahead of work instead of behind it.

"Well, I'm proud of you. I know this was a long-term goal for you, and there is no way your boss would have promoted you into a position she didn't have full confidence in you being able to kick ass at. Who would have imagined my little sister would be a senior account executive at the ripe old age of twenty-seven? You're making us all look bad." He patted her on the back.

"Thanks, Jamie." Claire could tell the praise was sincere, and her heart warmed at it. She was grateful that she had maintained a close relationship with her brothers as they grew up. Jamie was easily her best friend in the family, but she shared something special with each of them. She knew that was a rarity, especially considering how they had grown up. Her eyes welled with tears at the thought.

"Now, before you start to ugly cry tears of joy into your beer and make it all salty, tell me about the view from your new office. Can I see it?" Jamie deadpanned, "Does your lunchroom need a froyo machine?"

"You know...I think maybe it does."

"Yes!" Jamie cheered. "Good thing I know a pretty decent marketing chick to help me sell the idea to those kind people at Clear View."

"Good thing." Claire laughed, thanking the bartender as he placed their burgers on the bar. She lifted her burger and tapped it to Jamie's in their ritualistic food cheering tradition and bit in. "God, these burgers are good."

"Yup, tastes even better when you're paying," Jamie said around a bite.

Claire shook her head. She would happily pay for every drink and dinner with Jamie for the rest of her life if she could guarantee he'd always be by her side. "Enjoy, James."

CHAPTER THREE

Samantha stalked closer to Lucinda, and that familiar tightening in her stomach occurred, like so many times before, intensifying when she slipped her hand under Lucinda's shirt and caressed her side. "Just consider it." Samantha's mouth was dangerously close to Lucinda's ear now.

"I can't consider anything when you are clearly trying to influence my decision." Lucinda turned her head and captured Samantha's lips with hers. She halted Samantha's venturing hand at the level of her ribs and gently pulled it out from under her shirt.

"You're no fun." Samantha's mock pout turned to a soft moan when Lucinda's tongue slipped into her mouth.

Lucinda pulled back and looked at Samantha, her eyebrow raised in challenge.

"I take it back—you're the most fun. Keep kissing me." Samantha slid her hands into Lucinda's long blond hair and pulled her closer again. "How much time do we have before your meeting with Claire?"

Lucinda groaned as Samantha's hand dropped from her hair to gently run across the seam of her crotch, pressing in as it glided up and down in a taunt. "Not enough. And you didn't lock the door this time."

Samantha sighed. "I hate it when you are so damn logical and right. Mostly the right part, though."

Lucinda held her close and kissed her long and slow, savoring the taste of her tongue and lips while they still had a moment to themselves. "That's why you're marrying me, though, because I'm so damn logical and—"

"And hot." Samantha winked. "Don't get it twisted."

Lucinda laughed and ran her thumb over the engagement ring on Samantha's finger. Samantha had proposed first, but Lucinda made sure to surprise her as well, eager to show her appreciation to her persuasive bride-to-be with a custom-designed cushion-cut diamond with pavé band. "Yes, dear."

"That's what I thought." Samantha purred into one final kiss before she stepped back and leaned against Lucinda's desk.

"So." Lucinda tried to quiet the buzzing feeling originating from her pants as she settled into her chair. Samantha was still close enough for her to stroke up and down the exposed skin of her thigh, selfishly prolonging the stimulated sensation. "You were saying?"

Samantha closed her eyes as Lucinda slid her fingers along the hem of Samantha's dress, toying with the fabric a little. "Well, that makes it very hard to concentrate."

"Funny. I had a very similar thing happen to me just a few moments—"

Samantha slapped Lucinda's hands away from her thigh. Her finger on Lucinda's lips silenced her teasing. "Hands to yourself, Moss."

Lucinda nipped at the finger on her lips and held up her hands in surrender.

"Anyway"—Samantha rolled her eyes—"I think it's a great idea. You've been talking about increasing the number of classes offered by the studio and updating some of the facilities. Not to mention purchasing that adjoining building and expanding like you've always dreamed."

"I'm listening." Lucinda reclined in her chair, clasping her hands at her lap to keep them from wandering back to the smooth skin of Samantha's thigh. It occurred to her that the shortness of Samantha's dress paired with those thigh-high boots was a little provocative for a workday. "Did you work today?"

"What? This morning, yes. But I went shopping." Her eyes followed Lucinda's gaze to her boots. "The boots are new."

"I noticed."

"And I may have hiked up my dress a bit while you were distracted on the phone to convince you to agree," Samantha admitted shamelessly.

"I noticed that as well."

"What do you think?"

"About the boots? And the amount of thigh you're showing? I approve."

Samantha laughed and shook her dark hair, leaning in to Lucinda again, her voice low as she momentarily glanced down at Lucinda's crotch. "I can practically taste the approval from here. I meant, more specifically, what do you think about the fundraiser?"

Lucinda let her head fall against the back of her chair in a dramatic fashion. "You're going to force this issue until you win, aren't you?"

"Yes." Samantha smiled brightly and leaned back against the desk, putting some space between them. She held up three fingers and gave Lucinda a solemn nod. "But I promise to make up for all the teasing later, Scout's honor."

Lucinda warily eyed the hand Samantha held in front of her. "Promise?"

"Of course." Samantha nodded as she slowly counted out each figure dramatically before making a suggestive hand gesture. "At least three times...maybe all at once."

Lucinda was a moment away from being a puddle and she knew Samantha knew it by the triumphant gleam in her eyes. "Fine."

"Yay." Samantha smiled. "How's Tuesday the fifteenth shaping up for you?"

Lucinda nudged Samantha's hip off her desk calendar and flipped ahead to the date in question. "There's a hip-hop dance class that I can shift to Thursday night without much difficulty. But I'd have to make sure I could get the specs for the plan in place from Elijah before then."

Samantha nodded, looking very serious. "I'm sure that won't be a problem. I talked to him earlier and he said he could have the preliminary drawings to you by the start of next week."

"Why am I not surprised that you already talked to him?" Lucinda mused as she reclined into her chair again, admiring the way Samantha's chest looked as she leaned back on her hands against Lucinda's desk.

"Because you know how resourceful I am." She blinked flirtatiously.

Lucinda's phone lit up with a call from her admin. Lucinda pressed the speaker button and replied, "Yes, Amanda."

"Claire is here for your one o'clock meeting, shall I send her in?"

"Just a second, I'll come get her." She disconnected the call and looked back up at Samantha. "Looks like we'll have to continue this discussion another time."

"No way, Luce. I have some planning to do and need to make some calls this afternoon before I, uh, prep for tonight's date night."

Lucinda smiled. "It's Thursday, isn't it?"

"Best day of the week," Samantha replied with a nod.

"Okay, what else?"

"I know we talked about Shelly a little bit last night, but I had an idea."

"Go on."

"Since our little powwow at your dance lesson with her on Tuesday, I've been brainstorming with Andrew, and I'd like to pepper a few dating prospects for Shelly into the attendees of the fundraiser."

"You want to do what? I thought things didn't work out with Abby and Sasha." Lucinda was confused.

"They didn't—well, I'm not so convinced about the Sasha thing, we'll revisit that. You know, maybe we should talk about this later— Claire is waiting."

"Oh." Lucinda had almost forgotten. "Okay, fine. Start whatever ball you need to be rolling and we can iron out the details later."

"I'm five steps ahead of you, love. No worries." Samantha gave Lucinda a quick peck on the lips and walked toward Lucinda's office door, adjusting her dress a little before opening it. She paused with her hand on the door handle and looked back at Lucinda with a mischievous glance. "Those windows are awfully reflective today, aren't they?"

Lucinda's office had two walls of floor-to-ceiling windows, one of Lucinda's favorite things about her office. Today was sunny and clear, no clouds obstructing the view, and Lucinda had fully opened and pulled back the blinds prior to Samantha's arrival. She'd considered closing them when their conversation heated up. Before Lucinda had a chance to question what Samantha meant by that statement, Samantha was opening the door and greeting Claire.

"Hey, Claire, I was just leaving."

"Hey, Samantha." Claire smiled and reciprocated Samantha's one-armed hug. "What are you doing here?"

Ever since Claire had taken the lead on Samantha's PR incident a few months ago, seeing it to a smooth conclusion, Lucinda had noticed a warmth between them. She knew Samantha was grateful for Claire's hard work and her discretion with the matter. It had been one of the weightier reasons she had pushed the board to promote Claire on an accelerated path. She had been pleased with Claire's performance for months before the Perfect Match controversy arose, but her skillful coordination of the crisis plan with such short notice was impressive. It had cemented Lucinda's original plans. She'd still had to convince the board, but that wasn't too hard in the end. Her original decision to hire

Claire had been the right one; Claire was shaping up to be a fantastic executive.

"Oh, you know, just discussing a little business. Oh, I almost forgot my purse." Samantha glanced back at Lucinda and made a subtle nod toward the windows as she turned and bent down to pick up her purse from the floor. Lucinda saw it then, the reflection of Claire clearly checking out Samantha's ass as she crouched forward, definitely longer than was necessary. Suddenly, Samantha's convenient arrival before Claire's scheduled meeting made a lot of sense.

"Samantha." Lucinda's tone dripped with warning.

Samantha stood, slipping her purse strap onto her shoulder as she raised an eyebrow at Lucinda in defiance. "Oh, Lucy, right. Good idea. Claire, here, sit. Sit. What are you up to on the fifteenth?"

Claire looked between them with a laugh, confusion on her face. "Of next month? Nothing, to my knowledge. What day is it?"

"A Tuesday." Samantha stood near the window, a perfect smile innocently plastered on her face. Lucinda was too captivated by the preparation this must have taken to be mad. Yet.

"Tuesdays are usually open," Claire provided easily.

"Is there another day that is usually filled?" Samantha was prying and Lucinda knew it.

"Wednesdays I play softball with my brother, unless you need me to be available." She glanced over to Lucinda.

"Softball? You don't say." Samantha stepped forward and leaned against the front of Lucinda's desk, glancing back to add, "She plays softball, Luce."

"Do you play, too?" Claire looked up at Lucinda, her expression friendly. Lucinda stifled a cringe. This was like leading a lamb to the slaughter.

"No, sorry, Claire, I don't." Lucinda supplied with a sigh. "Samantha, you were just leaving, right?"

"Right. Absolutely." Samantha stood and took one step toward the door before turning and sitting abruptly in the chair across from Claire. "Before I go, though…"

"Shit." Lucinda cursed under her breath as Samantha leaned in and placed a hand on Claire's forearm.

"I was just talking to Lucinda about hosting a fundraiser at her dance studio for some of Boston's most successful businessmen and women to help her expansion program get off the ground. I have quite a few clients eager to help support the arts. Anyway, I'll be hosting a little mixer and auction at the studio on the fifteenth and I'd like you to attend. You know, to rub elbows with some of Boston's financial elite. It'd be a great opportunity for you to expand your client portfolio. Not to mention a great way for Clear View to do a little promotion as well."

"Oh, wow. Sure, that sounds great." Claire smiled and leaned forward.

"Great." Samantha stood and clapped her hands once in enthusiasm. "Lucinda will get you all of the information. Won't you, Luce?"

Lucinda used all her strength to keep her face blank, her eyes locked on Samantha's. "You don't have to, Claire, it's not required."

"It sounds like a great idea. I've been hoping to branch out and bring in some of my own clients now that the dust has settled around Richard's departure. I'm in if you're okay with it."

"Claire deserves a chance to build up her portfolio and have some free drinks at a fun event, don't you think? Think of all that hard work and those long hours she's been putting in, Luce."

Lucinda forced a smile. She would talk about this with Samantha later. Devious little minx. "Absolutely. It'll be great."

"Well, glad we all agree. I'll see myself out. 'Bye, ladies." And just like that Samantha walked out of Lucinda's office with a casual wave and disappeared behind the closing door, effectively ending the conversation.

Chapter Four

Samantha took a step back and admired her handiwork. The room looked amazing. She had splurged on the flowers and lighting because she knew these things were important to Lucinda. They had been talking about expanding the dance studio for months—in fact, Lucinda had mentioned it one of the first times Samantha had ever stepped foot in this place. The adjoining space was owned by a cute elderly couple that had been there for decades. Just after Lucinda and Samantha got engaged, the husband came over and told them they were planning on selling and moving south to be closer to their grandchildren. Lucinda had started making phone calls that night to get the acquisition rolling. The positive relationship Lucinda had fostered with her neighbors over the years had made the transition smooth and seamless, and within a few weeks, Lucinda owned the space next door.

Part of Samantha felt a little guilty that the space still remained unused. And she knew a good part of that was because they were planning a wedding. But this event was important, and she wanted to make sure it was done right. The idea for the fundraiser had come to her long before the sale was finalized. Combining it with a matchmaking mixer was a new revelation, though. She laughed to herself as she remembered the look on Lucinda's face in her office that day when she'd realized that Samantha had intentionally stopped by right before her meeting with Claire. She was too proud of herself to feel sorry for her underhandedness. She was doing it in the name of true love, after all.

When Shelly had come to her office a few weeks before and they'd decided to start from scratch, her mind immediately ran through the catalog of eligible bachelorettes in her system. But finding what Shelly wanted was going to be a little more difficult this time around—

she needed a new approach. She had been idly fooling with some paperwork on her desk when she received a fax of her updated contract with Clear View. Claire's signature was on the boilerplate welcome letter that accompanied the fax.

She liked Claire. She was tenacious and capable. Lucinda spoke so highly of her—she was a prized pupil. And, Samantha had noted, she appeared to like women. More specifically, she had caught Claire staring at her assets more than once. And when she'd casually tried to make small talk with Claire, she noticed a few other key things: Claire was very close to her brothers and she was unattached, and maybe, just maybe, Samantha had wandered onto social media and seen a picture of Claire kissing some other girl. None of that mattered, though. She just had a feeling that Claire and Shelly might hit it off—the hard part would be getting them in the same room. Then, voilà, enter the fundraiser. Shelly would do anything to help Lucinda, and from what Samantha knew of Claire, she would do anything to prove herself. It was a win-win.

Convincing Lucinda had been another matter entirely. Samantha had done her best to reiterate that sometimes fate had to be helped, sometimes divine intervention was necessary. Lucinda had laughed and asked her if she had considered herself divine. That night, she'd done her best to prove she was indeed celestial. It seemed to have worked.

"What are you thinking about?" Lucinda's arm wrapped around her waist from behind.

"You." Samantha turned and kissed her fiancée sweetly. "Thank you for agreeing to this."

Lucinda gave her a small smile. "You know I don't often disagree with you, Samantha. I'm just a little unsure about this. Do you really think it's a good idea to set Shelly up with—"

"Do you trust me?" Samantha ran her hand along the side of Lucinda's face.

"Of course."

"And do you think that I am worthy of the title Miss Match?"

"Samanth—"

"Do you?"

"You are the best. I concur," Lucinda relented.

"Then believe me when I tell you this is just a chance for me to observe their dynamic without either one of them knowing they are being observed. And let me do what I do best."

"Make the impossible possible?" Lucinda's air quotes got her a gentle shove.

"Exactly." Samantha snuggled close to Lucinda and rested her head on her shoulder. "The more I think about it, the more I think they would be perfect together. Just something in my gut—I can't explain it. And if I'm wrong, then we still raised funds for the studio, Claire still made some business connections, and Shelly still got to practice her socialization skills in a controlled environment. She's come so far, Luce. I want this for her."

"All right. I have to admit, it was a stroke of genius. I can't believe I never noticed Claire checking you out before."

"Well, full disclosure, I may have picked out that outfit that day with the intent of setting her up for failure. I look great in that dress. The boots were a complete on-the-spot guilty pleasure purchase, though."

Lucinda pressed a kiss to Samantha's head. "What am I getting myself into?"

"A lifelong adventure, I suppose."

"I'm okay with that." Lucinda sighed. "This place looks great, Samantha. Really. You pulled out all the stops."

"Thanks. I happen to think you're worth it."

"Aww." The hand that had been gently caressing Samantha's shoulder paused. "Wait, what else do you have in mind for tonight?"

"So many accusations." Samantha stepped out of Lucinda's embrace with that same mischievous smile from her office that day. "Well, since you asked..."

Shelly stood in front of the mirror on her closet door and exhaled. This event was entirely out of her comfort zone. She had agreed to attend because Samantha and Lucinda had asked her to. And she loved supporting the arts. What was the point of having her wealth and not sharing it? As she looked at herself in the mirror again, she frowned. This outfit was not working.

She walked back toward the bed and tossed the blazer onto the duvet. The pants were fine, the shoes Andrew had picked out, so they must be perfect, but the shirt and blazer combo was off. She headed back to her walk-in closet and looked at the clothes: organized by color, all dry cleaned, and neatly arranged with care. This had been

Samantha's doing—but Shelly secretly loved it. Before Samantha and Andrew, Shelly had dressed in what she would refer to as nerd-chic. She was promptly educated that her natural style was actually decent, but the fabrics she chose and the fits were not flattering. In came the tailor and the personal shopper, and now everything fit her perfectly.

She walked over to the casual leather jacket section and ran her fingers along the soft leather. Whenever she was insecure about her clothing choice, she found herself back here. Something about the warm softness of the material drew her in—and it made her feel bold and edgy even if it was made to be worn indoors and was lightweight. Leather made her a little more confident. Tonight was a leather night, she decided.

"Hedy," she called over her shoulder as she pulled down a crisp black dress shirt. She shrugged off the white pinstriped shirt and let it fall to the floor. She caught a glimpse of herself in the mirror as she slipped the black shirt over her shoulders. Samantha had also overhauled her bra and panties selection. She had resisted this at first, but there was something about a matching set that made her feel sexy. Of course she still had her favorite Spider-Man boyshorts and requisite granny panties for her monthly cycle—she wasn't a savage, after all. But it was nice to have adult things. She admired the way the open fabric encased her slim frame, though the muscles defining her stomach were new. Lucinda had recommended she pick up something athletic besides their weekly dance lessons to help harness her anxiety, and she had chosen racquetball. The first few weeks were brutal; she had spent the better part of her life behind a laptop or tablet skipping meals and the sun in favor of working. That drive made her business with D'Andre extremely successful, but it also resulted in her having some bad loner qualities and social anxiety that she didn't have in college.

"Seriously, where are you?" She shrugged on the olive green faux leather jacket that she knew made her eyes look their best and walked into the bedroom again. "Hedy!"

A pair of emerald eyes that nearly matched her own appeared at the door frame, blinking at her expectantly.

"There you are." Shelly fastened her watch and ran her hand once through her hair. "What do you think? Do I look okay?"

Hedy sauntered into the room and jumped up onto the bed with the grace and ease of a ninja. She looked at Shelly for a moment and flopped onto her side, uninterested.

"No comments from the peanut gallery?" Shelly leaned forward to inspect her eyeliner application and gave herself a mental high five that her eyes appeared to match. "I'm getting better at this straight line thing. All right, I'll be home a little late. Gotta stop off and see Old Man Louis before the event tonight. Don't get into any trouble. And stay out of my closet, ya dig?"

Hedy blinked once more, this time yawning once before rolling onto her back, her arms and legs extended.

"Worst. Support. Cat. Ever." Shelly ruffled her belly and forced a kiss onto Hedy's face resulting in an annoyed meow. "She speaks. I'm outta here, Kit-Kat, see you in a few hours."

Shelly walked down the front stairs of her spacious three-bedroom house and started the car. She slipped into the driver's seat and dialed her father on the Bluetooth.

"What?" he grunted over the line.

"Hey, Dad, good to hear from you, too." She looked left and right before taking the turn onto the main road. "Did the food get delivered today?"

"I'm working, Sheldyn, I don't know."

Shelly cringed. She hated when he used her full name. Really, she hated the fact that he'd named his only child, a daughter no less, Sheldyn to begin with. Who names their daughter after a Nobel Prize–winning physicist? Someone hoping for a son, she presumed. She took a steadying breath to keep her blood pressure from rising. "Can you take a quick break and check the front door? I'm on my way there now and I'll set up dinner for you, but I have plans tonight, so you have to finish what I start, okay?"

"Maybe. We'll see. 'Bye." He disconnected the line abruptly.

She sighed and used the button on the steering wheel to activate the loud, angry rock music she had queued up in the cloud. For some reason, listening to this kind of music made her have fewer homicidal thoughts toward her moody and cantankerous father. She sat in his driveway nodding her head to the last verse of a Paramore song before finally shutting off the vehicle. Her father lived in an aging and deteriorating Victorian by himself, about ten minutes from her. That had been her choice, though. He had lived here his whole life—she chose a home close to him when she moved out because she knew he would never travel to her. She had not been incorrect.

As she walked up the uneven paver stones to the front door, she noticed a piece of the front gutter to the left of the door had detached and was inefficiently hanging at an awkward angle. The pane along the door frame was chipping, the original white a dusky gray now. The house almost looked haunted. She got to the front step and noticed the Peapod delivery of food still sitting there. She glanced over the railing and saw the cooler she had hidden tucked under the brush with a note on it. *Shelly, your dad didn't answer. I left the perishables in here with some extra ice I swiped from the store. Hopefully you get to this before it goes bad. Great idea on the cooler, by the way—Ramon.*

She made a mental note to leave a monster tip for Ramon on the next delivery. Her father had been getting less and less reliable about bringing the food inside in the last few months. That's where the cooler idea had come from. She knew Ramon was going above and beyond by using it—the delivery service had strict rules and he was breaking most of them to help her out. She was grateful. She picked up the grocery bin and keyed into the house she grew up in, walking into complete darkness, as usual. She hit the foyer light and walked to the kitchen, heading back to grab the cooler and unpack. The next delivery wouldn't be until next week. Ramon had circled the estimated date and time. She made a note in her phone to swing by that day and make sure the groceries made it into the house.

"Dad?" She called down the hall toward the study, where a whisper of light shone beneath the door. Again, the only light on in the house. It even felt haunted inside when it was like this.

She put the perishables in the fridge and freezer before washing the vegetables and drying them with care, rewrapping the ones she wasn't using now and putting them into glass containers with plastic lids. If things weren't easily accessible, her father wouldn't eat. Washing and drying fruits and vegetables was a step too far, and she knew it. She put the pot of water on the stove and clicked on the gas burner to bring the water to a boil.

"Dad! I have to leave, c'mon!" She looked around the kitchen and grumbled at the stack of papers obscuring the kitchen island, and as she stepped toward them to move them, her father appeared in the doorway.

"Don't touch those. They're important." He huffed and shuffled into the room. His gait was a mess, his steps stuttered and halted—his Parkinson's was progressing.

"Dad, did you shower today?" Shelly looked over his disheveled appearance and knew the answer. His hair was uncombed and standing straight up in the back. His shirt had a stain along the front lapel and his tweed sport coat was fraying at the right elbow patch.

"What are you, the hygiene police?" He adjusted his fingerprint-smudged glasses and pushed them up his nose. "I've been working."

"You mentioned that," Shelly replied as she finished cutting the peppers and onions, dropping them into a pan of olive oil. "Can you clear some of those papers off the island? Dinner is almost ready."

"I'll eat in the study."

"You'll eat at the island like a civilized human being before you go back to your cave." Shelly stirred the pasta and reached for the strainer.

"When did you get so bossy?" The sound of shuffling papers behind her indicated that her father was at least cooperating a little bit.

"Oh, about the time you stopped functioning like a normal human." She lowered her voice. "I'd say about the time I was nine years old."

"What's that?"

"Nothing, Dad. What do you want to drink?"

"Tea."

"Okay." She was grateful she had started the kettle when she arrived. Her father loved tea, but he only drank water from his mother's old iron kettle. It must have been a hundred years old and weighed at least that many pounds. She had bought him numerous kettles over the years—electric ones, aluminum, ceramic—but he swore the water tasted different and he turned his nose up at each of them. The woman at Bed Bath & Beyond had actually thought Shelly kept returning kettles just to hit on her. She was pretty but, alas, taken. Shelly didn't have the heart to tell her that her frequent trips were more to do with her aging father than her desire to get in the girl's pants. But it was kind of flattering nonetheless.

She poured the warmed sauce onto the strained pasta and stirred in the sautéed vegetables. She added just a pinch of salt and pepper before making two plates, a small one for her and a larger serving for her father. The rest she put into the glass containers that lined the counter, depositing them into the fridge.

"Here you go, Dad." She placed the larger plate in front of him and climbed onto the stool across from him.

"Why don't you have more food on your plate?" He spoke into the pasta between the bites he shoveled into his face.

"I have somewhere to be in a bit. I'm not starving and I'm sure there will be passed hors d'oeuvres."

"This is good. It needs more salt, though." He still had not bothered to look up from his plate.

"You know the doctor put you on a low sodium diet, Dad."

"Just saying." He reached for his tea and took a swig, finally looking up. "You look nice."

"Thanks." She finished her last bite and wiped her mouth before standing to clear her plate and load the dishwasher. "Greta will be by tomorrow morning to clean and do the laundry. That patch on your elbow needs to be fixed, so leave it out and I'll text her about fixing it."

"The jacket doesn't need fixing." He crossed his arms like a defiant child, making the tear more obvious.

"Okay, Dad. Whatever you say." She glanced at the clock once more. "I'll be over tomorrow or the next day, depends on how my meeting with D'Andre goes tomorrow. I will call you regardless, though, okay? I made extra pasta and put it into the fridge—just toss it into the microwave if you get hungry. Three square meals, Dad. Remember that."

"What are you doing tonight?" His expression was curious, his arms uncrossed now.

"What?" She paused in the doorway, her keys jingling in her hand at the sudden stop in forward motion.

"You're dressed…differently. And you have makeup on. Why?" Before she had a chance to answer he added, "When did you stop wearing glasses? There's nothing wrong with glasses."

"I'm going to a fundraiser for my friend's dance studio." She ignored the glasses comment and turned to go but he stopped her again.

"The blond one? What's her name? Lucille?"

"Lucinda. And yes." She was a little surprised he sort of remembered her name.

"I like Lucille better." He continued eating. "Have fun."

"Uh, thanks." She walked out the front door and shook her head in confusion. That was the most interest he had shown in her life in so long it felt foreign to her to share with him. She texted Greta to tell her to get him out of that jacket and repair it by any means necessary, before driving toward Lucinda's studio. She was actually looking forward to social interaction now. Spending any amount of time with her father tended to do that.

CHAPTER FIVE

Claire stepped through the door of Lucinda's dance studio and took a moment to appreciate how gorgeous the space was. There were white lights and paper lanterns hanging from the high ceilings, the glow from the polished wooden floors giving off a luminescent quality as the one mirrored wall reflected back to her. A soft melody played over the speakers, hidden from sight by lots of lush, towering flower arrangements.

"Can I take your coat, miss?" A young attendant met her with a warm smile.

"Yes, thank you." She slipped out of her trench coat and adjusted the collar of her shirt. Lucinda waved from across the room, motioning that she would be by shortly.

"Claire, champagne?" Samantha was a vision in a white pantsuit with matching heels. A loosely knotted red silk tie hung around her neck, disappearing into her cleavage, a shirt unnecessary for such an occasion, apparently. Claire did her best to keep eye contact; she really needed to stop checking out her boss's fiancée. But it felt a little impossible.

"Absolutely." She took the glass with a smile. "There are so many people here—this looks like a success already."

Samantha nodded and looked out at the growing crowd. "There are quite a few people here that owe me a favor or two. I have full confidence that the fundraiser will be a raging success. Have you been here before?"

Claire shook her head. "No, truthfully I didn't even know that Lucinda owned a dance studio until you mentioned it. It's beautiful, though. The space is so open and welcoming."

"Be sure to swing over to Elijah's table by the temporary door into the new space. Elijah is the architect—his vision is what we're celebrating tonight. We'll do a little walking tour into the new area in a bit. In the meantime, let me introduce you to a few people." She looped her arm with Claire's and guided her into a group of people off to their right.

"Ladies, gentlemen, this is Claire Moseley. She's the marketing whiz at Clear View I was just talking about." Samantha turned Claire toward the group and rattled off a few introductions. "This is Bette Taylor, owner of Chic Boutique on Newbury Street. Sylvia Augustus, her family is in the paper business. This is Chelsea Hanscombe, the much more attractive and charming better half of Dennis Waldorff, he works at—"

"Main Stage Productions. My brother used your studio space when filming his restaurant commercial." Claire turned her attention to the small blushing man to her right.

"Did he? What's his name?" Dennis pushed his glasses up his nose and scrunched his brow in attention.

"James Moseley. He and my brother Jerry run Open Kitchen Express—"

"The take-out place, right? They just opened a branch in Cambridge, last month I think." Chelsea stepped forward with a smile. "I love that place. Fresh ingredients, prepared in front of you, quick and easy. Your brother's crème brûlée is fantastic. I was just talking about them to Dennis the other day."

"Oh, I'll tell him that. He's his own worst critic." Claire fell into easy conversation with the small group, immediately grateful that she had decided to come tonight after all.

"I see you'll be fine, have fun." Samantha excused herself as Chelsea took her place next to Claire.

"How do you know Samantha?" Chelsea stopped the passing waiter and handed Claire a fresh glass of champagne.

"Oh, she's engaged to my boss." Claire didn't mention that they had worked together in the past when Samantha was a client of hers. Nondisclosure agreements sometimes demanded sins of omission.

"Ah, so you're a friend of Lucinda's." Chelsea nodded, sweeping her light brown hair out of her eyes. She was younger than Dennis, and warmer, as Samantha had mentioned in jest. Dennis seemed funny, though sarcastic. She could see their clear attraction to each other. He was in what appeared to be some sort of debate with the other two women in their group. "I wasn't sure if you were using her services like the rest of the people in here."

"Not me, no." Claire bit her tongue. She knew Samantha was very successful in her matchmaking business, but the idea of using a matchmaker to find herself a partner horrified her a little. Even if she was looking for Ms. Right—which she wasn't because she just got promoted and her career was everything—she'd find a girl on her own, in the wild, thank you very much. Not that she would ever voice those opinions to Samantha—or Lucinda, for that matter. The last thing she needed was to offend her client, who also happened to be her boss's fiancée.

"Well, if you ever decide you're striking out left and right in the love department, be sure to let Samantha and Andrew help you out. Meeting Dennis changed my life, and I owe that to them." She was so sincere Claire felt bad about her inner monologue. Just a bit.

"Claire, you look nice." Andrew Stanley stepped closer as Chelsea kissed Dennis on the cheek, thanking him for rounding up some passed shrimp cocktail.

"Hey, Andrew." Claire saw him much less frequently than Samantha, but dealt with him almost exclusively when operating as their PR executive. She appreciated the differences they each brought to the table—Samantha was definitely more of the schmoozer, while Andrew handled more of the operations side of the business. But she had seen them together and could see the draw; they complemented each other in the most fascinating way, each magnetic and charming on their own. "You don't look too bad yourself."

"Oh, this old thing?" He flattened the lapel of his designer tux. "I'm just trying to keep up with Samantha." He stage-whispered conspiratorially as Lucinda walked over, "Did you see that suit she's in?"

"Gotta love a good suit on a pretty girl," Lucinda supplied easily. "How's it going, Claire?"

"Good. Andrew was commenting on how nice I look tonight," she joked.

"That's high praise coming from someone as dapper as Andrew." Lucinda playfully blew him a kiss.

"My three favorite people." Samantha appeared over Andrew's shoulder. "Claire, I've been meaning to introduce you to someone, can I borrow you for a minute?"

❖

Shelly slipped through the main door and smiled at the changes in the studio she was all too familiar with. She had been taking dance lessons with Lucinda for months now, the highlight of her week. At first when Samantha had proposed the dance lessons, she had been a little resistant, but there was something about Lucinda and the way she moved with such effortless fluidity across the floor that captivated Shelly. It made her want to know what it was like to be so unburdened by physics. Plus, she really liked dancing, and her dates loved that she knew how to lead them on the dance floor. Definitely one of the things that had helped her find new confidence.

She accepted the champagne flute from the passing waiter and made a beeline toward the architect stationed by the temporary door into the new space. She had really been looking forward to catching up with Elijah. She had personally referred him to Lucinda when Lucinda first mentioned that her neighbors were selling their property. She had contracted Elijah and his group to help her build the interior of her new office building with D'Andre. She still couldn't believe they had cut the ribbon on that place three years ago already. It felt like it was only yesterday.

"Shelly"—Elijah stood from his table and hurried around to embrace her—"how are you?"

"Hey, Elijah." She patted his shoulder lightly. Affection was still something she was getting used to. She had to admit she was much better with it the more she danced, but physical contact with another person was still a little foreign unless she initiated it herself.

"I'm so pumped you made it tonight. Did you see the specs?" He reached behind her and pulled over a portfolio with rich three-dimensional color photos and blueprints of the space next door. She immediately recognized a water feature that he had installed in the waiting area of her office.

"Nice water feature."

"I know, right? It's a little different than yours, but along the same lines. I feel like it brings something unique to the space, you know?"

Shelly nodded. People loved it. She realized she was so used to it that she had been taking it for granted. She made a note to sit in the waiting area and enjoy it after hours someday soon. No need to surround herself with people if she didn't have to; she'd opened up a lot in the last few months, but she wasn't an extrovert by any means.

"Shelly, can I borrow you?" Samantha's voice drew her attention away from Elijah and back toward the party behind them.

"See ya, Shel. Pop by to see me before you leave—I wanna show you something cool I was thinking about." Elijah shook her hand and turned back to the newly formed line at his table checking out the plans.

"Nice jacket." Samantha ran her hand over the zipper along Shelly's cuff.

"I do what I can." Shelly brushed the hair off her shoulder in an exaggerated flirt. "What's up?"

"I wanted you to meet Claire Moseley—she works at Clear View. I thought you two might be able to talk about that project you mentioned to me last week."

Shelly looked past Samantha and realized there was another person with her. She had completely missed her at first. Not that she could figure out how that was humanly possible since Claire Moseley was gorgeous. Her shoulder-length auburn hair fell in beautiful, straight layers and her blue eyes shone with warmth. And her teeth were that perfect, blinding white that was so—

"Shelly," Samantha repeated with a smile, "this is Claire. Talk amongst yourselves. I have to go flirt some money out of those rich people's pockets. See you later."

"Sorry, um, hi. I'm Shelly White." She extended her hand to Claire as Samantha glided away toward a group of well-dressed business-looking people.

Claire giggled when accepting her hand and returning a firm shake. "Yes, she mentioned that."

"Oh, crap. I kinda zoned out for a second." Shelly was blowing this already and she knew it.

"No biggie. It's fine. These types of events get pretty boring—I definitely zoned out twice tonight already."

"So, you work at Clear View, huh?" Shelly tried again to make herself appear like she could string two or three words together in a coherent sentence. Attempt number two was almost a success.

"Yes. I'm a PR and marketing executive there. It's fun work, I love it." Claire placed her empty flute on a tray to the left.

"All right, ladies and gentlemen," Samantha's voice sounded over the speakers. "It's the time of the night when you are asked to grab a partner and hit the dance floor. Lucinda and a few of her dance instructors will be going around and helping you improve your form and lighten your wallets." The background music increased in volume.

Wondering if this was her chance, Shelly decided to try on that flavor of bold Samantha always coached her about. "Would you like to dance?"

"Oh, sure." Claire looked surprised, but not put off. That was a good sign.

"Great." Shelly awkwardly handed her glass to an unsuspecting Elijah walking by, as she guided Claire toward the center of the room. She could do this. She could dance and flirt and talk. She'd been training for months. It was go time.

As the music picked up and transitioned into a new song, Shelly rested one hand gently on Claire's midback and clasped Claire's hand with the other, slowly initiating a sway from side to side.

"You're a pretty good dancer." Claire looked amused.

"I've had some practice." Shelly turned them toward a quieter area of the dance floor. "You're good, too, though."

Claire smiled. "So, Shelly, besides dancing, what do you do?"

"I run an IT company with my partner. Well, I'm supposed to be doing the background work and he's supposed to be running the business side of things, but he's been a little absent lately, so…Sorry, I'm rambling. I work with computers. Clearly, I'm still mastering the art of socialization."

Claire laughed and Shelly swooned a little at the sound.

"Is it a company I might know?"

Shelly led them into another turn, pleased she was managing to keep them moving while trying to speak. "It's called Boston Pro App. We make templates and apps for people to use in order for them to—"

"Build their own businesses and websites. I've used your products a million times. You create that stuff?" Claire's excitement was palpable through the loose grip she had on Shelly's hand.

"I do. I found I spent more time in college showing my friends how to use their devices and technology than I actually did in class. So when D'Andre and I were fooling around in business class not doing the assignment, we figured we might as well try to make a living off of it."

"D'Andre is your partner-partner or…?" Claire was looking right at her when she asked. It was a little intimidating.

"Dre? He's a business partner. Really one of my oldest friends. It's not like that, I'm single." Shelly felt like that last bit was rushed out and forced, but she couldn't take it back.

"Me too."

Claire was so cute, and Shelly was having a hard time focusing. She tried some of that brave on for size again. "Well, that guy over there seems kind of interested. Maybe Samantha can make something happen for you."

"Which guy?" Claire looked to her left. Shelly had been bluffing just to find out if she was gay but pointed to poor, innocent Elijah just because he was in that direction. "Oh, he's cute. But that's not my thing, I'm not into—"

"Architects?" Shelly hoped her voice wasn't too hopeful.

"Not specifically, but I was referring to men in general. I like women. So I guess maybe Samantha could help me..." She paused for a moment and Shelly thought it was because that gulp she tried to stifle had actually deafened her dancer partner. Claire seemed oblivious though and leaned in closer, lowering her voice. "Hey, so, can I ask you something?"

"Yeah, of course." Shelly moved them a little farther away from the dancers. She could see Samantha watching her from the distance, her expression unreadable. Lucinda wove between the couples around them and cued a little here and there. She looked up at Shelly and smiled but headed in the opposite direction. Shelly assumed this meant she must be doing an okay job. But she thought maybe her hands were sweating. Probably. Definitely. Her hands were definitely sweating because her adorable dance partner was into women and they had been dancing for well over four songs now and it didn't look like an end was in sight and what if she ran out of topics to discuss?

Claire saved her from the imminent panic attack, her voice a mere whisper. "So, Samantha is a matchmaker and she's engaged to Lucinda..."

"Yeah. Wait, you work at Clear View, so you must know Lucinda, right?" Shelly had to turn her head to hear Claire over the music and the laughing couples around them.

"Lucinda's my boss. That's what I'm getting at. Did Lucinda get together with Samantha because she joined a matchmaking service?"

"What?" The question caught Shelly so off guard that she missed a step and nearly stepped on Claire's toes. "Sorry."

Claire didn't seem to notice, instead waiting for Shelly to start them back up again. "Well, do you know? Did she?"

Shelly laughed. "No. They met at a wedding."

"Oh." Claire looked disappointed. It was adorable.

"What makes you ask?" Shelly dipped Claire as the song ended and blended into a slower one. She chanced moving her hands to hold them a little closer, settling one hand on Claire's hip like she had seen Lucinda do a million times with Samantha when they thought no one was watching.

"Well, I've been here for a while now and more than half of these people have used Samantha and Andrew's services and rave about them both. I guess I'm surprised so many people need the crutch of a matchmaker to find happiness." Claire shrugged and continued to follow Shelly's lead.

"You think it's a crutch?" Shelly tried not to stutter. She stuttered when she was anxious. She wasn't sure this was a line of questioning she was comfortable with. Especially since she thought she might be about two songs away from asking Claire out.

"Sort of, I guess. I don't know if I would be caught dead filling out the applications to be put into the system or whatever. I was listening to some of them talk about the algorithms of a perfect match and it just seems so insane to me. What do you think?" Claire looked at her expectantly.

Shelly froze. "I, uh, I think everyone takes a different path in life. I don't know it's my place to judge."

As the song came to a close, Samantha's voice filled the room again, announcing that the last tour of the new space would be happening in a few minutes. The couples clapped and broke apart all around them, Shelly and Claire following suit.

"That was a lot of fun. You're a great dancer. Thanks again." Claire reached into her pocket and pulled out a business card, handing it to Shelly. "Samantha mentioned you have a new project you may want to consult on, right? Give me a call. I'd like to hear more about what you do."

"Sure. Great. Will do." Shelly wasn't quite sure how to thank Samantha for interrupting the train flying off the tracks a minute ago.

"It was nice meeting you, Shelly." Claire pulled her into a quick hug before heading off toward the last tour of the evening at the other side of the room.

"Yeah, me, too."

"You, too, what?" Samantha appeared at her side like a matchmaking ninja.

"Jesus. You scared me." Shelly's heart was racing but she wasn't sure if it was because Claire just hugged her or because her dating guru had magically appeared like a mist next to her and caught her talking to no one in particular.

"So?" Samantha pressed.

"So, what?" Shelly looked from the card in her hand to the disappearing form of Claire as she went through the door to the new space.

"So, I noticed that you danced with Claire. How'd that go?"

"Fine. Actually really well, until it didn't."

"What do you mean, it didn't?"

"I mean the dancing was fine and the conversation was going well and then it took a turn and then there were flames and screaming and the cruel death of a dream. That's what I mean." Shelly pouted as she put Claire's card into her pocket for no other reason than to have something to do with her hands.

Samantha looked alarmed. "Flames and screaming, huh? That sounds serious."

"Yeah, it was a mass casualty kinda thing. No survivors. *Titanic*-like failure."

"So in other words, *it didn't*." Samantha nodded in understanding.

"Yup." Shelly scuffed her shoe on the floor as she exhaled.

"Well, what if I told you what I saw, as a casual and innocent observer?"

"Something tells me that you were not all that casual or innocent. But I'm game. What did you see?"

"I saw two people smiling and laughing, having a conversation while in close proximity to one another, in an intimate position for the entire duration of the dancing portion of the evening. And I saw her hug you when it was over and give you her number." Samantha shrugged as though it were obvious.

"Except what you didn't observe when you were creepily watching us from across the room was the part where she told me that she thought matchmaking was a crutch for people unable to find a partner on their own in the world, like failures." Shelly rolled her eyes in a huff.

Samantha laughed and shook her head, slipping her arm around Shelly's and resting her head on Shelly's shoulder. "Shel, everyone says that. That's what people say when they have given up hope or are jaded. Don't let that blind you from the fact that she gave you her number."

Shelly rested her head against Samantha's with a sigh. "She gave me her business card for business purposes. Not for dating purposes."

"I beg to differ. She gave you her business card because she had a good time with you and wants to spend more time with you. Business or otherwise. You just need to look at it with an open mind."

Shelly considered this for a moment. "You know, she did mention she was into women."

Samantha squealed and turned to wrap Shelly into a twirling hug. "I knew it!"

Shelly laughed and shrugged Samantha off, pretending to dust herself off. "That doesn't mean she was coming on to me, Samantha. It means when I asked if she had any interest in Elijah, she corrected me."

Samantha stopped in her tracks, her mouth opened in surprise. "Wait, you actually asked if she was interested in guys? Why specifically Elijah?"

Shelly could feel the blush on her cheeks. "Well, I told her I was single and she said she was too and we were sort of facing Elijah so I might have pretended like he was interested in her and told her he was checking her out and *maybe* then she told me she was gay."

"I. Am. So. Proud. Of. You." Samantha rested her hands on Shelly's shoulders and shook her. "You sly dog, you. I think I'm rubbing off on you."

Shelly shook her head and let herself fantasize that maybe Samantha was right about Claire.

CHAPTER SIX

Claire sat in her new office, staring blankly at the wall. Today had been an endless day of meetings and client file reviews. She was looking forward to the chance to flex her creative muscles again soon, something that her new promotion had limited for the past few weeks. She leaned back and let her chair spin around a little, using her foot to speed up and slow down until it made her dizzy and her stomach protested.

Her head was still swimming when her office phone rang. She lurched forward to grab it and nearly fell off her chair.

"You are a moron, Claire." She held her head and composed herself before connecting. "Claire Moseley."

"Oh, I thought I might get your voicemail, hi."

"Hi." Claire looked at the phone number on the screen, but didn't recognize it. Or the female voice on the line. She paused, waiting for the mystery woman to identify herself.

"How are you?" No clues here. The plot thickened.

"I'm good. You know, just, uh, working." That wasn't even remotely true. She was absentmindedly spinning in her chair considering if she should put some more personal touches in her new work space. She felt like something was missing from her desk, but she couldn't quite figure out what it was.

"Right, right. I don't mean to bother you, sorry. I was hoping to talk to you about that, the working thing." The sound of typing in the background became audible and continued after the woman stopped speaking. Then there was a long pause. And silence.

Something about this was amusing to Claire and she had no idea why. She decided to play with it a little bit. "Yes, I'm happy to talk about the working thing...But what exactly are we talking about?"

"Oh, right. Well, when we met last week you told me to call you about that project I had coming up if I thought you could help, and I think maybe you can." The woman's voice was soothing, almost a little husky. Sort of. Like she was speaking quietly. The typing sound was back again, this time faster, louder.

Claire considered this statement—the only real schmoozing she had done recently was at the fundraiser last week. Or at the bar the other night after softball. Or at that froyo tasting over the weekend. Come to think of it, Claire had given her card out a lot over the last week. Maybe she ought to see how many she had left. Was she a card whore? Just how many people did she offer to help this past week? Gosh, this was a little embarrassing. How was she supposed to narrow down the sultry voice on the line if she was a card whore to half of Boston? She weighed the options a bit. It was most likely that this was someone from the fundraiser, but there *was* that blonde at the bar, with the martini and the three olives and long legs—

"Claire?" *Click, click, click.*

"Right, sorry. Who am I speaking with again?" She gave up after having been caught in a daydream.

"Oh." The typing stopped. "What's the matter with me? Duh. Um, this is Shelly, Shelly White."

"Shelly, hi. How are you?" Claire reached forward and grabbed a pen and paper from her desk.

"I should have started with that, my bad. I'm sort of in the middle of something on my end. Maybe I should call you some other time, you're probably busy." There was a faint knocking sound in the background and some shuffling. Claire heard Shelly tell someone, "Put the package over there."

"No, I'm free. I just was trying to make the voice connection— epic fail on my behalf. What's in the package?" Claire twirled the pen between her fingers as she remembered how masterfully Shelly had moved her around the dance floor. It was funny, she'd been talking about the fundraiser to Jamie and almost skipped right over mentioning it. She hadn't done it intentionally; it was more that it had felt like such a routine experience that it didn't stand out to her as something to talk about. Jamie had pointed out that she hadn't danced with anyone else that night. And since when was dancing with a complete stranger not something to make note of? She didn't have an answer for him—just that it was fun and that Shelly had the most amazing green eyes and that it had felt like a totally normal thing to be doing at a work function. Which made absolutely no sense.

"What package?"

"The one that someone just put over there."

"Are you spying on me?" Shelly sounded a little paranoid.

"No, you called me, remember? I'm just showing you that I'm paying attention. And you just told someone to put something down. A package, more specifically. So what's in it?"

Shelly hummed. "You know, I have no idea. Let's check." More shuffling, followed by the sound of cardboard being cut open and a light thud. "Well, that's convenient. It's a few pieces of equipment that I need for a prototype I'm working on. And a travel mug. But I have no idea how that got in there."

"What does it look like?" Claire found herself starting to spin in the chair again. She halted her progress as soon as she realized she was doing it.

"Pieces of metal and some circuit board. Wires. A USB stick. It looks kinda...gray? I guess."

Claire decided that Shelly was adorable. "I meant the travel mug."

"Of course you did." Shelly sighed with a small laugh. More adorable. "It's blue, with a black handle and matching lid. Looks big enough to hold about sixteen or so ounces. Dishwasher safe."

"Sounds like a good mug." That was it, that's what her desk was missing, a mug. "Now that that mystery has been solved, what can I help you with?"

"I had forgotten that was why I called. Right, sorry." The previous typing resumed. "I am working on a new project and I was hoping to get together with you to get your opinion on it. It's kind of a new venture for me and I would feel more comfortable working with someone who has a different perspective than I do. Sometimes I get stuck in my own head."

Claire nodded along to Shelly's voice, making spirals on the notepad in front of her. "Sure, how about we meet. What's your schedule like tomorrow?"

"Tomorrow?" The typing ceased. "Yes, okay, great. I have some meetings. Can you swing by here? Is that okay?"

"Of course. What's the address?" Claire jotted down the information and gathered a few details from Shelly before disconnecting. She looked up at the clock and fist-pumped the air—the day was over and at least some of her card whoring had paid off. She shot off a quick email to Lucinda letting her know about the connection made from the fundraiser and powered off her laptop, deciding to swing by the mall on the way home to look for fancy mugs for her desk.

❖

Claire stepped out of the elevator into the lobby of the Boston Pro App office and took a moment to soak in the scene in front of her. The space was well lit and clean. The walls were white and the furniture was modern; brightly colored pillows accented the comfy couches that lined both walls, the colors complementing the designs of the gray area rug that covered a majority of the industrial slate floor. A metal and fiberglass chandelier, with bulbs artistically placed throughout the piece, illuminated a water fixture inset into the table below. The table was the height of an average coffee table in a home or apartment but was made out of the same slate material as the floor, giving the appearance of being both a water fountain and a fire pit in the midst of the modern office space. It was quite the contrast but, at the same time, felt completely appropriate.

The table was round and the surface not taken up by the water fixture was covered by neatly stacked tech magazines and brain teasing toys: a Rubik's Cube, interlocking rings, and a colorful triangle with moving parts. She thumbed through the magazines and found a sudoku puzzle book on the bottom, a pen slipped into the book, holding a spot on the page. This was obviously a work in progress. There was even a little Zen sand garden with a rake on the table, a swirling pattern woven between the rocks matching the shapes in the carpet below.

The sound of a college-aged male speaking into a headset drew her attention to the large frosted glass desk positioned at the other end of the room. As she stepped closer, Claire noticed his fingers were hitting invisible keys—there wasn't a keyboard on the desk. Instead, a green light shone from the base of his monitor, casting a laser outline of a keyboard onto the frosted glass below. This was something she had heard about and seen in sci-fi movies, but not experienced in real life. She couldn't help but stare.

"Yeah, most people get mesmerized by the Non-Keyboard." He disconnected his call with a tap of his headset and looked up from the screen with a smile. "Hey, I'm Toby. What can I help you with?"

"Is it accurate? Like, does it really work?" Claire was fascinated.

"It takes a while to get used to and it doesn't work all that well on some surfaces, but this cool opaque glass is the perfect surface. And the cleanup is super easy—you know, 'cause it leaves fingerprints all over the desk." He opened the drawer to his left and pulled out a bottle of organic cleaning spray. "I start and end my day with a little spritz and it's good to go. It helps keep down on desk clutter, too. Can't type if there are papers everywhere, right?"

"Yeah, I suppose that's true. Wow. Is it cool working here?" Claire had a lot of questions for Toby. She had spent a good portion of last night researching Shelly White and her business partner D'Andre Johnson. Their success story was exciting research fodder. They had been classmates at MIT who started a small technology company right after graduation that took off first locally and then nationally. They'd started with templates and making things more user friendly; then they expanded to making actual software programs and began hosting seminars on college campuses and at high schools. Their template and software programs were incredibly cost-effective and so easy to use that they cornered the market in education and self-development, empowering youth organizations and fostering entrepreneurial spirit in middle school and high school aged students.

Although now they had dozens of apps available to their clients, the one that got them to where they were today was simple: Their initial app was run on a server that they monitored from their office. It allowed students to keep track of the due dates on their assignments and input the grading criteria and requirements into the server as a sort of digital planner for academics. They first started it at a local high school and quickly expanded it to be available to college students before making a version for businesses and professional life. They used this knowledge to expand internationally when smartphone use began to boom, and soon almost everyone was using their original algorithm for one app or another. The fairy-tale story didn't end there—all of her research indicated that the employees at Boston Pro App almost never left and the morale in the office was always high. There were stories of extravagant parties and Nerf gun fights between deadlines with free pizza for lunch on Fridays. She imagined someone like Toby would relish working here. She had to know if it was all true.

"It's the best. I was originally placed here as an intern when I was a freshman, but I asked to stay on while I finish up school. It's the best place to work, ever. Shelly and Dre are so chill. They're flexible with my finals schedule and even let me do some administrative stuff from home during exams week. They're the best." He was smiling from ear to ear, his enthusiasm infectious. "Sorry, I didn't catch your name. You are?"

"Claire, Claire Moseley. I have a meeting with Shelly at two p.m." Claire glanced up at the clock above Toby's desk. She was early—that's how she preferred things.

"Of course. Cool. Let me page Shelly and let her know you're here." He typed into his Non-Keyboard and pressed the button on his headset, speaking into it excitedly. "Shelly, Claire's here. Should I send her back?...No?...Sure. I'll tell her." He paused and blushed. "Yeah, for real?...Yes!...Oh, right, cool, thanks."

Claire waited with a broad smile on her face. She couldn't help it—Toby was like a happy puppy. "Everything all right?"

"Yeah, yeah. Shelly said she would come out to get you in a minute or two."

"That's it? It sounded like there was more." Claire teased him as his blush deepened.

"Yeah, I'm seeing this new girl—she's so cool—and Shelly told me she got me some tickets to a ballet for next weekend. It's our one-month anniversary, and I'm so pumped because the ballet is expensive and I have no idea what any of it is about, but Shelly knows, like, everything, so I asked her and—I'm rambling. Sorry. She told me not to ramble."

Claire laughed and leaned against the desk, "Hey, can I try that keyboard thing?"

"Sure." Toby hopped out of his seat and took off his headset, motioning for her to sit. "It's pretty sensitive at first, but you get used to it. Shelly made an app so that you can use your phone as the monitor and carry a little pocket projector around so you can work without a clunky screen. See this little green light?" He pointed to a small LED light on the monitor stand. "This is a new prototype. They're trying to do away with the need for a little projector and put the technology into the stand itself. Fewer parts, less cost, more desk space. Genius, right?"

Claire looked up at the screen and tried the keys, watching the cursor move on the page in front of her. Toby was right, it was sensitive. She spent more time trying to hit the backspace than actually getting a full sentence on the page. He gave her a few cues and advice on how hard to hit the non-keys and after a minute or two she had nearly three whole sentences on the screen.

"Toby, I'm sure Ms. Moseley has better things to do than type your essay." Shelly was leaning against the frame of the door to the right of Toby's desk. Her smile indicated her teasing, but Toby blushed nonetheless.

"I asked to try it out, fancy-shmancy." Claire stood and thanked Toby for letting her tinker away. "I promise you, I only delayed his essay writing, not enhanced it. That is harder than it looks."

Shelly nodded. "It takes a little practice, but Toby and his fellow millennials seem to love it." She reached into her pocket and pulled out two tickets that she handed to Toby. "Okay, Lucinda sent these over, so don't get into any trouble or get kicked out, cool?"

Toby took them and gave her a serious nod. "Aye, aye, Captain." He paused and adjusted his collared shirt. "Is Samantha coming by later?"

"She's taken, champ. And so are you." Shelly pointed to the blinking headset. "Feel free to get that call."

Toby gave her a thumbs-up and plopped back into his seat, answering the call and turning his attention to the screen in front of him.

"Sorry to keep you waiting," Shelly said to Claire as she stepped forward and extended her hand. "How are you?"

Claire shook her hand and motioned around her. "I'm good. This place is so fun. That water table thing is awesome."

Shelly beamed. "I'm glad you like it—want a little tour?"

"Absolutely." Claire followed Shelly toward the center of the lobby where she told her about how the chandelier was the idea of one of her clients' students and used LED technology to put out more light with less energy. She pointed down to the table next.

"Elijah, you remember the architect from the dance studio? He designed this table. I wanted the waiting room to be relaxing and kinda fun, too. Nobody likes to wait. He felt like this was a tranquil addition while also warming up the cold, industrial floor space. Mostly Toby complains it makes him have to pee more often, but I think that's just an excuse to leave the desk to call his girlfriend."

"I heard that," Toby replied from the desk, his attention on the screen in front of him.

"Lucinda sent over the ballet tickets and your receptionist knows Samantha? You guys are pretty friendly, huh?" Claire watched as Shelly stiffened a little. She wanted to ask about it, but Shelly changed the subject.

"Yeah, we're close." Shelly picked up the Rubik's Cube and

twisted it while she spoke. "Anyway, I thought we could meet in the conference room and chat. It's just through those doors." She nodded toward the door behind Toby from which she had first emerged, but Claire didn't bother to look. She just stared at Shelly's hands in awe.

"Did you just solve that Rubik's Cube?" Claire almost couldn't believe her eyes. They had been standing there for less than half a minute, and Shelly had lined up all the colors without even pausing in their conversation.

"Oh, yeah. I'm not a big fan of idle hands…" She shrugged and placed it back on the table, putting her hands in her pockets nervously.

"How did you do that?" Claire looked down at the cube and then back up to Shelly as if something magical had transpired.

"It's really not a big deal. With enough practice, it's easy."

Claire picked the cube up and spun the columns around, mixing up the colors. She handed it back to Shelly. "Do that again."

Shelly glanced up at her and gave her a shy smile. "Shall we time it?"

"Shut up. You can do that faster than last time?" No way. No way did Claire think that was humanly possible. She had to see this.

"Definitely. I wasn't even trying last time. And Toby mixed the last set. He's been trying to stump me for years."

"It's true. She's a freak," Toby supplied from behind his monitor, his fingers moving on the glass in front of him.

"What are you saying, I didn't mix the rows up enough?" Claire balked and took the cube back, spinning and twisting a little more in hopes of making it more challenging.

"I'm saying, it probably doesn't matter." Shelly smiled and took the cube back. "What was our last time, Toby?"

Toby stopped typing and glanced up. "Nine seconds. You're getting slow."

"Nine seconds? You can finish this in nine seconds?" Claire replied incredulously. "No way."

"My record is just under five. I'm a little rusty." Shelly shrugged.

"Are we doing this or nah? I'm trying to finish my midterm over here," Toby teased.

"Ready, set, go." Shelly's hands whirled around the cube, pieces rotating and gliding in a choreographed movement that blurred in front of Claire's eyes. "Done." Shelly tossed the cube into the air and caught it as Toby clapped from the desk.

"Seven point eight, Boss. Nice."

Shelly dropped the cube back onto the coffee table and motioned for Claire to follow her through the doors to the rest of the office. She paused to give Toby a high five before holding the door open for Claire.

"I can't believe I just witnessed that." Claire shook her head in disbelief. "That was insane."

"You're easily impressed. I think the record for a three-by-three square is like three seconds or less. I'm a sloth compared to that." Shelly walked them through rows of cubicles toward the back of the building. Each cubicle was inhabited by someone working in front of a monitor or talking quietly on a headset. Each work space was decorated with photos or little action figures. One woman had a pink feather boa along the top edge of the cubicle and twirled a glittery princess wand while she talked to her neighbor. Everyone waved or smiled at them as they passed.

"So, everyone works from a cubicle?" Claire asked as she took in the open floor plan.

"Yup, myself included." Shelly pointed toward a slightly larger corner cubicle by the window. From their position Claire couldn't see the contents of the desk, but could tell it was messier than most. "We'll meet in here because it's quieter and more private." She walked them toward a large enclosed room, with the same frosted glass as the door behind Toby. In fact, all of the doors and rooms she saw, four in total, were of that same material.

"I like this glass." Claire ran her fingers along the cool pane of the door. "It's so different."

Shelly nodded and held the door while Claire walked into the conference room. "The building is long, so in order to help get light to all of the areas, we didn't want to close off any windows. The glass gives us a chance to get light in the conference areas and help the cubicles toward the back get some semblance of natural light as well."

"Makes sense." Claire settled into a comfortable leather seat on wheels and looked out the window that ran along the far side of the conference room. "This is a great view."

"It's the back of the Public Gardens. This is my favorite room." Shelly sat at the head of the table and looked at Claire.

After a few moments, Claire cleared her throat. "So, you wanted to meet with me?"

Shelly blinked. "Right, right. Okay, sorry. Yeah, let me grab a folder off my desk." She stood and ducked out of the room without another word.

❖

"Shit." Shelly shuffled the things on her desk in a frantic way, trying to remember where she'd put the file she was holding when Toby had called to tell her Claire was here. It had to be somewhere—she just had it.

"Looking for something?" D'Andre stood at the edge of her desk, holding a folder. The folder.

"Yes, thanks. Where did you find this?" Shelly took the folder and skimmed through the contents making sure it was all there.

"You left it on the sink in the bathroom. With your cell phone." He held up her phone with a smirk. "Distracted?"

Shelly snatched the phone back from him and glared. "I've been a little stressed lately." She motioned to the mountain of paperwork on her desk. "Not that you've been much help. Where were you yesterday?"

"I meant distracted by the pretty girl in the conference room." D'Andre frowned. "I took a personal day. I'm allowed. I'm the boss."

"You are one of the bosses. Not *the* boss. And you missed a conference call to California." Shelly tried to keep her voice even, but this was becoming a more frequent thing than she liked. This was the third call he'd missed in the last month. She couldn't remember him taking so many days off like this in, well, ever.

"Wendy knew I would be out. She was plenty prepared to run the call." D'Andre nodded toward the woman with the glittery wand two cubicles over.

"Wendy is not you. They were expecting you. Next time, shoot me an email so I can do damage control, would you?" Shelly huffed and brushed her hair out of her face. "I don't like being left high and dry, D'Andre."

"Sure. I'll do that." D'Andre gave her a tight smile and sighed. "I have a meeting off-site, I'll see you tomorrow." And with that, he turned and walked away, leaving Shelly frustrated. Things had been weird between them for a month or so. Actually, right when he'd started taking more time off. She made a mental note to schedule a meeting with him sometime soon and see what was up.

She walked back into the conference room to find Claire finishing a call. She held up her hand in apology and mouthed that she would be done in a second. Shelly sat quietly at the head of the table and chanced a glance at Claire while she was still looking down. Claire looked great.

Her hair was tied up today, exposing her neck and showing off the soft indent of her clavicle visible through the opened top button of her dress shirt. She was in a skirt and cute but sensible heels that Shelly had first noticed when Claire was hanging out with Toby in the waiting area. She must have taken off her blazer and draped it over the back of the chair while Shelly had been gone. She was almost disappointed to have missed the undressing.

"Did you find it?" Claire smiled and nodded toward the file Shelly was clutching.

Crap. She was daydreaming. "Yeah, sorry. Can I get you some water or juice, tea? Coffee?" Shelly stood and walked toward the minifridge and kitchenette in the corner. She pulled out a bottle of water for herself and held one up to Claire.

"Sure, thanks." Claire took the water as Shelly sat back down. "So, where were we?"

"Right." Shelly nodded, took a deep breath, and opened the folder. "I wanted to talk to you about a new project I was working on. I'd like to try something a little different and I wanted your opinion on it."

She handed the contents to Claire to review as she reached into the messenger bag by her feet that contained her tablet. She powered up the tablet and grabbed the remote off the table, turning on the television that was mounted on the far wall. She pulled a keyboard and mouse out of the little drawer she'd had installed into the conference room table and started typing. "We have a few new products we want to put out into the world—you saw one earlier at Toby's desk. Lately we've been a little busy with the ongoings of the business and I want to make sure that we have everything ready to launch for the upcoming tech expo."

Claire looked up from the documents in front of her and gave Shelly a curious expression. "I'm with you. But why aren't you using the Non-Keyboard software thingy?"

"Oh." Shelly paused her typing. "I like the sound of the keys—I find it relaxing. I tried the keyless approach but found myself getting frustrated. The rhythm of the movement and the texture of the keys help me with my typing. I have a bad habit of typing when I'm nervous. That's how the idea of the laser keyboard came about, a way for me to silently code and work without people realizing I was busying myself. But I never really got into it like I hoped I might." Shelly frowned. "I have no idea why I just told you that."

"Well, I sort of asked," Claire pointed out with a small smile.

Shelly quirked an eyebrow in her direction. Claire was teasing her. "That you did." Shelly considered that a moment—she wasn't really prone to such verbose interactions with people she was just getting to know. In fact, she usually just shut down and stopped talking completely when someone asked her something that delved a little deep. She wasn't quite sure why she was oversharing with Claire.

She motioned toward the screen for Claire to follow along. "I'd like to show you some of the ideas we have and what we are working on. You can keep the contents of the folder for review later on. There are some kinks to work out before the Expo that will require the team to put in some long hours. I'm hoping that you will be able to work on the PR and marketing stuff in tandem. We don't have a lot of time, so there will have to be some overlap between the business and the development side as we get closer to the event."

Shelly watched Claire study the screen. She slowed the movements of her cursor to allow Claire to see the three-dimensional depiction of the products they were finalizing. She could feel herself getting a little anxious; she felt completely out of her depth. This project was something D'Andre was not supportive of—that was the primary reason Shelly had decided to seek outside help. She had never been at the helm of a product launch; she was strictly the nerd behind the keyboard. That's how she liked it. But somewhere along the way their mutual understanding of the path this company was on had started to deteriorate. D'Andre seemed more interested in making a profit than making things easier for people. In the beginning, that was their entire business plan: help people help themselves find success in everything that they did. Lately it seemed that D'Andre was only interested in his own success, and she had never felt more alone.

"These are great." Claire stood and walked toward the monitor, her fingers hovered over the images and the short CGI video that played on the split screen. "You made all of these?"

"Well, not yet, not completely. And not without help. They were just some ideas I had been throwing around with the engineers for a bit, something fun and different. When it was announced that Boston would host the annual tech show, it seemed like a good time to try our hand at it." She leaned back in her chair and let that statement settle with her a bit—she must have been crazy when she started this.

"How much time do we have before the Expo?" Claire strode back to her chair with a determined look on her face.

"Three months, give or take a few days." Saying that out loud made Shelly's stomach turn. She wasn't sure they would finish all the work on their end, let alone teach Claire about all of the products she would need to promote. This was sort of her last shot—if she didn't finalize her plan within the next week, they would have to pass on the Expo altogether. "What do you think? Is this something you would be interested in? Are you up for the job?"

"I'm in." Claire extended a hand to Shelly and gave hers a firm shake. "Let's get started."

CHAPTER SEVEN

Claire sat at her desk with a frown on her face that had been there for the better part of the last fifteen minutes. She was completely stumped on where to go next with the Boston Pro App situation. She and Shelly had been logging long hours in person and on Skype to get some of this work squared away before her initial pitch, but she wasn't sure what to do with the third mystery project. She couldn't spin anything for it if she didn't know anything about it. Shelly had promised to give her a little more information once it was closer to development, but they were at a standstill.

In Shelly's defense, Claire had noticed she had been even busier than usual. They had been meeting once or twice a week for over a month, but the last two sessions had been over the webcam. Which, although better than not meeting, wasn't very helpful. She texted Shelly to find out if she was free to chat. Shelly replied immediately, like always.

Hiya. What's up?

Busy?

Not too busy for you. Everything okay?

Claire smiled as she typed a response. Shelly's texts were always full sentences with punctuation and usually inquired about how she was feeling. It was sweet.

Fine. Not fine. Stuck. At the office?

There was a pause before Shelly replied, *Le sigh. Yes.*

Coffee? Be there in 15

Sure. Tell Marshall I'm expecting you. Call me when you get to the office door.

Great. C-ya

:)

Claire grabbed her purse and the files off her desk, dropped her laptop into her bag, and ducked out of the now dark office toward the elevator. She pressed the button and waited, waving to the cleaning woman as she walked past with the vacuum on, earbuds firmly in her ears. Claire let out a long sigh and glanced at her watch—it was after seven. The ping of the elevator door drew her attention away from the time and she stepped into the empty elevator, leaning against the far wall, her fatigue evident. This was the fourth time in the last two weeks she had been at work after five. She had nearly missed her softball game last week because of it, and even then she didn't play well; she was just going through the motions. Her workload had increased exponentially in the past few weeks, and her work with Shelly was taking up a good portion of her free time in addition to her work time.

She stepped out of the elevator and into the parking garage below the building. The remote starter beeped as she got closer, the doors unlocking when she stood outside the driver's door for a moment. That was a nice perk from the car upgrade that she finally committed to this year. She had been driving her high school Chrysler, which she affectionately called Elaine, until it died on her last year. She'd loved that car. It was the first car she had ever bought on her own—hours of saved pennies from odd jobs and working at the Smoothie Stand in the mall on the weekends when her school friends were partying and dating. She'd picked the old beater up secondhand but essentially brand new, barely driven by the elderly woman who had owned it before her. Retiring Elaine had been hard for her. Jamie practically had to carry her out of the junkyard. She was inconsolable.

As she settled into the contoured leather seat and pulled the car out of the spot, she let her mind wander. The heated seats and fancy stereo of her new car had helped the transition, a little. But she had a lot of memories with Elaine: her first girl kiss, the first time she rounded off the bases in the backseat, that time Brittany the cheerleader did that thing with her tongue—

A honking noise broke her from her reverie. She was sitting at the garage exit, the automatic arm already up and waiting for her to drive through.

"Get it together, Claire." She gripped the steering wheel before waving apologetically to the impatient looking man in her rearview.

As she pulled out onto the street in the direction of Shelly's office building, she was grateful they worked relatively close together. The drive was quick; the streets were surprisingly quiet. She wondered if

there was a Red Sox game in the area. Even the foot traffic was light—
maybe everyone was up by Fenway. At the next light she took a hard
left, slipping into the back entrance of the company parking lot behind
Shelly's building. She pulled into the spot that she knew belonged to
D'Andre. Shelly said he was traveling this week. She seemed annoyed
by it—not that she verbalized it explicitly, she didn't do that often. She
was sort of quiet about her relationship with him. The silence made
Claire more curious.

She popped into the coffee shop that was on the ground floor
of Shelly's building and ordered the usual fare—her latte with light
foam, Shelly's overcaffeinated iced monstrosity. On her second
meeting with Shelly they came down here to decompress after the tech
geeks debriefed her on the science of the products for the expo. She
remembered how her head was swimming. Shelly had taken pity on
her and encouraged her to take a walk with her. That's when Claire
first found out how bad Shelly's sweet tooth was.

Marshall smiled at her when she entered the building. "Ms.
Moseley. Another late night?"

"Seems like it." Claire set the coffees on the security desk and
signed in. "Game tonight?"

"Oh yeah, big one." He stood and stretched. "Sox up by four,
bottom of the sixth."

"Explains the empty streets. I'm good to go up?" She nodded
toward the elevator.

"Yeah, sure. She know you're coming?"

"I sure hope so—I don't think I can drink both of these myself."
She held up the large iced cavity that Shelly preferred with a playful
look.

"Tell her that shit is going to give her diabetes." Marshall sighed
and shook his head.

"I will, promise." Claire stepped into the elevator and glanced
back at him as he called out to her before the doors closed.

"Ms. Moseley, make sure you call down before you leave, one of
us will walk you to your car. 'Kay?"

"Thanks, Marshall." The doors closed and she started her ascent.
She liked Marshall. She liked this building and how friendly everyone
was. The coffee here was exceptional, too. And for whatever reason,
they never charged her when she ordered something for Shelly and
herself. She made a note to ask Shelly about that.

She stepped out of the elevator and texted Shelly to let her know she was outside the door, waiting for her to unlock it. The barista downstairs had flirted with her a little until she placed Shelly's coffee order, but then she said, "Oh," and smiled briefly before drifting away to make the drinks. That had happened before, too, last week. It was peculiar. She added that to the list of things to ask Shelly.

"Hey, she brings gifts." Shelly opened the door with a wide smile and motioned for Claire to enter.

"I was always told never to show up to a party without provisions." She stepped into the now familiar waiting room as Shelly locked the door behind her. She walked over to the water feature, checking the pattern in the Zen sand garden. It was different today, just like every time she was here. "An exclamation point today. And the rocks are in the shape of a smiley face, with its tongue sticking out."

"I'm not sure that this constitutes a party." Shelly looked tired. "And yes, the Zen garden gnome strikes again. One never knows what to expect from that little joker."

"You look like you need this." Claire passed Shelly the jug of sugar water and added, "Marshall is worried you are becoming prediabetic."

"Marshall has a soft spot for warm Cronuts and a tendency to put too much cheese on everything." Shelly laughed, "I'll take my chances with insulin resistance."

Shelly led them through the waiting area toward the back conference room. This was where they usually met; Shelly had taken it over after Claire had signed on to work with her. When Claire inquired why, Shelly had told her that she needed a space to spread out that had a lock on the door. Claire just assumed that it had something to do with the prototypes Shelly and her team were working on. Not that Marshall or anyone else would let a stranger up to their floor. Everyone seemed to like Shelly around here, maybe except for that barista girl.

"How come they never charge me downstairs when I order that sludge drink for you?" Claire plopped into her usual chair, the space in front of her seat clear of paperwork, like it had been left waiting for her to occupy it.

Shelly glanced up from where she was studying some papers on the table, the straw still in her mouth as she mumbled something unintelligible.

"What?"

"Sorry." Shelly finished her sip and sighed contentedly. "We own them. Well, that's not entirely true—we own the space. Anytime you get coffee or anything there, just tell them you're with me and it'll be free."

"You own the space?" Shelly's nonchalance never ceased to amaze Claire.

"Yup. There was a coffee chain here a few years ago that served this nasty, watered-down garbage that was just not cutting it. When we bought the building, we shopped around to find a better coffee shop to rent from us. We found this great local guy, Micah, a total bean guru. Ever since then he gives me my coffee for free." She shrugged and took another hearty sip. "This is like crack."

"That's because it is crack and corn syrup. So much corn syrup."

Shelly stuck her tongue out. "You're worse than Marshall."

Claire leaned back in the chair and cracked her neck. She watched Shelly's brow furrow as she leaned closer to the table, that laser focus erasing the playfulness from a moment ago. Shelly was like that—sarcastic and fun one minute but totally engrossed the next. It was one of the things Claire liked about her. She enjoyed working with Shelly; maybe that's why she had texted her and not waited until the morning.

"So you own the building?"

"What?" Shelly didn't look up. She was lightly chewing a pen now, while the fingers of her left hand drummed the table a bit.

"The building. You own it?" Claire sipped her latte and watched Shelly swipe at her long dark hair, brushing it out of her eyes and tucking it behind her ears. The soft layers razored throughout complemented the shape of her face even when combed haphazardly with her fingers. When Shelly didn't look up, Claire continued to let her gaze trickle over her. Shelly was wearing a starched white dress shirt, the sleeves rolled up to the elbow. She had loose satin braces attached to the high-waisted black slacks she wore. This was a fancier outfit than Claire had seen her in before, and she looked great. Really great.

"Yeah, we rented for the first few years but then the owner got greedy when we started to make real money. The reason Dre and I chose this location from the start was because of its proximity to our homes. It was clear that we would be spending a lot of time here, and we wanted something convenient. Toss in the formal parking lot and coffee shop downstairs and we thought we'd hit the jackpot." Shelly pushed the paper she had been staring at to the side and grabbed her pen, twirling it as she looked at her tablet screen, appearing to be stumped by something. "We decided that the location was too good to pass up, so we made an offer on the building. Now we rent the floors we don't use. It was a hassle in the beginning because I didn't want to be anyone's landlord, but it's turned out to be a big blessing. We expanded quite a bit and now have full control over all the building materials used and waste management. Green living and working, you know?"

Claire nodded. She hadn't noticed how perfect Shelly's teeth were before this, but as she chewed her bottom lip in concentration, their brilliance was on display. When Claire realized Shelly had stopped talking, she shook her head and broke her trance. "Why does that barista downstairs with the side ponytail act funny when I order your coffee?"

Shelly looked up at her this time, the green of her eyes glinting as her eyebrows rose in response. "Tara acts funny?"

"You know her?" Claire tried to contain the amusement in her voice.

"Sure, she works here." Shelly broke eye contact and shuffled some papers around.

"Uh-uh. No way. I saw that look in your eyes—I want the real story. Why does she give me stink eye when I order that drink?" She nudged Shelly's coffee with her index finger, leaving a line of condensation on the conference table.

That got Shelly's attention. "Stink eye? She gives you stink eye?"

Claire shrugged. That same intensity was in Shelly's look again. She had noticed the color of her eyes when they first danced at that fundraiser, but she hadn't really had the chance to admire them like she could right now. They had flecks of light and dark green scattered throughout, the coloring almost giving the appearance that they sparkled. "You have really pretty eyes."

"What?" A blush formed on Shelly's cheeks. "Thanks."

"So, about Tara?"

"Oh, I was hoping we had moved onto how beautiful you thought my eyes were," Shelly teased and tried to change the subject.

"Nope. Still on the bean girl. Spill." Claire leaned back in her chair and clasped her hands behind her neck, smiling broadly.

"We used to date. It didn't last long. I thought it ended amicably. Evidently, I was wrong. I guess that's why there's stink eye." She nudged her cup back toward Claire. "Do you think she spit in this? Now I'm paranoid."

"You two used to date? Tell me more." This was an interesting revelation. She leaned forward and tapped her fingers together excitedly.

Shelly sighed and plopped back into her chair with a huff. "It was a few months ago. I was going through a thing. It was brief, she was nice, I wasn't that into it." She pouted. "I'm going to have to get my coffee somewhere else now, aren't I?"

"I watched her make it. She didn't spit in it, I promise." Claire made a heart-crossing motion with her hand. "I didn't know you were into women."

"You never asked." Shelly shrugged and eyed the remnants of her coffee. "Can you taste it? What if she spit in it and I'm so used to her spitting in it that I don't know the difference anymore?"

Claire blinked. "You're worried she spit in it and you want me to taste it to tell you if it's safe or not?"

"Yes. Yes, I do." Shelly nodded and pushed the cup closer to Claire. "Please?"

"This is completely ridiculous." Claire shook her head with a chuckle.

"So that means you're not going to do it?" Shelly sounded so defeated that Claire felt bad.

"Fine." Claire reached out and took a sip of the drink, cringing as the sweetness overpowered her. "No spit. But this is disgusting. How do you even get that sludge through the straw?"

Shelly breathed a sigh of relief, taking her cup and leaning back in her chair as she took a sip. "I have a pretty talented mouth, lots of practice."

Claire felt herself flush this time. Not sure what to say in response, she just stared at Shelly. That had escalated quickly. Did Shelly really just say that? Why couldn't Claire stop looking at the way Shelly's mouth wrapped around the straw?

"What?" Shelly looked confused, then alarmed. "Oh God, I meant lots of practice because I drink these all the time." She burst out laughing and coughed on her drink. "Your face right now is priceless."

Claire reached for her own cup to occupy her hands and her mouth, because she was all kinds of flustered at the moment. She nervous-laughed and hated herself for it. "Okay, got it. So, I had a business question."

Shelly was clearly trying to stifle her remaining giggles and nodded, attempting to look serious. Claire decided she hated her in that moment. "Oh, right. What's up?"

Claire composed herself and tried to remember why she was sitting in Shelly's office so late during a weeknight. Meeting with Shelly never really felt like work, and considering this was her first solo project for Clear View, she often worried she was doing something wrong. At first when she'd sent Lucinda the heads-up email about Shelly contacting her, she had been a little nervous that Lucinda would put someone else on the case since Claire's workload had increased so quickly. But when Lucinda gave her the thumbs-up and told her she would be working this project alone, she wasn't quite sure what to think. She knew that no matter what, she had to prove that she was capable of handling a big fish on her own. Prior to this, most of her client portfolio had been inherited from her predecessor. It was time Claire flexed that creative muscle and showed that she was capable of not only catching the big clients but representing Clear View well in the process. And with the technology expo right around the corner, there was no client bigger than Boston Pro Apps. This was her chance to prove herself, and she knew it.

"I've been working on the marketing specs for the Expo and think I have a really good grasp on the *Star Trek* keyboard and the nifty little glasses things…"

"Don't let the techies hear you call them nifty little glasses things." Shelly smiled. "They're very sophisticated video documentation devices that are both streamlined and lightweight in addition to being Wi-Fi enabled to transfer video footage to any device with the supporting app."

"Precisely what I said." Claire reached into her bag and pulled out the papers she had been working on at her office. "Now I know that the Non-Keyboard and the space glasses have something to do with the third mystery object that you are keeping under lock and key, but I need to know what it is and what kind of cool science-y thing it does so I can make a little bundle package of awesome for the Expo."

Shelly laughed and stacked the papers in front of her into a neat pile, clearing off the space on the table between them. "First of all, the laser keyboard isn't anything new or exciting per se, it's just a little easier to manage and a newer model, without the need for a third-party projector. The new app we designed can project the laser from a computer or television monitor, or you can use your smartphone in a cradle. Secondly, the space glasses, as you call them, are hugely important on their own but would work really well with the mystery object. Thirdly, I kept the mystery object a secret because, in truth, it wasn't fully realized until two days ago and I'm still working out the kinks, but I think we can plan for it to be ready in time. Hopefully."

"That doesn't sound very encouraging." Claire frowned. "Perhaps you being a little more enthusiastic and confident would help me work my magic. Just saying."

"Meh. I've seen what you're capable of, and I think you'll be fine." Shelly shrugged and pointed to Claire's phone. "Can I borrow that?"

"What do you mean you've seen what I'm capable of? That sounds a little Big Brother-y. Can you hack into things and spy on me?" Claire was half kidding. Half.

"Not all computer nerds are hackers, Claire-Bear." Shelly gave her a playful glare as she unlocked Claire's phone with a few quick swipes. "Of course, when you set your cell phone passcode as one-two-three-four-five, you make it kinda easy."

"Hey!" Claire tossed a pen in Shelly's direction that she easily dodged. "It's the fastest way to get it opened in a pinch. Wait, did you just call me Claire-Bear?"

"Hmm, seems like I did. That cool?"

"Yeah, my brothers call me that. That's my childhood nickname."

"It's cute." Shelly was typing something onto Claire's phone, her fingers a blur on the touchscreen. "You're right-handed, right?"

"Yes."

"Can I borrow your right thumb and then your left thumb?" Shelly didn't bother looking up.

"For what?" Claire was already extending her thumb toward Shelly. She was asking more as a formality. She trusted that Shelly wouldn't harm her.

"Just put it over the home button and keep it there for a few seconds." Shelly held Claire's hand in place, gently rubbing her own thumb along the back of Claire's hand. "Good, now the other thumb."

Claire complied, as she considered how warm Shelly's hands were, given how large and cold her so-called coffee was. It seemed unreal. "What are we doing right now?"

"We are setting up a new password for your phone because you're better than one through five." Shelly took the phone back and scrolled through the security screen for a second before pausing to show Claire what she had done. "See? Now to unlock your phone in a hurry, you just put your right or left thumb on that spot and give it a second or two, and then the phone unlocks. You should still change your passcode, but this is a marginal improvement."

"Hey, that's pretty cool. Does it really work?" Claire peered down at her phone incredulously.

"Give it a whirl." Shelly nodded toward the door, "I have to grab something to show you how the mystery object works, BRB."

❖

Shelly stepped into the darkened hallway outside of the conference room and let out a sigh. She couldn't believe she had accidentally inserted a blatant sexual innuendo into their work meeting. She was pretty sure that could be considered sexual harassment. And it was entirely unintentional. Of course she might have subconsciously been thinking about Claire in a not-so-work-appropriate way when she caught Claire checking out her outfit. And she was pretty sure she saw Claire gulp when she mentioned having dated the barista downstairs. It was kind of the perfect segue to tell Claire she was into girls, even though now she probably had to have a conversation with Tara, or the owner of the café—like she needed anything more on her plate.

She headed to her recently abandoned cubicle and rifled through the drawers, pulling out the supplies she needed. Since she had relocated to the conference room, her desk space looked much more organized. She could actually see the picture of Hedy she kept next to her monitor. The photo was suspended in a hand-blown glass paperweight that she had found when digging through her mother's things so many years ago. It was one of the only things she had of hers. There weren't many material items left behind when she'd abandoned Shelly and her father. Shelly had been only eight at the time, but she remembered it like it was yesterday. She tapped the top of Hedy's photo affectionately and made a mental note to work from home one of these days to spend time with her favorite little beastie. She had been working long hours the past few weeks to get everything ready for the Expo, and Hedy had been giving her the cold shoulder because of it. It was well deserved, and she knew it.

As she approached the conference room she glanced at the clock on the wall and was surprised it was already well past nine. Time seemed to fly when Claire was around. But it never felt like it was unproductive. It just felt…easy.

"Okay, ready to play a little game?" she asked as she walked to find Claire typing away on a laptop that she must have unpacked while Shelly was out.

"I'm at the ready." Claire tapped her fingers on the keyboard in a drumroll fashion.

"Good. The mystery object is actually a type of projector—"

"I thought the entire point of the *Star Trek* keyboard app was to eradicate the need for a projector," Claire replied.

"Yes, for that it is. But this is something different." Shelly put the superglue, clear tape she'd borrowed from Wendy's desk, a box cutter, and a jewel case for a compact disk on the table.

"Why does this game involve sharp things?" Claire pointed to the knife. "This does not sound like a friendly game, Shel."

Shelly laughed. "It's for demonstration only, I promise. I am the only one who has to wield the sharp thing."

"That really is no comfort considering how much caffeine I know was in that slush."

Shelly scrunched her nose at Claire and took the front of the CD case off, placing it on the table. She drew a series of shapes with a pen and used the box cutter to cut clean edges until the pieces fell through to the surface below. She lined up the pieces and put stabilizing tape on the edges as she used the superglue to line up the seams. "What took me so long was to figure out the easiest way to make a prototype to display the functions of the new app. I needed to find a way to make a quick and easy projector that could demonstrate the technology at the Expo that was small and compact while still being efficient. I figured out that I can use a 3-D printer to make the shell of the device and test the program's efficacy."

She looked up to find Claire watching her intently. Claire had such a childlike exuberance when Shelly showed her some of the tech gadgets they were working on—today was clearly no different. It was intoxicating to hold her attention. Shelly tried to ignore the butterflies it gave her. "Pull up a gif on your phone for me. Something that's not too complicated, like a hummingbird hovering or lightning striking on a blank background."

"First you brandish a knife and MacGyver some wild little clear, topless pyramid and now you tell me to go find nature gifs? What madness are you up to, Shelly White?" Claire teased as she scrolled through her phone for a moment. "Okay, done. Lightning wins. Wow me, Dumbledore."

Shelly took Claire's phone and placed it on the table, screen side up. Then she put the little handmade projector over the screen so the exposed top of the topless pyramid, as Claire called it, was resting above the center of the gif. "In order for you to understand the aim of the app and the programming that goes into it, you first need to understand the basics of a hologram. I assume you've heard of or seen a hologram, right?"

"Oh this is definitely some *Star Trek* shit now." Claire rubbed her palms together in anticipation. "Yes, I've seen it on television and I've seen those creepy hologram people at the airport security line telling you to throw away the water you just bought when you walked in."

"Right. Well the hologram is actually just a series of images taken from multiple angles that is projected on clear or mirrorlike surfaces that give the illusion of multidimensional existence—so they look like real people, even though you know they aren't. Close your laptop for me, will you?"

Claire complied as Shelly walked over to the conference room door and clicked off the light, casting them both in total darkness.

"This is a lights-out kinda party? I should've brought my glow sticks."

"I made this out of a CD case, so the darker the better for the demo. I promise, no hanky-panky." As soon as the words left her mouth, Shelly regretted saying them. What was it about Claire that put her mouth and mind in the gutter?

Before she could retract her statement, Claire laughed. "So that little plastic thing is going to project a hologram?"

"Yup. A lightning show, in fact." Shelly took the seat next to Claire and scooted as close as she could. She touched the screen to activate the gif and placed the projector over the image, casting a hologram of the lightning up into the inverted base of the pyramid.

"Shut the front door." Claire reached out and touched Shelly's arm in the dark. "You did not just make that with superglue and tape."

Shelly suppressed a shiver at the contact. She was pleased that Claire's hand stayed on her forearm as she spoke. "It's not some big secret—you can find a DIY on YouTube and try it yourself later."

"You've obviously never seen my World's Best Mom arts and crafts projects from kindergarten. One word: abomination. I should never be allowed near a glue gun, ever."

As the lightning storm raged on in the little box in front of them, Shelly had an idea and reached for her own phone to see if she could find what she was looking for. "Isn't kindergarten a little young to use a glue gun? Isn't that the eating glue sticks phase?"

"See? This is what I'm talking about—that kind of genius would have been useful when my brothers were poorly chaperoning my activities. I still have a glue burn on my wrist." Claire moved her arm from Shelly's forearm to point to the faint scar illuminated by the glow of Shelly's cell phone screen.

"You have brothers? How many?" Shelly found what she was looking for and cued up the video, swapping out their phones and scooting closer to Claire again before the show started.

"Four. Two much older, and twins a few years older. Do you have any siblings?" Claire yawned in the darkness beside her.

"Nope, just me."

"They stopped at perfection, huh?" Claire nudged her with her elbow. "That's what I tell my brothers—I was last because I was the best."

"Yeah? Does that go over well with them?" Shelly shifted so their arms were sharing an armrest, skin touching skin. So what if she was using her little toy as a way of maximizing her closeness to Claire?

The video on Shelly's phone started to play and Claire squeaked with excitement. "Fireworks? Hell, yeah, I'm watching a fireworks show indoors."

Shelly mentally fist pumped for finding the Fourth of July video from Boston Commons that she shot from the office rooftop last year. She thanked nerds everywhere for making the cloud so easy and convenient for data storage. The colors popped and trickled along with the gentle sounds coming from the phone, and in this darkness, it was gorgeous. "This is last year's fireworks display from down the street."

"Really?" Claire reached forward and passed her hand over the top of the projector, interrupting the image briefly. "How did you get this footage?"

"There's a little rooftop platform on top of this building that they use for maintenance. I found it by accident shortly after we became owners. The view is spectacular up there." When Shelly looked over at Claire she could see from the reflected bursts that Claire looked mesmerized, smiling and happy. "You like fireworks?"

Claire turned toward her voice and this was the closest their faces had ever been to each other. Shelly held her breath, wondering what would happen if she leaned forward just infinitesimally and kissed Claire. Would Claire kiss her back? She could have sworn Claire's eyes flicked down to her lips briefly. She wet them with her tongue out of nervousness, and this time Claire's eyes definitely jumped to her mouth before returning her gaze.

Claire said softly, "Fireworks are my favorite. There's something about all the bright colors and chaos of the explosions that fade into soft rainbows of light. The celebration it represents, it's—"

"Beautiful," Shelly supplied, unwilling to break their eye contact, those butterflies from earlier making their presence known in her abdomen. Just as Shelly began to lean in, she was interrupted by her own voice coming out of the speakers on the phone, drawing Claire's attention to the projector. Fuck. She had forgotten how she'd ended the video. A hologram of her with the fireworks in the background appeared, a recorded message to her father that she had forgotten she had made.

Hologram Shelly smiled and pointed behind her head. "See, Dad? This is what you're missing spending all of your time in that study. Happy Fourth."

Hologram Shelly gave them both a brief wave and refocused on the finale of the fireworks, the bright colors and smoke from the video floating over Shelly's phone like a tiny live display, accompanied by the faint sounds of music and cheering in the background. When the video cut away she chanced a look at Claire, who was sitting quietly next to her, staring at the empty space above the projector, her expression vacant.

"You okay?" Shelly placed her hand on Claire's arm, worried she might have made her uncomfortable, but immediately regretting the action when Claire twitched and looked over at her.

"Yeah, sorry. Totally spaced out for a second there." Claire looked a little rattled but when Shelly began to withdraw her hand, Claire stopped her, squeezing her fingers gently before letting go. "Thank you for that. That was so, I don't know, *magical*. I've never seen fireworks like that. From a cell phone, no less. You really are so gifted, Shel."

A multitude of emotions passed over her as she looked at Claire in that moment. She appreciated the praise but felt it was unwarranted. Really though, what concerned her was how quickly Claire seemed to deflate in front of her, like she was sad. How had she gone from almost kissing Claire to making her sad? "Thanks, look, I didn't mean to make you uncomf—"

"You didn't, really. I think the day just caught up with me a bit." Claire dismissed her concern, reaching out to squeeze her hand once more before she opened up her laptop, casting them both in the light blue glow of her screen. "That was a cute message for your dad."

Shelly merely smiled in response, unsure of what to say. She stood from the table and flicked on the overhead light, walking back to her seat a few chairs away. She blinked as her eyes adjusted to the change.

"What about your mom?" Shelly looked up to find Claire watching her.

She felt anxious, and not the good kind of nervousness she felt before when they were so close. This was the kind of nervousness that made her feel uneasy, vulnerable.

"It's just me and my dad. And he needs to get out more."

Claire nodded, but didn't say anything. Shelly sighed. This evening had her feeling all sorts of things.

"So"—Claire powered down her laptop and organized the papers in front of her—"the mystery object is actually a hologram projector. Right?"

Right, they were working. "Sorry, I sort of went off on a tangent there. No. That's a part of it, but no."

Claire gave her a confused look. "I'm lost."

"I know. I'm completely at fault." Shelly settled into the seat and organized her thoughts. "The mystery object is an app that formats home videos and webcam footage into data that can be converted into holographic images. In order for you to see a hologram, it needs to be filmed or photographed from multiple angles and then transmitted over a series of surfaces to give it the illusion of being there in front of you, and not a two-dimensional thing. My goal is to give everyone the ability to make their own holograms, just like I showed you today. I wanted to have a little prototype viewer for the Expo, but the real trouble has been getting the software up to snuff."

"Can people use the space glasses to film stuff that the mystery app can then convert into a hologram?" The light returned to Claire's eyes as she leaned forward excitedly. "They are all connected, aren't they?"

"Yes, they are." Shelly felt a level of validation that she didn't think she ever would with this project. It had come to her in a daydream a few months ago, when she was playing with Hedy. "The idea is that someone can record events in their life as they are living them, with hands-free, live-action memory recording. The glasses will help them live to their fullest and get little clips of their day-to-day, and the app will help them relive them as though it were real time."

"Memories brought to life as vividly as they first occurred." Claire nodded. "And the *Star Trek* keyboard?"

"A way to instantly upload or categorize the information without having to be chained to a desk or computer. All you need is a smartphone and the glasses to make the whole thing work. But you saw—they can make the projector on their own. Or just use footage from the smartphone to record the memories. They don't need the glasses, but I just think they're kinda—"

"Cool." Claire shook her head. "Yeah. Wow. Holy crap. This is unbelievable. Will it really work?"

Shelly frowned. "The glasses work but can only store limited little clips at the moment. They need more memory for storage, but I want them to still be lightweight and not bulky. But so far, they're doing what I ask them to do, yet I'm not a hundred percent satisfied. The Non-Keyboard is all set and can function as a standalone. The app is another story. I have to iron out some rough patches. I can get it to work, but I'm having some issues with background images and blurring. It needs work, but I think I'm on the right path. I just need a little more time."

"All right. You keep doing all those little genius things you do and I'll work on finishing that draft of promotional stuff." Claire glanced at her phone and yawned again. "Oh jeez, I've kept you far too long at work. I gotta hit the hay, otherwise tomorrow is going to be brutal." She finished packing up her stuff and slipped on her blazer. "This was great, Shelly. Thank you, that was so fun."

"Yeah, thanks for popping by—that was an unexpected surprise. And sorry about the stink eye thing."

"It's fine. I'm in the know now." Claire smiled as Shelly joined her by the conference room door. "You apologize too much." Claire paused and reached out, gently tugging on Shelly's braces. "I like these. This is a good look on you."

"I've heard that before, on both accounts." Shelly went to hold open the door for Claire but stopped when Claire gave her an unexpected hug.

"Thanks again, for the fireworks." Claire pressed a quick kiss to her cheek and slipped out of her arms before she even had a chance to respond.

And just like that, Shelly was alone in the conference room at an ungodly hour on a work night and was suddenly feeling very much awake, speaking to no one in particular. "You're welcome."

CHAPTER EIGHT

S o, yea or nay on the toasted coconut?" Jamie asked as he dipped his spoon into his light pink frozen yogurt concoction and tasted it.

"Yes, this is fantastic. Way *yea* on this. With the dark chocolate chips, those are a must." Claire closed her mouth over the spoon and savored the contents a moment longer. "I love this."

"I'd say so," Jamie replied. "It looks like you and the spoon need a room."

Claire laughed. "How's the Bubble Gum?"

Jamie shrugged and pushed the tasting cup toward her. "It's good. Tastes like bubble gum. But it's not my thing. I'm sure someone out there would love it, though."

Claire put a small spoonful into her mouth and nodded. "It's very sweet. Shelly would love this."

Jamie looked up at her with a small smile. "That's the second time in the last ten minutes you've mentioned her. Wanna tell me why?"

"What? I have not." Claire pushed the pink yogurt away and reached for the coconut, but her plans were foiled when Jamie moved it out of her reach.

"No more deliciousness until you spill. Go." Jamie took a large spoonful.

"Jamie, don't eat it all, it's mine." Claire pouted and halfheartedly tried to get it back from him.

"You're deflecting." Jamie helped himself to some more, the contents of the cup dwindling before her eyes.

"I almost kissed her last night."

Jamie stopped his teasing and gaped. "You almost what?"

Claire capitalized on his distraction and stole the cup back, leaning out of his reach and nibbling on the remainder. She decided this was her favorite new flavor; she particularly liked the small toasted coconut flakes on the top—the texture was a nice bonus. As she scooped another bite into her mouth, Jamie cleared his throat impatiently. Oh, right, the kissing thing.

"We were working late at her office and she has the most gorgeous green eyes and she dated the female barista downstairs and there were fireworks and I almost kissed her." Claire rushed it all out, afraid if she didn't she would chicken out.

"Slow down, let's try that again." Jamie pushed aside his yogurt and folded his hands in front of himself in a professorial fashion. "You went to her office late last night to have a meeting."

"Yes."

"And at said meeting you noticed that she has green eyes?"

"No, I noticed that the night we danced at the fundraiser. I was just reminded of it again at the meeting last night."

"She asked you to come by her office after hours?"

Claire paused. "Uh, no. I sort of invited myself over."

"Hmm."

"What does that mean?" Claire crossed her arms.

"Nothing." Jamie cocked his head to the side. "Did you mention fireworks?"

"Oh, yeah. Right. Yes, there were fireworks. The room was dark and there was nerd science-y learning and the building of a mystery thing and then fireworks, a real hologram show of last year's fireworks from the Commons. You could hear the sounds of them popping and almost see the smoke clouds—it was incredible." When Claire noticed her brother's amusement at the way she was talking with her hands moving excitedly, she stopped and crossed her arms again.

"You know that none of that makes any real sense, right?" Jamie was giving her that triumphant smile he had when he knew she was trying to minimize something, and she decided in that moment that he was out of her will.

She sighed. "We're working on this product launch for the tech expo that's coming up in Boston."

"Oh right, Jerry wants to go check out some of the video game stuff there."

"You're going to be there?" Claire hadn't heard Jerry mention it. This was news to her.

"Probably. All depends on the tournament results."

"Oh, shit." The tournament. Claire had completely forgotten about the end of season softball tournament. It was scheduled for the same weekend as the tech expo. They weren't guaranteed to make the finals, but Jamie's home run streak had remained intact this entire season and they were undefeated. Assuming they did well in the playoffs, their appearance in the finals felt almost guaranteed. "I probably have to work at the Expo. Shit, Jamie, I may miss the final game."

"We haven't made the finals yet, Claire, so let's worry about that later." He patted her on the hand and nodded toward her frozen yogurt. "Finish that and finish the part about the kissing."

Claire frowned. She hadn't expected to be so disappointed about the prospect of missing the finals. They had come so close to winning the whole thing last year, and she had been ecstatic when Jamie's home run streak started up—they had a real chance this year. But she had been so distracted with work and Shelly that she hadn't even considered one interfering with the other. She knew that Jamie was trying to make her feel better but could tell he was a little disappointed. She was, too.

"Claire. Stop overthinking the Expo thing. We'll figure it out. You're the backup pitcher anyway." He poked her in the arm.

"I'm not going to tell you anything about Shelly's perfect teeth if you keep teasing me."

"She has perfect teeth? This is getting good." He rubbed his hands together in excitement. "Go on."

"We're working on this product launch for the Expo, like I said. But one of the products is still in the development stage. So I texted her to see if she was working late because I'm kind of stumped about how to market it."

"You two have a texting relationship?"

Claire thought about that momentarily. Shelly was incredibly quick with text and email responses. It was their preferred communication method. "Is that weird?"

"Do you text your other clients?" Jamie was watching her so intently right now it was nerve-racking.

"I guess not, no."

"Continue." He waved his hand at her.

"Anyway. She said she was at the office, so I popped by and picked up her favorite coffee from downstairs, but the barista stopped flirting with me when I ordered it so I asked Shelly why and she told me it's because they used to date."

"Why do you know what her favorite coffee is?"

"Jamie. I just told you that my client is gay and I almost kissed her and you want to know why I know her favorite coffee? Why is that even at the top of your list of questions?"

"Because that feels like an intimate thing to know." Jamie shrugged.

"I know how you like your coffee. I know that Jerry likes green tea, lukewarm with a little milk. Does that mean we're intimate?"

"No, it means we're family." Jamie paused. "How does slutty Nikki take her coffee?"

"Barfly Nikki?"

"Yup. Heartbreaker 101 class president. One and the same."

"I have no idea."

"Exactly. Intimate." Jamie patted himself on the shoulder. "So, Shelly's gay."

"Well we didn't get into specifics, but she dated the girl at the coffee shop. Which rents the space in the building that she owns, by the way, but that's a discussion for another day. Anyway—the new product involves some hologram technology, and she literally constructed a projector with glue and a CD case in front of me and turned off all the lights and sat next to me and put on this fireworks display and it was amazing, Jamie. She is so smart and funny, and it was amazing."

"And then there was almost kissing?"

"Well, yeah. She was right next to me and her arm was touching mine and she looked at me and those green eyes were so close and she had on this lip gloss that just glowed when the fireworks went off. Then there were the little silk braces. They were so hot how they framed her chest and clipped to her pants. I mean, who wears silk suspenders? And I swear she was leaning in to kiss me, but then the hologram started talking and I lost the moment."

"The hologram started talking?" Jamie looked puzzled.

"It was a recording she took from the rooftop of her building of last year's fireworks. But at the end of the video, she turned the camera onto herself to record a message for her dad. It sort of killed the moment for me."

"Oh." A look of understanding passed over Jamie's face. "Well, had that not happened, do you think you would have kissed her?"

"Probably." Claire flopped back into her chair with a sigh. "I wanted to."

"So can we safely say that since you text her, know her favorite coffee flavor, know she's at least dated women in the past and put on a private fireworks show for you in her office late at night after you initiated a meeting, a meeting at which you almost kissed her, can we agree that you like her? Because all signs point to yes."

"Crap." Claire gave her brother a helpless expression. "I think I like her."

Jamie looked down at the empty toasted coconut cup and nodded. "I think we're going to need some more of this."

"Add more chocolate." Claire let her head fall back against her chair and tried to quell the panic threatening to bubble up inside her. Shelly was her client; she couldn't like Shelly. Except, she totally did.

❖

Shelly stretched out on her bed and let herself daydream a little. The sun was coming through the windows, the birds were chirping, and she was blissfully working from home today. Well, supposed to be working. At the moment she was contemplating a catnap. She had put in a few solid hours before lunch and felt like she needed a quick recharge, so she padded into her room and crawled under the covers.

Her phone buzzed next to her—it was a text from Claire. She was letting her know that she had sent an email with some preliminary marketing specs for her review. She signed it with a smiley face and ended it with *Let me know what you think*. Shelly already knew it was going to be fantastic. She had mentioned such to Claire last night when she had come by the office. Before she had picked up the business card to call Claire, she had done a little research on her and the projects she had completed in the past. Even though she was initially attracted to Claire at the fundraiser, that didn't mean she was willing to put this new project in her hands unless she was more than capable of helping it be successful. And her research had uncovered that Claire was plenty talented. And funny. And cute. She was definitely cute.

Shelly let herself remember last night. Claire was so bubbly and playful when she arrived. It was such a breath of fresh air—she had been struggling with some little details for the app but felt a sudden clarity when Claire arrived. After Claire left, when she kissed her on the cheek as she was leaving, Shelly felt invigorated. That bug that had been plaguing the coding process vanished—she knew the resolution. Being around Claire made her feel like she could do anything. Being around Claire…made her feel a lot of things, actually.

She became aware of the warmth of her right hand resting on the skin below her tank top, just above her boxers. Her fingers wandered as she thought of how it felt to be admired by Claire. She liked the feeling it gave her when she caught Claire observing her, and she was glad she had chosen that outfit to wear that day. She knew the tight dress shirt and braces were flattering. It was one of those outfits that Samantha had personally selected for her wardrobe. She flashed back to the look Claire had given her when she arrived. It was almost lustful. That was it, that was the look Shelly had seen when she was so close to Claire that night, when Claire's eyes were on her lips, it was lust. Claire wanted her. And she wanted Claire.

She slid her hand lower, underneath the band of her boxers, under the flimsy barrier of the silk panties she still wore from last night. She had been aware of their dampness after Claire had left. A dampness that was similar to right now. Just thinking about being close to Claire, the way her neck and collarbone peeked out from her dress shirt last night, how soft her skin was when she touched Shelly's arm and squeezed her hand, all of that made Shelly a little hot, a little wet.

She dipped her fingers down and felt the wetness she knew would be there. She played with herself a little, teasing and stroking the skin gently, gliding over her clit and then away. She let herself imagine what would have happened if she'd leaned in, if she had kissed Claire when she wanted to. Would Claire have kissed her back? Would she cup her jaw and open her mouth and let Shelly slip her tongue in, exploring her? Would Claire moan a little? Did she make noises when she kissed? If she had taken control, in that moment, would Claire have battled her for dominance? Or would she submit, taking all that Shelly would give her?

Shelly increased the pace of her fingers now, moving them in more deliberate motions, sending buzzing sensations across her core with each swipe, stronger and stronger as she let her daydream escalate. Would Claire's mouth be as hot and wet as Shelly imagined it to be? Would she whimper if Shelly sucked on her tongue or tugged on her lip gently with her teeth? Would Claire pant into her mouth when she palmed her breast through her shirt? Would she tolerate all the teasing that Shelly so desperately wanted to subject her to?

As the familiar pressure started to build, Shelly gave in to it, letting herself imagine the taste of Claire's tongue against her own, the notion of it pulling her past the precipice of her climax and into the blissful torture of the tremors that would follow, prolonging her sensations, sating her momentarily.

She let out a contented sigh and let the warmth of her orgasm wash over her. Her muscles were relaxed and her body felt heavy and tired. Suddenly this catnap idea was even more brilliant than she had originally thought. She lay there for a moment or two considering what just happened. There was no doubt that she was attracted to Claire, but not once ever in Shelly's life had she masturbated to the idea of someone else. Especially not someone that she was in a working relationship with. Not someone like Claire. But she hadn't ever met anyone quite like Claire, had she?

A soft thump at the bottom of the bed drew her attention away from that thought as Hedy made her presence known.

"Well, that was good timing. That could have been awkward for the both of us." Shelly laughed and stretched.

Hedy let out a little purred meow and curled up at the foot of the bed, gently kneading the blanket before plopping onto her side. She looked up at Shelly with those lazy green eyes and blinked at her.

"What?" Shelly nudged her with her foot and patted the space next to her with her left hand. Hedy stared at her a little more.

"I'm sensing judgment. Look, it's not like I planned for that to happen. It just sort of did. Seriously. I was just going to nap." Hedy seemed unimpressed. "Okay, maybe I'm not upset about it. Maybe I want it to really happen."

Hedy stood and started to slowly walk up the outline of Shelly's form below the blanket, stopping just short of Shelly's left hand, just out of reach.

"I know, I know." Shelly sighed. "Okay. I like her. It's true. I like her and I think she's pretty and I want to do more than nap with her. Okay? Fair?"

Hedy slammed her head into Shelly's side and scooted up closer, settling under Shelly's hand and purring as Shelly petted her.

"I think she likes me, too," Shelly said as she scratched behind Hedy ears. "Maybe I should ask her out. What do you think?"

Hedy squeaked and rolled onto her back, exposing the soft fur of her belly, her purring almost deafening at this point.

"You're right. I'll just do it. We can make it casual, see if it goes anywhere. Maybe it won't. Who knows? Can't know until we try, right?"

Hedy squeaked once more and head-butted her hand again, seemingly agreeing.

"Here goes nothing." Shelly grabbed her phone and shot off a quick text asking Claire what she was up to later, saying that she needed a distraction from working and asking if she was free.

A few minutes went by and Shelly panicked a little. What if she had made the wrong choice? Before she could fully freak out, Claire texted back.

I have a softball game later on, at the Arbo. You can swing by if you'd like. We do drinks and dinner after the game.

Shelly wondered who the *we* was. She texted an affirmative reply that she'd stop by, and got the details before putting down her phone.

"Well, there's no taking it back now, Hedy. Looks like I'm going to be brushing up on the rules of softball...after our nap, of course."

Hedy snuggled closer in agreement and Shelly decided to ignore the flutter in her stomach for now. She would worry about all of the touching and the daydreaming later. Right now she was going to catch some z's with her favorite fur baby and rest up. Maybe if she was lucky, she would have a long night.

CHAPTER NINE

"Hey, Shel. How are you?" Samantha's voice sounded happy. It always sounded like that these days. It was nice.

"Great. Good. I don't know. What do you know about softball?" Shelly turned up the Bluetooth volume on the steering wheel and clicked on her blinker.

"I know lots of hot ladies play softball. But the high socks are a total turnoff. The face paint-y stuff is kinda sexy though."

"So, I did a thing." Shelly glanced around to find parking. She was surprised by the number of cars at the field.

"I'm listening." Samantha laughed on the line.

"I sort of asked Claire if she was busy tonight and she invited me to come by and see her softball game. There may be drinks and dinner later. With or without someone else. She mentioned a *we*, but she told me she was single a few weeks ago. Do you think she has a girlfriend?"

A clicking noise sounded and suddenly Samantha's voice was closer. "Sorry, you were on speaker, and I thought I misheard you. Did you just say you asked Claire out?"

"Well, not exactly. I sort of inquired as to what she was doing later and agreed to be in the same place that she would be." Shelly pulled into the open spot at the edge of the field, slightly hidden by an overgrown shrub.

"This is new and exciting. Tell me more."

"She came by the office late last night. We were working on the Expo thing and I was demonstrating one of the new products, but I shut the lights off in the room and put on a little fireworks display and I think we almost kissed." Shelly shut off the ignition and checked her mascara in the rearview mirror. She had sprung for mascara and some pink lip gloss today, casual but clearly intentional. That was her aim tonight.

"Ooh, this is juicy. Like, are we talking about a literal fireworks display or a figurative one?" Samantha teased.

"Literal. Well, holographic. Not pornographic. But maybe it could have led there. I wore the dress shirt with the braces."

"Say no more. I have excellent taste. And you look great in that ensemble. I assume she noticed?"

"She tugged on them before she left and told me I looked good in them. Then she kissed me on the cheek and thanked me for the fireworks."

"The literal fireworks? Or the figurative ones? One would assume both at this point." Samantha's voice was smooth, contemplative. "I think this is good news."

"Right. Me, too. So, I'm sitting in the car at the edge of the softball field second-guessing my decision to come by, but I'm on to something, right? She must like me, a little."

"I'd say it's worth a shot. Anything else I should know about?"

"She didn't bat an eye when I told her I used to date that barista downstairs. She seemed excited by the information."

Samantha sighed. "Well, I'm glad something positive came out of that. You know how I feel about the bean girl."

"It was a moment of weakness. Lesson learned. I will not stray from the path you have laid out for me again." Shelly nodded, properly chastised.

"Well, so far I'm batting a thousand. Is that a softball or a baseball term? Couldn't tell you. I'm more into dancers, myself." Samantha had that dreamy air in her voice again.

"So I've heard. How's the wedding planning going?" Shelly unbuckled her seat belt and checked her hair in the mirror, just in case it had moved from two seconds ago.

"It's good. We're almost done. Just the countdown now. Well, that and the dreaded seating chart. Any interest in sitting with my mother?"

"Uh, sure." Shelly knew how Samantha and her mother struggled to see eye to eye. She had been surprised when Lucinda had let it slip that the mother was coming to the wedding at all. There had been a little concern that she might make a stink.

"I'm kidding, Shel. I wouldn't subject you to that kind of crazy. She can sit with my brother's brood and my father. In the corner, by the bathrooms." She laughed again, that boisterous carefree chuckle that was so charming. Shelly smiled at the sound.

"I'm so happy for you two. Truly. This is exciting stuff." She meant it. Lucinda and Samantha were just so right for each other. It gave her hope.

"Thanks, Shelly." Samantha sounded genuinely touched. "And just so you know, I have you down for bringing a plus-one. Keep me posted on tonight's events."

"Will do. Catch you later." Shelly disconnected and took a deep breath. She could do this. She could be totally normal and sit in the stands and watch Claire do her athletic thing and it wouldn't be weird. At all. Right?

❖

"Why do you keep looking over at the bleachers?" Jamie elbowed Claire in the ribs before adjusting his batting glove.

"I'm not." Claire totally was. But whatever. She didn't need him pointing it out.

"You are. Who's here?" Jamie did a mini squat and stretched his leg out along the bench. He was up at bat next.

She had spotted Shelly at the top of the third inning. She was seated along the rear of the bleachers, high up and to the center. She noticed that Shelly was wearing the space glasses. They had briefly made eye contact when Claire hit a double at the bottom of the fourth. Shelly gave her a cute little wave and a smile. Claire was glad to have performed so well, though she was aware she wanted to impress Shelly. She'd sort out those feelings later.

"You're staring. Who are you staring at?" Jamie was leaning so close to her that she jumped. Why didn't she notice him creeping up on her? Because she was staring, that's why.

Claire ignored him and tried to look at anyone but Shelly. Too bad he caught her.

"Cute girl in the glasses. Dark hair. Holding a tablet. Who brings a tablet to a softball game?" Jamie squinted in Shelly's direction, a look of recognition washing over his face. "Ha. That's Fireworks, isn't it?"

Jamie had been calling Shelly *Fireworks* since their little discussion at the froyo shop earlier. Claire had taken a half day at work and spent the remainder of the day tasting all her brothers' new flavors. When Shelly texted her asking what she was doing later she had nearly knocked over Jerry's orange cream cup. Since she had admitted to Jamie that she liked Shelly, she had been on her mind. The text felt serendipitous. Not that she believed in that sort of thing.

"It's Shelly. Please don't call her *Fireworks*—I'll die."

Jamie was called up to bat and Claire thanked the softball gods because she knew she was blushing. He just gave her a wink and headed to home plate with an exaggerated strut. To her horror, he turned toward the bleachers and pointed to Shelly, before pointing toward the sky and mimicking a little burst with his hand.

"I'm going to kill him," Claire mumbled as Jamie widened his stance and waited for the pitch.

Strike one.

The bleachers booed. Jamie's home run streak was attracting fans. Tonight was mild, and the sun was setting later and later as the season progressed. There was a good crowd. Shelly was in that crowd.

Strike two.

Jamie stuck his tongue out at the opposing team's pitcher and wiggled his shoulders, waiting for the pitch. Second and third had runners on base. Their team was winning, but only by two runs. They needed to put this game away.

The pitcher shook her head once, twice, then nodded. She wound back and Claire was on her feet, her teammates cheering from the little park's home team dugout.

Boom. Contact was made and the ball flew past the infield and off to the far right. Claire's team leaped into action and Jamie flew around the bases, sliding into home after the other two runners just as the ball soared over the pitcher's mound in his direction.

Claire high-fived her teammates and slapped Jamie on the butt as he jogged by. She looked up to see Shelly standing and clapping, giving her a little wave. She was up at bat next, but it didn't much matter. Jamie had clinched the win, and she just had to finish up clean.

❖

"Shelly!" Claire called out as the bleachers started to empty. They had won 9–5 by the end of the game. She dusted herself off from her race into home and tried to brush back any flyaways that her hair might be doing.

"Hey. Great game." Shelly flashed her those perfect teeth and swept her hair behind her ear.

"Thanks for coming." Claire couldn't figure out why she was a little nervous. Shelly had never made her nervous before. But that was before she realized how kissable her mouth looked with that lip gloss on last night. Which she noticed Shelly was wearing again today, in the daylight, right in front of her.

Shelly walked down the steps and paused, almost hesitating. After a moment she stepped forward and embraced Claire in a soft hug.

"I probably stink, sorry." Claire squeezed her back, but not long enough for Shelly to find out if that assertion was true. She had some pride, after all.

Shelly brushed a little dust off Claire's shoulder and leaned against the railing at the bottom of the bleachers. She had on dark jeans and low-cut boots that she'd paired with a gray and black softball shirt and a leather jacket. She looked...delicious.

Claire reached out and tugged on the bottom of the softball shirt. "Do you play?"

"Play what?" Shelly's gaze was on the hand still holding the fabric of her shirt.

"Softball." Claire tugged a little more, mostly to see what Shelly would do.

"Oh. No. Honestly, I picked this up on the way here—I had no idea what one wears to these things. In fact, I think the tag is still on it." She shifted in her jacket and pulled the collar away from the skin on her neck. "Help?"

Claire laughed and stepped forward, reaching up to extract the tag that was indeed still attached. She braced her other hand along the curve of Shelly's shoulder to break the tag without disrupting the fabric of the shirt. "This is a very soft shirt," she commented absentmindedly as she pulled out the plastic tag attachment and smoothed the material, her fingers dancing along the skin at the nape of Shelly's neck.

"That's why I bought it." Shelly's voice disrupted her from her examination of the silky baby hairs on the back of Shelly's neck, at the base of her hairline. When she looked up, she realized how close they were standing. Shelly smiled, her voice low. "I'm glad you like it."

"I do." Claire became aware that her hand was still at the back of Shelly's neck, gently caressing the skin. She mentally slapped herself to stop and straightened Shelly's collar, sliding her hand along the sleeve of Shelly's leather jacket. "You look nice."

"Thank you." Shelly reached out and squeezed her hand as it reached her cuff, but dropped it quickly as Jamie's voice sounded behind Claire.

"You must be Shelly." Jamie wiped his hand on his pants before extending it toward her. "I'm Jamie, Claire's big brother."

"Littlest big brother." Claire elbowed him in the side, simultaneously annoyed and relieved he interrupted her roaming hands and distracted groping. Although Shelly didn't seem to mind, so there was that.

"Semantics. Anyway, Shelly, are you busy tonight? We always celebrate after I perform like an absolute champion." Jamie gave Shelly his most flirtatious smile; Claire wondered if she could elbow him in the face without it being too obvious.

"Ah, so this is the *we*." Shelly's smile seemed genuine. "I'd love to."

"Great." Jamie clapped and dust flew up into the air. "I think tonight's game got a littler dirtier than I was expecting. What do you say we head back home to get cleaned up and order in some pizza?"

"Uh…" Home? Like bring Shelly to the house Claire grew up in? Claire did her best to convey her panic to Jamie in the subtlest way possible. His encouraging nod meant that he had received the message and then promptly ignored it.

"C'mon. You know how busy Connelly's gets on the second Wednesday of the month. Not to mention, you have a smear of dirt on your face. You a mess."

Claire's hand immediately went to her cheek and he laughed at her.

"You're so gullible." He shook his head and pulled his phone out of the gym bag that was on his shoulder. "We live like ten minutes from here, Shellz. What do you say? Extra cheese and pepperoni okay?"

"Throw in a side salad and I'm in."

"Healthy. I like that." Jamie turned to Claire with a smirk. "Last one to the house has to use Craig's shower."

"Ew. No, Jamie, no." But her complaints fell on deaf ears because Jamie was already jogging back to his car, leaving her in the literal dust again. "Shit." Claire reached out and grabbed Shelly's arm, tugging her to the parking lot. "I am not showering in Craig's nasty stand-up shower. We gotta go. I'll drive."

"Yes, ma'am." Shelly laughed and, to her credit, kept up with the near sprint that Claire forced her into. Claire marveled that she wasn't even out of breath by the time they got to Claire's car.

Claire launched her gym bag in to the backseat and threw the car into reverse, cutting Jamie off at the exit of the park's parking lot. He leaned on the horn and flipped her off but she pulled out and made it through the adjacent traffic light, leaving him behind.

"That'll teach you to cheat," she said to herself.

"Competitive much?" Shelly's voice beside her reminded her she had company. In her car. In the passenger seat. And she had practically kidnapped her.

"Oh my God. Shelly, I'm so sorry. First, you are under no obligation to hang out at my brothers' house and get pizza right now. And secondly, I should have asked you if you wanted to drive yourself or have any real say in the crazy car chase I just forced you into. I am so sorry." Claire slowed her car to a normal speed and put her blinker on to pull over to the side of the road.

"Why are we pulling over?" Shelly looked left and right. "Are we here already?"

"What? No, I was pulling over because I sort of kidnapped you and I wanted to give you a chance to slap me and run away without the vehicle in motion. It's only fair. Go ahead, wind up, I can take it." Claire stuck out her chin for effect.

"Don't pull over unless you want to use Craig's shower. I'm in this crazy rat race to win. Are you a winner or a loser, Claire?" Shelly was teasing her. Claire decided she liked her even more than she did before she kidnapped her.

"I'm totally a winner." Claire turned off the blinker and pulled back onto the main strip, slipping down a side road and taking a hard left. "This will shave two lights off and get us to the back of the house before Jamie even figures out which end is up." She suppressed the urge to laugh maniacally.

"Good." Shelly leaned back in the seat and rested her head on the headrest. In her peripheral vision, Claire could see Shelly studying her. "So, who's Craig? And why is his shower so undesirable?"

"Ha-ha. Oh, right. I kidnapped you and you know nothing about me or the mess you are walking into. Let's start over a little—so, you know I have four brothers, right?"

"I remember this mentioned last night, yes."

"Oh, yeah. Anyway. Jamie and his twin Jerry live in the house I grew up in. My other brother Austin also lives there, but travels a lot for work, so he's not usually home. My oldest brother, Craig, moved out a few years ago and is married with kids. But Craig's room was in the unfinished basement and he has the nastiest and creepiest shower/bathroom setup. No matter how many times we clean and scrub that thing, I swear, spiders reproduce down there and stains continually pop up like they are burned in by ghosts. This shower is so nasty you don't even want to step in there with flip-flops—you would need rain boots and a hazmat suit. For real. Gross." Claire was giving herself the heebie-jeebies just talking about it. She shuddered involuntarily as she banked the last turn a little wide and nearly hit a curb.

Shelly squeaked and covered her eyes. "I was really trying to put on a brave face for you, Claire, but the remainder of this ride will have to be eyes closed if we come that close to a tree again."

"Sorry, almost there, I promise I'll make it up to you later." Claire nearly bit her tongue once the words came out. Well, couldn't take it back now.

As she pulled into the driveway with a screech of her tires, Jamie's car nowhere in sight, she cheered. "Booya. No spider shower for me."

"Uh, Claire?" Shelly looked a little paler than Claire remembered from when she first got in the car. She pointed toward the porch at Jamie, standing there with a huge grin on his face, his hair wet and sloppily combed back.

"Are you freaking kidding me?" Claire was out of the car in a huff, "How did you—"

He started laughing and shaking his head. "Gotcha."

Claire groaned and grabbed her bag out of the backseat, jogging over to Shelly's side to help her out of the passenger seat.

"We lost?" Shelly still looked a little pale. Claire wanted to apologize, but she looked so disappointed about the potential of losing that Claire decided she wanted to kiss her instead.

"No. We won." Claire placed her hand at Shelly's low back and led her toward the porch. "Shelly, this is Jerry, Jamie's identical twin."

"Hi. Nice to meet you." Jerry grinned. "You are so screwed when Jamie gets back. I saw you take that one-way backward—that's cheating."

Shelly stopped walking and whipped her head toward Claire. "When did that happen?"

Claire bit her lip. "Uh, about the time you closed your eyes. That was a wise idea, by the way."

"Your face was freaking priceless, Claire-Bear." Jerry took Claire's bag from her shoulder and shook his head as he laughed. "Jamie called ahead and told me to wet my hair and pretend to be him—he's picking up the pizza instead of having it delivered. Man, you make it too easy..."

Claire huffed and motioned for Shelly to enter before her. "Be glad you're an only child. They terrorize me."

"Only because we love you," Jerry called over his shoulder. "Go shower, I can smell you from here."

Claire winced and gave Shelly an apologetic look. "I will be super quick, I promise. Don't believe anything they tell you. It's all lies, seriously."

Shelly gave her a solemn nod. "I will merely be polite and immediately disregard everything I'm told as hearsay. Promise."

"Thanks"—Claire squeezed Shelly's hand as she turned to go upstairs—"and sorry again for the whole unhinged driver thing."

Shelly's voice stopped her on the bottom step. "It's okay, you can make it up to me later."

Claire stood there for a moment, unable to will her legs to move or her head to turn. She'd set herself up for that one. Game on.

CHAPTER TEN

A nother beer, Shel?" Jamie's voice sounded from the kitchen as Jerry's character in the first-person shooter game jumped from behind a short wall of debris and unloaded holy hell on Shelly.

"Shit." Shelly's character's screen went red, obstructing her ability to see the closest health checkpoint. She was doomed. "Uh, sure," she called over her shoulder as Jerry whooped beside her.

"I thought you would be some gaming genius," he teased as he took a sip of the beer in front of him. "I had higher expectations, to be honest."

Shelly gave him a playful glare. "I'm just warming up. It's been a while since I've been tag-teamed by game sharks."

"Who are you calling a shark?" Jamie plopped onto the couch next to her, handing her a cold beer. "I thought Jerry and I made it plenty clear that we were on a quest of game domination and you were merely target practice. It's important that we hone our skills on peons like you. How else will we remain undefeated? Jerry knows all my moves and vice versa. Bring on the fresh blood."

Shelly laughed into the top of her beer bottle. It had been a long time since she had played war games on the couch with boys. Most of her nights in college started like this. Of course, most of her nights in college ended with her seducing her guy friends' girlfriends. She was both popular and unpopular because of it. Those days felt like ancient memories, though. Somewhere along the line she had developed a nervous stutter when she was around beautiful women—that was what had brought her to Samantha's office so long ago. It had taken lots of introspection and reflection, and therapy, for her to realize it was a defense mechanism, her brain's way of protecting her heart. She had forgotten about the stutter she had developed when her mother had left—she'd struggled for years to overcome it. Distraction was the easiest way to engage her brain mentally, and that's how she had gotten into gaming. Not that she was doing herself any favors in this moment. Jamie and Jerry were destroying her.

She cracked her knuckles and rolled her neck to loosen up. "All right, boys, this shit is about to get real. Give me room." She wiggled in her seat and nudged the brothers playfully to give her more space on the couch. She had been carefully watching their playing habits when her character died for the umpteenth time. Jerry's tell was that he smirked before he used his special skills weapon. Jamie snuck his tongue out of his mouth a little when he was nervous or when his health meter was getting low. She might not know the game terrain as well as them, but she knew how to dodge and deflect like a champ.

By the time Claire finally emerged from the shower and walked back into the room, Shelly had decimated the brothers' scores. Jamie's character had died no fewer than ten times and Jerry had tossed his controller down in disgust about five minutes ago. Last she heard he was freshening up their beers and putting the now cooled pizza back into the oven.

Claire sat next to Shelly with a fatigued huff. "I had dirt in places that I would rather not discuss."

Shelly leaned back against the couch as Jamie cursed next to her, his character dying yet again. "I think that's enough carnage for one night, don't you, Jamie?" She handed him her controller and gave him a soft punch to the arm. "Maybe you'll win next time, champ."

"Looks like I missed all the good stuff." Claire angled her body on the couch so she was facing them both. "Jamie, did Shelly kick your ass?"

"No comment." He frowned and stood with a stretch. "Beginner's luck. I'm going to rinse off since Claire is finally done wasting the world's resources. What were you doing up there, letting off a little steam?" He paused, holding up his hand. "You know what, don't answer that. I don't want to know."

Shelly nearly choked on her sip of beer as Claire launched a couch pillow at Jamie's retreating form, a deep blush spreading on her cheeks.

"I didn't, I mean, I—" Claire looked mortified. Shelly felt a little bad for her.

"It's none of my business what you did up there. No judging here." Shelly extended the still cold beer toward Claire. "Thirsty?"

"Sure." Claire took the bottle and sipped it. "I didn't take you for a beer drinker."

"Meh. I'm pretty go with the flow about things. There were promises of video games and beer. I succumbed to peer pressure. Usually I'm a bourbon girl." She leaned back and turned so she was facing Claire more fully. Claire had on a loose T-shirt and yoga pants, and mismatched socks—one electric blue and the other hot pink. Her hair was still damp in a side braid, which was surprisingly perfect. Shelly reached out to touch it. "How did you get the braid so even?"

"Years of practice. Being the only girl left me with a lot of responsibility to self-groom. It's so much easier nowadays thanks to YouTube tutorials for every little thing. The miracles of modern technology." Claire smiled easily, her blush gone now. She propped her head on her hand and rested her elbow on the back of the couch. She looked so comfortable here, like she was at ease. Shelly was glad she had come over.

She caressed her braid for a moment longer before deciding that this was an oddly intimate thing to be doing in a house where either of Claire's brothers could walk in at any moment; and yet at the same time, she didn't really care. Maybe the beer was catching up to her. She let her hand fall back to her lap, and Claire's eyes followed it.

"Didn't your mother help you with your hair and stuff?" Shelly almost never asked about people's parents because she hated talking about her own. She preferred to pretend she wasn't abandoned and now left to care for a father who was quickly declining. But it had struck her as odd that none of the Moseleys had mentioned their parents. She had seen their portrait in the foyer when she came in. It was curious that Claire's brothers lived in the home she grew up in, and yet no one talked about the missing parents.

"Oh. Not really." Claire looked up at Shelly, her expression sad. "My parents died in a car accident when I was pretty young. My brothers raised me, so a lot of my youth was kind of trial and error."

"Claire, I'm so sorry, I didn't know." Shelly hated herself for asking. The comfortable, peaceful Claire from a moment ago was gone. The Claire who sat before her looked hurt and defeated. Shelly scooted closer, placing her hand on Claire's thigh and reaching up to touch her face. "I'm sorry. That must have been awful."

When Claire closed her eyes as Shelly skimmed her fingers along her cheek, she nearly pulled back, wondering if she had overstepped.

But Claire merely sighed, a few tears escaping. She didn't pull back, she didn't recoil. She was very still, silent. Shelly wasn't sure what to say. She could feel herself starting to panic, feeling a little responsible for how things had changed so quickly. Just like last night when her hologram self had left that message for her father. That was it—that must have been what happened last night, too. The personal message to her dad had affected Claire in that moment as well.

She stuffed down her own anxiety over the moment and tried something that Lucinda had taught her many months ago. She tried to lead by touch, she tried to soothe. She stroked her thumb along Claire's cheek, tentatively at first, her confidence growing as Claire leaned into the contact. She shifted a little, closer still, squeezing the hand on Claire's thigh gently as she spoke. "I'm so sorry. I'm here if you ever want to talk about it. And although the circumstances were less than ideal, I think you should know that you really have perfected the art of the side braid."

Claire laughed and the constellation of tears on her lashes shook loose as her expression lightened. She pressed her hand to the one on her face and squeezed Shelly's fingers with her own as she brushed away the rest of her tears with the back of her other hand, which still loosely held Shelly's beer. "You know just what to say to make a girl feel better."

Shelly caressed her cheek once more before leaning back and pointing toward the beer in Claire's hand. "Can I borrow that for a second?"

Claire nodded and wiped the rest of the tears away as Shelly placed it on the table in front of them. She turned toward Claire and opened her arms. "The hug you gave me at the end of the game today was less than satisfactory. Now that we know you aren't all covered with sweat and athleticism, let's try again."

Shelly mentally high-fived herself when Claire giggled and cuddled closer, slipping easily into her arms and melting there. "You grew up here?" Shelly asked into the still wet hair above Claire's ear as Claire rested her head on Shelly's shoulder.

"Yup. My bedroom is at the top of the stairs to the left. Jamie and Jerry have never lived anywhere else. Austin broke up with his girlfriend last year and moved back in. I couldn't take all the heaviness of living here still. I have an apartment about fifteen minutes away, but I still come hang out here a few nights a week. Even though it's hard sometimes, it's still home, you know?"

"Yeah, I get that." Shelly used to feel that way about her father's house when she was younger. Now the house was old. Just like he was, older now, sicker. She dreaded going over there, and she wondered if Claire felt the same way sometimes about this house. "Sometimes the memories can be too much."

Claire lifted her head from Shelly's shoulder and looked at her. The intensity made Shelly want to retreat. She couldn't remember the last time someone had looked at her so intently—she felt a little exposed, vulnerable. "That's exactly what it feels like."

Shelly held her gaze, studying the blue eyes in front of her. Claire had the longest eyelashes she had ever seen. She hadn't noticed the soft spattering of freckles on the bridge of Claire's nose before. They were so faint you could miss them if you weren't looking closely. "Would you like to have—"

"Dinner!" Jamie and Jerry came into the room shoving each other and laughing as they juggled the now hot pizza and plates. Claire shuffled out from under Shelly's arm but not fast enough.

Jamie gave them a knowing smile. "You two look cozy. Should we eat this in the kitchen? Alone?"

Jerry had the decency to look at least a little embarrassed that they had interrupted them. He cleared his throat and glanced away. Shelly decided she preferred Jerry in that moment.

Claire leaned forward and drank from the beer she and Shelly were apparently sharing now before changing the topic and teasing her brothers. "So, Shelly tells me she pulverized Team Moseley. Care to state your side of the case?"

"Say what? I mean, pulverized is a pretty serious word." Jamie scoffed and plopped into the seat to the left of the couch, placing the pizza on the coffee table and tossing a few napkins at the girls. "I feel more comfortable with *helped us to see our weakness.*"

"Jamie's right. It was an eye-opening experience for sure." Jerry put a slice on his plate and motioned toward Jamie. "Let's be honest, of the two of us, you were really the loser tonight."

Claire held up her hands to block Jamie from throwing his wadded-up napkin at Jerry. "Boys. We have a guest. I think the only way this can truly be settled is by a friendly but competitive game of Mario Kart after dinner. Deal?"

"If you drive your go-kart like you drive your real car, I'm out." Shelly reclaimed the shared beer from Claire and laughed when Jamie hooted.

"Ooh, harsh." Claire handed Shelly a clean plate. "Don't worry, I'll let you win once or twice."

"She's got your number, Claire. Watch out," Jamie said as he took a bite of his pizza and moaned. "This is so good. Best. Pizza. Ever."

Shelly took a bite and had to agree. This was the best pizza and game night ever.

❖

"I'm really glad you texted me today," Claire said as she put her blinker on. Much to Shelly's relief, the return ride to the ballpark to get her car was a much more civilized one.

"Thanks for inviting me to come hang."

"Of course." Claire switched lanes to the left and drummed her fingers along the steering wheel as she hummed quietly. She paused and glanced over at Shelly. "Did I see you in the space glasses earlier?"

"You did." Shelly patted the messenger bag on her lap with her right hand. "I'm still working on finalizing the app for the Expo. I was taking some footage to toy with later on. Daytime recordings require a little more finesse than those taken in dark spaces. This seemed like a good opportunity to test the space glasses out."

Claire nodded and pulled them into the now abandoned parking lot. Shelly's car sat at the edge of the lot, next to a large shrub, right where she had left it. Claire pulled up next to Shelly's car and put the car in park. "I'd like to see it sometime. The footage, I mean."

"Sure. Actually, I have to thank you. After you left last night, I was inspired and figured out a way to get around one of the issues I was having with the app. I worked a little from home today and fixed it. I'm really excited to see how today's footage translates. So thank you." Shelly meant that sincerely.

"Wait, you're thanking me because you were inspired when I *left*? As in, my departure was an inspiration for you? Because that's not really a compliment, Shel." Claire's expression was blank. Shelly couldn't decide if she was joking or really offended. She decided to backtrack.

"No, gosh. No, no. Far from it. I meant that seeing you last night really helped me unlock something that was blocking me. I was inspired. Your *presence* inspired me." Shelly ran her hand through her hair and tried again. "I'm trying to say that you sort of rescued me last night and I'm really grateful. You were the muse I needed in that exact moment."

"I don't think anyone has ever called me their muse before." Claire gave her a small smile.

"I'm happy to be the first." Shelly gave Claire her cheesiest grin. "Just like I was first in Rainbow Road on Mario Kart tonight."

Claire wrinkled her nose at Shelly. "I can't believe you pulled that off. You were third place the entire level." Claire shook her head. "Dethroned by Yoshi, of all characters. I'll be the laughingstock of all Moseley events moving forward. The horror."

"Hey, Yoshi is the cutest little dinosaur ever. You should respect the Yoshster."

"See? Right there? You lost me. Totally nerded out and lost me. All your cool points went out the window."

"Even though I just called you my muse and told you that you totally saved my nerd ass? That's got to get me some brownie points for a later date."

"That's fair." Claire gave her that easy, relaxed smile from earlier tonight. It was quickly becoming Shelly's favorite smile. Claire was watching her closely, her voice a little softer this time. "I knew what you were trying to say before about the muse thing. I was just teasing you."

"You do that an awful lot, don't you?"

The softness remained as Claire asked, "Do what?"

"Tease me."

"I suppose I do." Claire's voice was barely a whisper now.

Shelly let her gaze drop to Claire's lips; they were parted slightly, like they were getting ready to say something else. She mentally implored them to wait, wait until she had a chance to ask what she had been dying to know since last night. "Did you want to kiss me last night?"

Claire's lips parted momentarily before closing again.

Shelly didn't wait for a response before she leaned over the center console of the car and spoke again. "Did you want to kiss me last night, the way I want to kiss you right now?"

Claire licked her lips, her eyes fixed on Shelly's now, her breathing shallow. "Yes."

Shelly felt emboldened. "When you looked at my lips and you were so close, did you want to know if they were soft?" She reached across the space between them and placed her hand on Claire's knee. "Did you wonder if I would kiss you back?"

The muscles of Claire's leg twitched beneath Shelly's fingers, and her knees parted a bit as she exhaled. Shelly massaged the tissue above her knee as she watched Claire's focus dance between her lips and her eyes. She leaned closer. "Tell me, can I kiss you?"

"Yes," Claire breathed out in a hush. "Shelly, I—"

Shelly closed the distance between them, pressing her lips to Claire's. Claire responded immediately, her hand threading up into Shelly's hair, pulling her closer. The kiss was warm and soft; Shelly tried to savor the moment, record it to memory. When Claire pressed into Shelly more forcefully, Shelly moaned at the urgency. She teased her tongue along Claire's lips until Claire opened her mouth and invited Shelly in, deepening the kiss. Claire's hand cradled Shelly's jaw as she reclined, pulling Shelly more onto her lap. Shelly braced her weight with her right hand on the frame of the driver's side door as Claire sucked on her bottom lip, teasing her. Shelly's left hand on Claire's knee rode up as Claire reclined even more into her seat. Shelly's hand now rested on Claire's upper thigh and she was acutely aware of the warmth coming from Claire's center, the thin yoga pants doing nothing to mask the taut muscles twitching and pulsing under her palm. Shelly nearly lost her balance from the precarious position she was maintaining when Claire's hand left her hair and slipped under her jacket, gripping her ribs.

Claire's mouth was insistent against her own and when Claire spread her knees apart that last fraction, Shelly lost her hold against the door frame, slipping back against the steering wheel, the horn honking from the pressure of her back.

Claire pulled back, startled. Her eyes were dark, pupils large. She still had Shelly's jaw cradled in her hand, while the hand at Shelly's ribs dropped to her waist. Her lips were swollen and kiss-plumped. They looked positively edible.

Shelly laughed. "Hold on a second." She kissed Claire quickly before shuffling over to the passenger side of the car again and grabbing her bag. She tossed her bag on top of her car and tugged open Claire's driver's side door. "Come here."

Shelly pulled Claire out of her car with a hand gently clasped at her wrist. She pressed Claire against the frame of the car and guided Claire's hands around her neck as she leaned forward and pressed a soft, lingering kiss to Claire's lips. This was much more gentle, more sensual than the impromptu make-out session in the car. Shelly leaned into Claire, their bodies touching as they separated to catch a breath.

"Well," Claire breathed out. "That happened."

"Mm-hmm." Claire held Shelly close, her hands toying with the skin on Shelly's neck, playing with her hair as they rested on her shoulders. Shelly wasn't sure Claire realized how sensitive that skin was. When Claire had pulled the tag out of her shirt earlier and caressed the skin, Shelly's knees had almost buckled. And here she was again, distracting her ability to function. "Let's make it happen again."

Claire's hand moved to Shelly's neck and Claire leaned in to kiss her. Her thumb slid down below the collar of Shelly's shirt and rested against her collarbone. Her kiss was playful; she teased and nibbled in between gliding her tongue along Shelly's. There was a definite spark between them, and when Claire's other hand abandoned Shelly's hair to pull her closer by her hip, Shelly thought that spark might ignite.

Claire moaned into Shelly's mouth when Shelly shifted, widening her stance so that their hips and breasts were touching as they kissed. Claire's hand was insistent on Shelly's hip, holding her closer and gently rocking them together. Shelly's lips moved from Claire's mouth to her neck when Claire's hand left her collarbone and slipped up under her jacket, grasping her back. Claire was holding her so close now that Shelly wasn't sure she could tell where she stopped and Claire began.

Shelly left hot, openmouthed kisses along Claire's neck as Claire continued to gently rock them together. Shelly became aware of her nipples hardening against the friction between them, making her stomach tighten with want. This was escalating quickly. They were definitely past the spark zone; she could feel that slow burn heating up.

"Shelly, I—" Claire circled her hips as she scratched along the fabric of Shelly's shirt, dragging her fingers down Shelly's spine and provoking a shudder that Shelly couldn't suppress even if she wanted to. "I need to, I—" She dipped her head and captured Shelly's lips with her own, her playfulness a thing of the past as she dominated Shelly's tongue. When Shelly's hand skimmed up Claire's side and brushed against the side of her breast, Claire whimpered and pushed back through the hand on Shelly's hip, separating them by a fraction. She panted into Shelly's mouth. "Okay, time-out, time-out. I need a second."

Shelly pressed a slow, prolonged kiss to Claire's lips, sucking on her bottom lip before she leaned back, letting Claire's hand guide her. Claire put space between them, but not much. Shelly's nipples ached against the deep breaths Claire was taking. The friction made them feel almost too sensitive, raw. Shelly surveyed Claire closely. "Are you okay?"

"What?" Claire blinked like she hadn't heard the question. Her breathing slowed as the hand she had at Shelly's back slipped out from under her jacket. Shelly missed it immediately, the absence of her warmth like a void. Claire rubbed her forehead as she leaned her head back against her car. "Sorry, what'd you say?"

"I asked if you were okay." Shelly stifled the urge to giggle. Claire looked all kinds of flustered.

"Yeah, no. Yes and no." Claire shook her head as she cursed. "How can you be so smart, and so creative, and have *those* eyes, and kiss like that? Like, how is that even fair? How can you have all of those things and still do whatever it is you just did with your mouth?"

"Are those rhetorical questions or—?" Shelly teased and Claire shoved her playfully before pulling her back for a sweet kiss.

"I had a really great night but I have to go before I... Yeah, right. Exactly. Okay." Claire looked like she was struggling.

"On the couch earlier, before your brothers interrupted us, I was going to ask you out. Can I take you to dinner, Claire?" Shelly took Claire's hand off her hip and held it loosely.

"My brothers? Oh, right. Dinner." Claire nodded and entwined her fingers with Shelly's for a moment before letting go. "Okay."

"I'll give you a call tomorrow, sound good?" Shelly knew she should probably try to restrain the grin that was taking over her face, but she didn't think she had the discipline.

"Yes, tomorrow. 'Bye." Claire kissed her quickly on the cheek and ducked back into her car, giving her a little wave before she backed out of her spot and pulled away.

Shelly laughed and ran her hand through her hair as she thought about how the night had unfolded. She grabbed her bag from the top of her car and sank into the driver's seat, the cool leather a stark contrast to the heat she felt just about everywhere. She drove home in silence, playing back the events of the day in her mind. It felt like only minutes before she was pulling into the driveway of her empty house. Tonight had been something else entirely. And it never would have happened if she hadn't taken a chance.

CHAPTER ELEVEN

Shelly found herself humming as the elevator climbed to the top floor, something she couldn't recall ever doing before. But then again, she'd never really had anything to hum about. Now she hummed about a lot of things, or rather, many parts of her hummed about one thing: Claire.

The elevator door opened to Perfect Match's lobby and the receptionist's smiling face met Shelly as she stepped off.

"Hey, Shelly." Sarah stood and gave her a half hug over her desk. "Samantha's just finishing a video call if you want to take a seat."

"Sure, thanks." Shelly walked toward the white leather sofa and eased into it. She pulled out her phone to check some emails when Andrew's voice drew her attention.

"Shelly White, in the flesh. What brings you to our humble penthouse today?" He leaned down and kissed her on the cheek, reaching out to run his hand along her jacket. "This is nice. Did you pick this out yourself?"

Shelly laughed. "No. It's one of those trial garments the personal shopper sends over every few weeks to see if I like the fit and the style."

"And? What do you think?" Andrew pulled her from the couch by her hands and had her turn for him.

"I love the sleeves and the zippers, but I'm not so sure about the chest pockets. I think the color complements my eyes, but I'm afraid it's too long and makes me look like my legs are too short."

Andrew gaped at her, as if unable to believe what she said. "I think the time has come for you to graduate to shopping for yourself. Bravo, my friend. I can honestly say I wasn't sure if this day would ever come."

She laughed and shoved him as Samantha came around the corner. "Hey, don't bruise him, I need him to emcee an event tomorrow." Samantha glided across the room and embraced Shelly. "God, this jacket is to die for. Did Christy send it to you?"

"She did." Shelly looked over at Andrew, who was giving her a silent thumbs-up and motioning for her to continue. "Do you think it's too long in the torso? Does it shorten my legs?"

Samantha stepped back and appraised her outfit more closely. "I think it's fine with dark pants and tall boots, no flats, no capris." She paused. "Wait, do you own capris?"

Andrew burst out laughing and Samantha shot him a look of feigned annoyance.

"Why do I get the feeling I just walked into something?" Samantha's plump lips spread into a casual smile.

Andrew cleared his throat and replied, "You didn't. Shelly came in here like a supermodel and I just wanted to see if she could confidently recite the same concerns to you that she did to me. I told her she's ready to shop for herself. What do you think?"

Samantha nodded. "You've come a long way, Shel. And as much as I'd love to talk about clothing and all things retail related, I have a feeling you're here to tell me about a certain auburn-haired PR exec."

"Ooh, I have a meeting at the Four Seasons." Andrew checked his watch and pouted. "Tell Samantha everything, with detail, so we can talk about you later."

"Okay, will do."

"You're the best." He kissed them each on the cheek and waved to Sarah. "Ciao, ladies."

Samantha grabbed Shelly's arm and pulled her into her office, closing the door and pointing to the chair across from her desk. "Sit. Spill."

Shelly sat down and tried not to nervously tap her foot. "So, the last time we talked I was going to watch Claire play softball."

"Check and check." Samantha sat at her desk and made a note on the paper in front of her. She pulled up something on her computer and glanced back at Shelly. "Go on."

Shelly took a deep breath. "Okay, so I went to the softball game and then we raced Claire's brother back to her parents' house where they live and we played video games and had pizza and then Claire and I made out in the car at the park later."

"You did what now?" Samantha's left hand dropped the pen and she looked up. "Back up—Claire's brothers live with her parents? You met her parents on your first date?"

"It wasn't a date. And no, Claire's parents passed away when she was younger. Her brothers are twins, well, there are four of them, but the twins live there still and one of the older ones, too, Austin I think it was, but his shower is off-limits, so I'm not sure how often he's there." Shelly was counting out fingers on her hand to keep track of everything. When she looked up, she noticed that Samantha had left the other side of the desk and was now perched in front of her, legs crossed at the ankles, giving her an amused look. "What?"

"You just rambled a ton of information at me, the gist of it being that you socialized with her brothers doing something that you enjoy and finding a commonality with them while doing it, and then you ended the night with some alone time with Claire that led to kissing. Am I following correctly?" Samantha's voice was smooth and even. Shelly got the impression she was trying to help her calm down and form coherent sentences. It was working—she felt better already.

"Yep, that's about right." Shelly nodded, grateful she didn't have to repeat herself.

"Good." Samantha smiled and unclasped her hands to rest them on the desk on either side of her hips. "Now, tell me about the brothers."

"The brothers?" Shelly was confused. Maybe they weren't on the same page. There was kissing and groping that should probably be discussed.

"Yes, the brothers. Did you like them? Did they like you? Was it uncomfortable?"

Shelly thought about this for a second. "I think they're great. Claire went to shower upstairs so she could avoid the haunted spider shower in the basement, and I hung out on the couch and played video games with them over beer while they warmed up the pizza. And then Claire came down and we had a nice quiet moment on the couch until they came back in and then we all played as a group for a bit until it was time to head home. Why do you ask?"

Samantha nodded and sat next to Shelly in the other chair. "I asked because you told me Claire had a significant family loss and that you met her brothers on your first date together. A date that ended well and involved you having a pleasant experience with them independent of her and as a group. Something that at times has been a struggle for you to be part of. So family is important to Claire. She invited you into her space, and after the evening ended, she felt comfortable enough to kiss you. Moreover, you felt comfortable enough to kiss her back."

"Huh. I hadn't thought about it like that." Shelly chewed her bottom lip while she considered that. "I still don't know that it was a date, though. I mean, we didn't explicitly define it as a date."

"Sounds like a date to me." Samantha shrugged and encouraged Shelly to continue. "Now tell me about the kissing."

Shelly smiled. She'd been waiting for this part. "It was great. Claire is a great kisser."

"Who initiated what? And was it rated PG or otherwise?"

"I leaned in to kiss her first, but I totally asked permission before I did. And yes, I know, that could have been a mood killer, but I just wanted to make sure because she'd been a little emotional earlier in the night when telling me about her parents and I just didn't want her to feel like I was taking advantage of her," Shelly reasoned.

"Consent is sexy." Samantha gave her a serious nod. "Go on."

"So I leaned across the center console and cupped her face and kissed her. And she kissed me back. It was like opening Pandora's box because the next thing I know she was reclining her seat and pulling me onto her lap and then the horn honked when I lost my hold on the door frame and then of course it made sense to continue making out outside of the car with less restrictions than the confines of the car."

Samantha agreed. "Obviously."

"Right. So there was more kissing. And a little groping. All in all, it was a success." Shelly sighed, remembering the way her lips tingled for hours afterward.

"And you asked her out, or where did you leave off?" Samantha asked.

"I asked her out to dinner. She seemed a little flustered but she agreed, so that's something." Flustered was an understatement. Claire looked like she might spontaneously combust. Shelly hoped it was from the kissing and not from regret.

"So by my estimation, it's been a little over a week. Have you talked to her since?"

"Uh, yes and no. We've been chatting via text and email about the upcoming Expo pretty regularly, but she mentioned she's been busy with work. To be honest, I've been, too. D'Andre has been a little sketchy lately, showing up when he feels like it, leaving early…I was planning on calling her at the end of the week to see if we can get together over the weekend. I don't want to come across as too eager, but—"

"But you like her." Samantha smiled. "I get it. Good. Keep me posted."

Shelly nodded, clasping her fingers in her lap for something to do.

"This seems different this time. Don't you agree?" Samantha leaned back in her chair, her expression curious.

"I'm not following."

"Do you remember what you said to me about Sasha?" Samantha asked.

"Sasha?" Shelly hadn't even considered the attractive firefighter, not once, in months. "What about her?"

"You told me you had great physical chemistry but that you weren't sure if you had anything else that could keep you involved. You said you didn't feel entirely comfortable around her. This thing with Claire, it's completely different, right?"

"Yes. Absolutely. It just feels right." Shelly looked up at Samantha, the realization making her heart beat rapidly in her chest. "She's the one, isn't she? This is what it was supposed to feel like all along. Oh, crap, what if I fuck this up?"

Samantha laughed and took Shelly's hand. "And what if you don't? Shelly, as long as you're honest and patient and give her the benefit of the doubt whenever she needs it, there is no reason that it won't work out. You obviously have a physical attraction and good chemistry, and she trusts you and can be vulnerable around you. Those are some of the hardest things to overcome in a relationship. You need to find out if you can match that vulnerability and then decide if it's right—these things take risks for both parties. Just be yourself, and if she's the right one for you, that will be enough."

Shelly let out a deep breath. "I hope you're right."

"Shelly"—Samantha flashed her that winning smile—"I'm always right."

Shelly smiled at that statement, willing it to be true. She did like Claire, and as far as she could tell, Claire appeared to like her back.

❖

Claire didn't remember anything from the meeting she just walked out of. In fact, she was pretty sure someone had asked her a question that she hadn't even bothered to answer. She was just glad that Lucinda wasn't in today to see her zone out, for a variety of reasons actually: first of all, because it was unbelievably unprofessional, and secondly, because she had hooked up with her client who also happened to be Lucinda's close friend. This was messy.

She closed the door to her office and sank into her chair with a heavy sigh. What was she going to do? She leaned back and let the chair swing idly left and right for a few moments while she tried to collect her thoughts. Everything had been a little off since last week, since Shelly came to her softball game and Claire had ended up in her lap crying on the couch. And then later on Shelly was in her lap in the car kissing her like she was some magical kissing deity sent down to show Claire all the things she had been missing in her previous make-out sessions. Forget about what happened next.

Claire groaned and collapsed forward onto her desk, resting her head onto her folded arms. The next part was what had been driving Claire crazy these past few days. Everything seemed to have gotten away from her. She'd nearly kissed Shelly at Shelly's office, then she'd invited Shelly to come see her play softball. Suddenly there were feelings and heavy conversations and Shelly had said all the right things. But Shelly really believed them, and she was so sincere that Claire wanted to ask how she could convey exactly what Claire had been thinking without being able to put it into words. Shelly was so sweet—she was affectionate and caring but not pushy, and Claire had nearly kissed her again on the couch before the boys interrupted them. Who almost kisses someone after crying on their shoulder? Especially if that someone is practically a stranger? But Shelly wasn't a stranger, not really. Claire had spent almost two months getting to know her through this project and she had found her to be sensitive and funny and unbelievably hot when she got all techno-geek and built a projector out of a CD case.

And then there was the way Shelly was with her brothers. She got along with them so well. She had annihilated them over video games. Her brothers had gone on and on about Shelly after that night. They really liked her. Claire couldn't remember any other time when her brothers liked someone she was interested in. But was she interested in Shelly? Or was she caught up in everything that happened?

No. She was definitely interested in Shelly. It was only compounded by the fact that her brothers liked Shelly and that she adorably bought a softball shirt to fit in with the crowd while still nerding out and collecting footage for the app they were working on together. Because they were colleagues. Working on a project together. Claire's first solo project, in fact.

"I'm so fucked." Claire lifted her head and pressed the heels of her hands into her eyes out of frustration. She cradled her head in her hands as she let herself acknowledge what the biggest issue was from the whole night. She had very nearly climaxed while making out with Shelly White.

It had started out innocently enough—she'd noticed Shelly's eyes and her sweet nature and her sense of humor. Then she was at her softball game and in her childhood home playing with her brothers. Then they were talking closely in the car and Shelly asked her if she wanted to kiss her and she admitted that she did. All of a sudden Shelly was kissing her and Claire was trying to find a way to get flat because Shelly's hand on her thigh was making her brain scramble. The next thing she knew they were outside the car and Shelly was up against her with that mouth doing unbelievable things to every part of Claire she could reach. Before she knew it she was grinding up against Shelly. She didn't even realize she was doing it. When Shelly's hand skimmed her breast she nearly lost it. What kind of grown woman nearly comes while kissing someone against a car like a horny teenager?

A knock at her door disrupted her train of thought. "Claire?"

Claire spun in her chair to find Lucinda standing in her doorway. "Lucinda, hi. What's up?" She did her best to sound like she wasn't having a breakdown: cool, calm, and collected.

"Hey. I was just popping in to pick up some files to review and I wanted to check on how things were going with Boston Pro App."

Of course she did. "Things are great, really good. I sent over some preliminary specs and projection ideas to Shelly and I'm just waiting on her feedback." That was mostly true. Except she already had Shelly's feedback—she loved it. They were supposed to meet once more this week to finalize a few things before the materials were ordered. That would be their first time face-to-face since that night. Claire wasn't even entirely sure she could look Shelly in the eye.

"Claire?" Lucinda sounded concerned. Shelly must have said something, crap.

"Sorry, I'm nursing a little bit of a headache. What did you say?" That part was true—she definitely had a headache, but she had a feeling it was from all the Shelly thoughts swirling inside her cranium.

"Are you feeling okay? I can call in one of the junior associates to help you out if you need to leave for the day." Lucinda's concern remained evident. Claire felt bad.

"No, I'm fine. Just a bad night's sleep." Or eight. "You were saying?"

"I said, I'm glad things are moving along so smoothly. Shelly mentioned to me she felt like you were doing great work. I'd like to see the final specs when they're ready."

"She said that?" The words tumbled out before Claire could stop them. She managed to stop herself from asking just when exactly this conversation had occurred. Whether it was before or after the kissing.

"She did. In fact, she told me you had been pivotal in the debugging process of the software she's working on. Something about helping her see something from a different angle. Good work."

Claire wondered if that different angle was the one where she was flat on her back in the driver's seat with Shelly on top of her, or the angle of Shelly's hip positioned against her clit when she was pinned to the car—

"Well, I've got to head out. I'm glad things are going well. Let me know if you need any help from me or the other execs. If that headache doesn't clear up, head home. No use torturing yourself—it's a Friday, after all. 'Bye, Claire." Lucinda gave her a brief wave and closed her door.

Claire stared at the closed door for a few moments contemplating what to do next. She couldn't focus because she felt like she needed to talk to Shelly. But she wasn't exactly sure what to say. She had agreed to have dinner with her, and yet, she hadn't responded to Shelly's attempt to schedule anything, instead choosing to hide behind work like a coward. The longer she put off this conversation, the worse her distractibility seemed to get. Her head throbbed and she felt sick.

"That's it, I'm calling it." Claire stood and immediately regretted the motion as the room swayed—she clutched at the chair back to steady herself. "I can't just sit here and freak myself out." She stood her ground and took a deep breath. "Good talk."

Claire packed up her belongings and called the main administrator to let her know that she was leaving for the day with a headache. She had to sort this shit out, and fast.

❖

Shelly sat in her recently commandeered conference room and thought about the benefits of having four walls and a door. She had worked out of a cubicle for her whole time running this company because she liked to be among her employees, working alongside them. D'Andre had always had an office. She'd felt a divide between him and the employees, and sometimes she assumed it was because of the walls he kept between them and him. But she was growing to like the walls. The privacy. It gave her a chance to think. Maybe that wasn't such a good thing these days, though, since all she ever seemed to think about was Claire and the soft little whimpers she let out when they kissed last week. That kiss. That kiss had been electric. It was everything and more than Shelly had expected, and yet Claire seemed to be avoiding her a little—something she became more aware of after Samantha asked about it yesterday at their meeting. She wasn't sure how to feel about that. So her mind wandered, behind these new walls, in a way that the cubicle would not have allowed. Alone with her thoughts in a conference room with memories of fireworks and Claire Moseley.

D'Andre opened the door while he knocked. "You busy?"

Shelly glanced around the empty room at the stack of papers in front of her. The screen to her tablet had gone black—that meant the screen saver had timed out. She wondered how long she had been staring off into space before he arrived. "No, I'm free. What's up?"

D'Andre came in and sat in Claire's seat. The thought would have amused her if it didn't mildly irritate her. D'Andre had been ghosting in and out of here for weeks. When he'd arrived this morning, he'd locked himself in his office and closed the blinds. Suddenly now, after months of skirting the issue, he wanted to talk.

"How's the project coming along?" he asked.

"Fine. Good. It's still got a ways to go, but…" Shelly wasn't sure why she bothered to say anything. He had made it very clear that she was on her own about this. That irritated her as well.

"Listen, I won't blow smoke up your ass and tell you it's going to be great, because we both know you are a mad genius scientist and will get it done in a way no one but you can, but regardless, I'm proud of you for trying something new. And I'm sorry I didn't support you earlier. You deserve better than that." D'Andre seemed genuine, but Shelly felt uneasy.

"Thank you." She shifted in her seat. "Why do I feel like there's a *but* about to follow that statement?"

"No buts." He shrugged. Something was wrong.

"What's going on? Are we breaking up?" Shelly tried joking to ease her tension.

His face dropped. "Maybe not breaking up. Just taking a break."

"What? I was kidding. Why are you not kidding back at me?" Shelly leaned forward, focused. D'Andre looked different—tired. He looked older and a little meek. Since when did Dre look anything but confident and cocky?

"I need some time off, Shel. I need a break." D'Andre folded his hands on the table in front of him. This suddenly felt very rehearsed.

"What does that mean exactly? You own half of this company, Dre. How exactly do you expect to take time off?"

D'Andre shrugged. "I don't know. I just am. I can't do this right now. You'll figure something out, I'm sure."

"Figure something out? What?" Shelly felt her blood pressure rising. She bit her tongue to refrain from saying something she shouldn't. Benefit of the doubt, she reminded herself, give him the benefit of the doubt. "Are you sick? Is something wrong?"

"No, I'm fine." D'Andre leaned back in his seat and crossed his legs. "I just need to get out from under all this responsibility for a little bit. You know, live some of what life has to offer. I need to reevaluate things."

Shelly just looked at him. She wasn't sure what to say. On the one hand, she completely got the fact that maybe he wanted to take an extended vacation to clear his head. She had thought about that lots of times. On the other hand, he was dumping this entire business in her lap. A business that he primarily ran while she worked on the products. They were a team. The Expo was around the corner; this could not happen at a worse time.

"Dre. While I appreciate your desire to live on a beach in Tahiti drinking mai tais with a beautiful woman or women, that's your business. But I have to ask, what brought this on? I mean, you have never had trouble taking extended vacations before, even for multiple weeks at a time. What's different now?"

He exhaled, the tiredness from before more evident now. "Because this time, I'm not sure I'm coming back."

Boom. There it was. This might not just be some time off. This might be *all* the time off.

"You're fucking with me, right? Like one of our nanny cams is hidden in that plant over there, right? Because you wouldn't just come into the room and tell me you were quitting *our* business like it was no big deal, right? Tell me I'm right, Dre. Tell me I'm not about to be the only captain of this ship."

D'Andre stood from the chair with a frown. "I'm sorry, Shelly. I'm not ready to make any final decisions, but I need to get away for a while. You'll figure it out. You're smart. The smartest. And let's not kid ourselves, you've been the captain of this ship all along."

"Dre, wait. Let's figure something out. We can work this out." Shelly wasn't sure what the point was—D'Andre was notorious for making his mind up about something and never revisiting it. He was so stubborn that way.

"It'll all work out. I'll be in touch. I drafted an email for the staff to let them know I'll be away for a bit. I'd appreciate it if you kept the details vague. I organized all my files and my schedule for you on this flash drive. Good luck with your hologram app, Shel. Really, super-innovative stuff. I'll have my lawyer call you." D'Andre placed a flash drive on the desk and gave her a sad wave before leaving and closing the door behind him.

"What. The. Literal. Fuck." Shelly stared at the flash drive for a minute before she launched out of her seat to grab it. She jammed it into her tablet, jarring it awake just in time to see D'Andre's email go out to the entire interoffice webmail. Within seconds everyone would know he was taking a sabbatical. Whatever that meant.

D'Andre's files filled the screen. Detailed notes in the sidebar lined all the pages. He had obviously been tying up loose ends. She flipped through his calendar and saw that it was essentially empty. She scrolled back to two months ago. He had been slammed. Every hour was filled with phone conferences or meetings. On-site and off-site. She scrolled forward a bit; gradually his days started to lighten, with fewer and fewer meetings popping up. Little notes about handing clients off to some of the employees were written in D'Andre's slanted script. Huh, he was using their writing technology with their scheduling system. The one they had worked on together. The one Shelly had slaved over to perfectly reflect D'Andre's idea of sophisticated note taking and agenda organization. D'Andre had effectively erased his position in the company right under her nose without her even noticing it.

She'd been so busy pursuing some pipe dream of developing new software to help capture life's moments in real time that she had fucking missed her business partner checking out on her. What was she going to do now?

CHAPTER TWELVE

Claire pulled up to the sports club and looked around a bit. Shelly's little coupe roadster was parked up front, but save for a few other cars, the lot was mostly empty. She exited her vehicle and walked toward the front door but it was locked. She leaned forward and peered through the glass. A young twentysomething guy was sitting at the desk, his feet up and his hands folded over his chest. He was watching something on the monitor in front of him. Claire could see bright blue Beats headphones on his ears. She looked back at the door and noticed the newly printed sign hanging on the inside of the glass—the gym was closed early due to a maintenance issue. That explained the lack of cars. And yet Shelly's car was there and this kid was obviously here, so...

She knocked on the glass and tried waving to get his attention. He laughed at the screen and continued to not notice her. After she'd left her office, she had called Shelly. Five times. She was afraid if she didn't see her today, she would lose her nerve and that was not an option. When Shelly didn't answer her cell or work phone, she shot her off a text. Then an email. Then she decided to swing by her office thinking that maybe she was just working with the engineers and computer geeks on the apps and was in the design space. At about the time she was walking through into Boston Pro App's waiting room she realized that her behavior was probably kind of stalker-like. And yet, she wasn't all that put off by it. Shelly never ignored her calls.

She banged on the glass again, louder this time. Beats boy looked up, alarmed. He fumbled out of his reclined position and stood, nearly falling backward when the cord of his headphones halted his progress. He gave her a bashful smile and jogged to the door.

"We're closed," he shouted through the glass, pointing to the sign.

"I know," Claire replied, pointing toward Shelly's car. "Is she here?"

His gaze followed her hand and he nodded, unlocking the door. "Yeah. Come in."

Claire stepped through the doors and looked up at him. He was much taller than he'd appeared while lounging. She read his name tag before addressing him. "Thanks, Max."

"Sure." He shrugged and locked the door behind her. "She's been at that for over an hour."

"Who has?" Claire followed him to the desk where he plopped down.

He pointed to the monitor. "Ms. White."

Claire looked past the laptop he had perched on the desk that had some clip paused on it. She recognized the frozen figure as an adult cartoon that her brothers watched, *Bob's Burgers*, or something. Beyond the screen was a smaller monitor—it had scrolling views of security cameras positioned throughout the complex, giving different angles with time stamps in the corner. The screen flickered and a new set of hallways and exercise rooms cycled through. They were all empty except for one corner room. Claire could see Shelly's outline feverishly hitting balls against the wall. She was relentless in her pursuit of the ball. The image shifted and a new view of the room vibrated, the picture distorted.

"What's with that one? Why is it moving?" Claire realized she was leaning way over the desk into his personal space; she leaned back.

"Oh. Ms. White likes to listen to music. Loud. She plugs it into the wall with the north camera. Usually the vibrations completely impair the video feed. Everyone else just uploads a playlist but she brings her own speaker unit." He reclined in his chair, propping his feet up again.

"What kind of music?" Claire realized she had no idea what Shelly would listen to, let alone work out to.

"Thirty Seconds to Mars, Panic! at the Disco, Fall Out Boy, Paramore, lots of alternative rock. The usual." He was scrolling through the laptop, half paying attention to her.

"That surprises me," Claire said to no one in particular, but he looked up at her.

"She always works out to rock music. She's probably the chillest person in this place." Max furrowed his brow. "Is she expecting you?"

"No." Claire wasn't sure why answering that made her a little panicky.

He sat forward and examined her briefly. "She knows you, though, right?"

"Yeah, yes."

"Cool." Max seemed convinced and began to put his headphones on before he stopped. "You can head down if you want. It's through the door over there. Tell her I'll lock up when she's all set."

"Thanks." Claire walked past him as he resumed his program, laughing under his breath as the cartoons moved across the screen. She went through the door he directed her to and walked along the empty corridors, following the sound of angry rock music. Shelly was in the last room on the left. All the other rooms were uninhabited and dark. Claire noticed that the corner room had fewer viewing windows, and a privacy screen was partially obstructing her view through them. Partially.

She bent forward to look through the exposed portion of the glass. Shelly continued her assault on the ball, lunging to the side to volley it and send it back to the wall to rebound. Her hair was swept up into a long, dark ponytail. She was in shorts and a sports bra. Her back and shoulders glistened with sweat as she darted to the side and then back to the middle again. Claire let herself admire the lean lines of Shelly's muscles, the ripple of her deltoids when she served. She watched Shelly's bicep twitch as she turned to the side to return the serve with a fierce forehand swing, banishing the racquetball to the corner. It occurred to her that she had never thought of Shelly as athletic. Although, considering she had sprinted or been dragged to Claire's car last week without even breaking a sweat, it shouldn't surprise her. Not like she could ever forget about last week even if she tried.

Shelly turned toward her and she instinctively ducked out of the window view. She realized she was kind of being a creeper. A little. Okay, a lot. And how did she also neglect to notice how cut Shelly's abs where? Like, seriously. The little bit she saw before she hid in the shadows like a pervert was really impressive.

A loud thump caused her to jump back from the window. The privacy shade retracted into itself and the small area of window exposed quadrupled. She leaned forward and peered and noticed Shelly on her knees, seeming to catch her breath. After a short period, Shelly stood and walked toward the speakers. She cut the music off abruptly and grabbed a towel off a bench in the corner, walking straight toward Claire.

❖

Shelly wound back and whaled the ball into the wall in front of her. She had been punishing herself for well over an hour, beating the sense out of every ball at the racquetball gym, doing drills as if her life depended on it. It felt like it did.

She grunted as the ball rebounded at an awkward angle and she had to chase it to keep it in play. The force with which her backhand hit the ball sent a violent vibration up her wrist to her elbow. She ignored the ache and swung again, this time sending the ball flying behind her, out of reach.

"Fuck," Shelly screeched, launching her racket across the court to the far wall. She slumped to the ground in a heap and let her head droop. She was exhausted. Emotionally and physically exhausted. She had replayed her conversation with D'Andre over and over until it started to blur together on her. She hated herself for not realizing something was wrong. She hated herself for being blindsided. She hated him for abandoning her.

Her legs burned and her shoulders felt like they were weighted with cement. She had tipped the guy at the front desk to make sure she could be in the corner court, the one with only one viewing window, for as long as she damn well pleased to be in here. Her body was fatiguing. But her mind still swirled—even in its weariness, it swirled and swirled. In that moment, she hated that part of herself, too.

She sat there for a few moments, catching her breath as she tried to calm down the waves of acid that burned inside her. It wasn't like her to lose her cool like that. She couldn't remember a time when she had thrown her racket in disgust before. Of course, she couldn't remember a time feeling this fucking alone either. Well, that wasn't entirely true; she had felt this way when her mother had left.

Shelly groaned as she stood from the ground, her body protesting, her muscles aching and throbbing. Slowing down had let the pain settle into her joints. Her adrenaline was wearing off. She stumbled toward the back wall to retrieve her racket, hoping it was still intact. Not that that mattered, she mused. She could always buy another one. Or a million. Because she had all this money and all this time and yet no one to share it with and no partner to celebrate her successes with. She had assumed that was why that stutter had returned when she had first met

Samantha. She was so desperate to find a mate, so desperate to find a partner in life, that she wanted it so badly, it seemed unachievable. The stuttering of her youth had resurfaced because she so wanted something that she didn't think she would ever get, so old habits reemerged. And yet, still, after all these months, she was alone.

She picked up the discarded racket. It was dented, but not destroyed. She would donate it to the club and pick up a new one on the way out. She looked at the wall for damage—nothing to speak of, but she had knocked the privacy screen off the only view window. It was askew, and she could see the corridor toward the locker rooms illuminated. The gym had been closed for some time due to the water issue with the showers. Max was undoubtedly asleep at the front desk by now. She probably should head out.

She shut off her music and grabbed a towel from the bench by the door and looked back at the carnage of balls strewn about. She must have taken two dozen in with her. They were everywhere. She would tip Max extra as she left, unsure if she could even bend and pick them all up. Not that she was particularly inspired to anyway.

As she trudged toward the door, a slight movement at the glass drew her attention. Claire was there, giving her a wave with a small smile. Shelly felt the dark cloud that was her mood lift a little—this was an unexpected surprise. She worried whether Claire had seen her little tantrum. She decided to pretend it never happened.

She pulled open the door and tried not to wince when her biceps burned. "Hi. This is a pleasant surprise."

"Hey." Claire stayed in the doorway.

"You can come in, if you'd like." Shelly stepped back and motioned for her to enter.

Claire stepped in and brought a rush of cold air with her. Shelly was only then aware that she was nearly naked, the sweat on her skin causing it to prickle and shiver with the temperature change. She imagined the room to be pretty dense with humidity from the amount of work she had exerted in there. It had become a regular habit of hers to jack up the thermostat in her court—the heat helped her stay warm and limber. Lucinda had taught her that little tidbit. It had really changed her training and her game play.

Shelly pressed the towel to her abdomen, more to slow the shiver than to absorb her sweat. The sweat meant she had done her work in there, the sweat meant she had earned that fatigue. She was aware of Claire's eyes on her, and the awareness warmed her a bit. She dried off her chest and face, draping the towel over her shoulder as she stood, unsure of where to put her hands now that she had stopped moving. They ached a little. She bet that blisters would form by morning—her hands felt raw.

"I didn't know you played racquetball. You know, come to think of it, I don't know what you do outside of coding and being a magical computer unicorn."

"You say all the right things, you know that?" Shelly crossed her arms just to give them something to do. Part of her wanted to take Claire's hand; another part of her wanted to be held. Today had been a long day. A thought occurred to her. "How did you find me?"

"Toby. I stopped by the office when you didn't return my texts—he told me you left early and said you were heading to the gym. I may or may not have tickled the details out of him. He may or may not have screamed like a little girl. But I've probably been sworn to secrecy, so you shouldn't ask me any details," Claire replied with a playful smile.

The smile was contagious, until Shelly realized Claire said she stopped by the office. She wondered what that was like. She had stayed after D'Andre left to do a little damage control, but she realized that she was feeling a little off. So she'd ducked out as well. Some captain, she thought.

"Oh. Sorry about the texts—my phone is off. How was Toby? You know, before you emasculated him with the tickling."

"He seemed a little distracted. Said something about everything going to shit. I assumed that was about his girlfriend or school. You know, come to think of it, he had been staring off into space when I got there. Did something happen at the ballet?"

"The ballet?" Shelly was lost. She should have stayed at the office. Leaving to go beat the living shit out of balls wasn't very leader-like.

"You gave him tickets to the ballet to take his girlfriend. I'm invested—how did it work out?" Claire leaned against the wall, her ankles crossed. Shelly thought she looked nice today.

"It went well. She thought he was a total stud, very romantic. Lucinda really came through for him." Shelly looked around for her shirt, suddenly a little self-conscious. She found it off to the side in a corner by her gym bag. It was a little damp. She grabbed her zip-up hoodie instead, shoving the damp shirt into the bag while digging out her cell phone. When she caught Claire watching her zip the hoodie closed, she stopped just above her navel, leaving it open a little. Because, why not?

"Right. Good." Claire's gaze met hers.

Shelly turned on her phone and watched Claire while it loaded, then slipped it into her pocket. Claire was giving her a friendly face, but she seemed a little preoccupied. Like something was on her mind. "Everything okay?"

"I don't think I've seen you with your hair pulled back—it's nice." Her smile didn't reach her eyes.

Shelly shifted uncomfortably. She zipped the hoodie closed a little more. Claire's eyes followed. "Why do I get the distinct feeling that's not the reason you came to find me?" After their impromptu make-out session, Shelly had worried that Claire was having second thoughts. They had texted back and forth, but Claire hadn't committed to dinner. In fact, the more she let herself obsess about it, the more Shelly was convinced that Claire might have felt like it was a bad idea. Something Claire seemed to be expressing right this very moment even if she didn't mean to. But then again, Shelly was pretty sure she had seen Claire checking her out a least twice since she invited her onto the court. She took a step forward and reached out for Claire's hand.

Claire took her hand and stroked it gently. She turned Shelly's palm over and gave her a pained expression. "You're bleeding."

Shelly looked down. Two blisters had formed on her hand and had opened. She didn't feel them, though; she was only aware of the warmth of Claire's hand. It was soothing. "Doesn't hurt." Shelly felt the sudden urge to cry. She couldn't remember the last time someone had shown her genuine affection and concern. The intensity of today stung at the back of her eyes; her exhaustion must have been catching up with her.

Claire cradled her hand and closed her eyes, letting out a heavy sigh. "Shelly, we need to talk."

Shelly felt a lump form in her throat. That was never a good start to a conversation. She couldn't get any more bad news today. She examined Claire, willing her tears to stay put. She and Claire were so close again—she never understood how they always ended up so close. And yet here they were, just inches away from each other. Shelly whispered, "Don't. Not today."

Claire gave her a confused look.

Shelly stepped closer, taking her free hand and running it along Claire's face. Her desire to be comforted overcame her fear of initiating contact with Claire. She paused at Claire's cheek and leaned forward to kiss her. Soft and pleading.

Claire kissed her back but kept her distance. She loosely held Shelly's hand in her own, but pressed her palm to the exposed skin of Shelly's chest when Shelly leaned forward. "Wait. I can't. I can't do this. I'm sorry. I can't date you, Shelly. I can't kiss you. I can't. I'm sorry."

Shelly closed her eyes and tried to compose herself, but the weight of the day was too much for her. Claire's statement was the very last straw and the tears flowed freely now. She kept her eyes closed for fear that if she looked at Claire, the image would never leave her. She didn't want to be heartbroken *and* haunted.

"Shelly." Claire's voice was soft. The hand on Shelly's chest slid up to cradle her head and jaw. Shelly turned into it, pressing her face against the soft skin of Claire's palm, letting it soothe her.

She chanced opening her eyes. Claire looked so concerned, caring. Her words didn't match her actions. Her face, that beautiful face, was close to Shelly's, examining her. Shelly released Claire's hand to hold the one to her cheek a little more firmly. She turned her head and pressed a kiss to Claire's palm, watching Claire carefully. Claire sighed, her thumb stroking Shelly's cheek. She seemed to be fighting with herself. Shelly couldn't take any more fighting today.

"Come home with me, Claire."

Claire's eyes widened a little but she stayed close, her hand still cupping Shelly's face. She opened her mouth to reply, but said nothing.

Shelly shifted forward, moving Claire's hand from her cheek to her chest. Her heartbeat raced under the pressure of Claire's hand, and she entwined their loosely held hands more tightly, pulling them closer. Her tears slowed. She wanted this. "Come home with me," she repeated. "I need you. Please."

Claire was watching the hand Shelly held to her chest. Her tongue ran over her still-parted lips as she looked into Shelly's eyes. Shelly decided this was her last chance.

"Come home with me." Shelly kissed her again, and this time Claire embraced her, her hands separating from Shelly's skin only long enough to wrap around her. Their kissing was unhurried, soft, needing. Shelly needed this, needed to be cared for tonight. She kissed Claire until she felt her tears were done falling. She sucked on Claire's bottom lip briefly before leaning back, appraising her. "Let's go."

Claire gave her a small nod. Shelly kept their hands clasped as she reached for her gym bag and led Claire to the door. They walked in silence through the corridors, up to the main entrance.

Max was yawning at the desk with his feet propped up, watching his laptop as they approached. He pulled off his headphones and gave Shelly a broad grin. "All done, Ms. White?"

She released Claire's hand to dig through her gym bag, pulling out her wallet and car keys. "You know I hate when you call me that, Max. It sounds like I'm a character from *Clue*." She placed two hundred dollars on the counter in front of him. "I left the court full of balls and my old racquet. The club can keep the racquet—I'm due for a new one. The privacy screen got knocked off kilter a bit. I'm going to leave my car here until tomorrow, so have the manager call me if he needs it moved."

Max looked from the cash to her and gave her a questioning look. "I'll clean up, no problem. You sure, Ms.—Shelly?"

She nodded, pushing the money toward him. "I'm sure. Thanks for keeping the gym open for me. Don't let them give you any trouble—if they balk about it, tell them I forced you."

Max took the cash and started to pack up his things. "It's all good. I clocked out and shut off the night monitoring systems forever ago—the cameras are doing security scrolls, but not filming. No one's going to be any the wiser."

Shelly was glad to hear that. She was sure the cameras had caught her and Claire kissing. She reached for Claire's hand and started to leave before pausing to ask, "How's school, Max?"

"It's good. Almost done. I'm having some trouble with one of my engineering projects but I think it'll work out." He gave her an optimistic shrug.

"If it doesn't, let me know and you can come hang with one of my engineers to go over it, sound good?"

"Really? Yeah, awesome, thanks." He pulled on a baseball cap and jogged over to the door to unlock it and let them out. "'Bye, Shelly, thanks again."

She gave him a quick smile and pulled Claire by her hand into the parking lot as he locked the door behind them and disappeared. She paused in front of Claire's car and kissed her once because she needed it to feel grounded. "Ready?" She wasn't sure if she was asking for herself or for Claire.

CHAPTER THIRTEEN

Shelly's hand rested on Claire's thigh as Claire drove. Shelly had quickly typed her address into Claire's GPS when Claire started the car, but otherwise she'd been quiet, and still. Except for the hand she had resting on Claire's thigh, which soothed and massaged intermittently. Claire glanced over at Shelly in her passenger seat, her eyes closed, her head back against the headrest. She wondered what Shelly was thinking. Really, she wondered what she was doing herself.

Claire had had every intention of seeing Shelly tonight and letting her know they couldn't be together. That she was far too worried about the consequences this would have on her career to be able to commit herself fully. But things hadn't worked out that way. She had been warring with herself for over a week, trying to figure out what to do. She could convince herself that she wasn't attracted to Shelly when they were apart, but the moment they were together, her brain stopped working. It was absolutely undeniable. She was attracted to Shelly with every cell in her body, and the minute they were near each other, nothing else really seemed to matter.

She turned her car onto a quiet street with perfectly manicured lawns and long sweeping driveways. The homes were spaced far enough apart for privacy but near enough to each other to remind her that they were still in close proximity to Boston proper. Shelly shifted next to her as they approached the GPS destination; it had only taken about fifteen minutes to get here. Long enough for Claire to get lost in her own thoughts, not that she thought of much else other than the way Shelly's hand felt on her leg.

"Pull up to the garage—we can go in through the front." Shelly's voice was soft; she sounded vulnerable. Claire had never seen her so exposed as she had at the gym. There was something almost desperate in the way Shelly told Claire that she needed her. It sparked something in her, a desire to protect her, to ease her, to take care of her. It made her realize that she *wanted* Shelly to need her. She wanted to be the one Shelly reached for. And since that realization, she had not released contact with Shelly for any significant period of time. It felt right.

Claire pulled up to the garage and turned off the car. Shelly's home was gorgeous, red brick with white shutters and polished black accents. A two-car garage was attached to the two-story home, its front as immaculately maintained as the house. The walkway to the front door was lined with blossoming flowers and shrubs, carefully shaped and cared for. Solar LED lights framed the path as they got to the front steps, flickering as the sun started to set on the day.

Shelly released Claire's hand long enough to adjust the bag on her shoulder and open the front door. She discarded the bag and her sneakers at the entrance, holding her hand out for Claire's as she waited for Claire to follow her.

As Claire took off her shoes and placed her purse on the table by the front door, a melodious little meow sounded to her right. Shelly slipped her hand back into Claire's as Claire said, "Well, hello there. What's your name?"

"That's Hedy LaMeow. How was your day, Hedy?" Shelly regarded the cat with affection.

The gray and black striped tabby cat wove between her legs, rubbing her head along the outside seam of her skinny jeans. The cat paused as if to examine Claire's mismatched socks. Green eyes looked up at her expectantly.

"Ah, you have green eyes just like your mama. Lady-killer." Claire stooped to scratch under Hedy's chin. "I see your judgment about my socks and choose to disregard it because you have the cutest face ever." She tapped Hedy on the nose. "Matching socks are the fashion of the uninspired, Hedy. Remember that."

"She's more of the nudist type, herself," Shelly said next to her. Hedy purred loudly as she circled their feet, pausing periodically to head-butt Claire's shin.

"She's so friendly." Claire resisted the urge to scoop Hedy up and take her with them. Claire realized she wasn't exactly sure where that would be. Or what they were going to do now.

"She likes you." Shelly gave her a small smile and pulled on Claire's hand. "Or she's hungry. It could go either way."

"Food-motivated affection? I can dig it." Shelly led them into an open-concept kitchen toward the end of the hall. Hedy bounded in after them and waited by her food bowl, purring and swaying slightly.

Shelly released Claire's hand and poured them each a glass of water. She filled Hedy's water bowl and put some food in her dish, scratching her little head as Hedy started eating. "Hey, princess."

"Hedy's a great name." Claire sipped the water Shelly had given her and leaned against the counter. She felt a little nervous, but not the bad kind of nervous, just, like, a low buzzing. Like she was excited sort of. She wasn't sure what she was at the moment.

Shelly leaned against the island across from her, their sock-covered feet touching. "I named her after Hedy Lamarr. She was a Hollywood starlet who moonlighted as a technological genius. She's credited with developing a frequency-hopping technology that went on to be the foundation of Wi-Fi and Bluetooth and digital communication as we know it. And she did this, and more, while using her good looks and talent to be a Hollywood legend. She was light-years ahead of her time and truly revolutionary."

"That's fitting." Claire watched with amusement as Hedy continued to purr while she ate. "How old is she?"

"Six or seven. I found her in my backyard one day. I guess you could say she chose me."

"She's perfect. And those eyes…" Claire looked up from Hedy to find Shelly watching her.

Shelly stepped forward and took the glass from Claire's hand, placing it on the counter. Her hand trembled as she traced her fingers along Claire's arm. Claire reached out and touched her face, trying to reassure her. Reassure her of what, though? That wasn't quite clear.

"What happened today? What's wrong?" Shelly was looking at her so intensely she felt bare. Shelly blinked, and her eyes looked wet. She decided Crying Shelly might be the most heartbreaking thing she had ever seen.

A few tears fell silently and Shelly shook her head. "I don't want to talk right now, Claire. Is that okay?"

"Okay." Claire nodded and caressed Shelly's cheek. "No talking."

Shelly let out a sigh of relief and kissed Claire once. She tugged on Claire's sleeve and motioned for her to follow. Shelly led them back toward the front door, up the wooden stairs to the second floor. The banister was cool to the touch, carved wood painted white with soft, rounded edges that her hand glided along easily. Shelly opened one of the large double doors leading into what Claire assumed to be the master bedroom. She walked to the large windows on the far end of the room and pulled the drapes closed before she headed into the en suite bathroom to their right.

A large two-person Jacuzzi tub enclosed in marble was on the left as Claire followed Shelly into the bathroom. An equally large and luxurious shower stall was positioned next to it. Claire watched as Shelly reached into the shower and turned on the water. The overhead rain shower started and two small wall jets kicked on as well. Within a few seconds, a light steam had formed on the glass.

Shelly turned and walked toward Claire, reaching behind her to close the bathroom door, containing them both inside. Claire's heart rate picked up when Shelly stopped in front of her. Shelly unzipped her hooded sweatshirt and dropped it to the floor. She shook her hair loose of the tie and stepped out of her shorts and socks. Shelly stood in front of her in her sports bra and panties looking a little shy.

"You're beautiful." Claire gave in to her desire to touch the skin of Shelly's abdomen. She had been thinking about it since watching her play earlier. Shelly was soft and firm at the same time. Her muscles toned and conditioned, her slender frame and narrow hips suited her so well. "I liked watching you play today. I hadn't seen that side of you before."

Shelly shuddered under her touch. She put a hesitant hand on Claire's hip, toying with the fabric of Claire's skinny jeans. "I want to feel your skin on mine."

Claire stifled a moan. Shelly was so direct and yet still so tentative. It was making her a little crazy. She felt simultaneously turned on and afraid to move too fast, take it too far. When Shelly began unbuttoning her pants, she decided there was no turning back at this point, and she gave in to her desires. She would let Shelly lead, but she would enthusiastically follow.

She let Shelly undress her, only stopping her progress when she hooked her thumb into the waist of Claire's panties. "Wait. This first."

Claire helped Shelly pull off her sports bra, reaching out to stroke the underside of her breast as Shelly's hand went to the clasp of Claire's bra. She pulled Shelly against her once the garments were free, appreciating their similar height and the contact it afforded their breasts. Shelly was so warm. She curled up to Claire's front, her lips finding Claire's neck. Shelly slid her hands up Claire's back, along her shoulders, releasing the clip in her hair and combing her fingers through the freed locks.

"Shelly," Claire breathed out as Shelly sucked on her pulse point, her hands scratching down Claire's back to her ass. She squeezed the flesh once before slipping her palms under the fabric of her panties and cupping her ass. She pulled Claire against her as she moved her mouth to the underside of Claire's jaw.

"I've been dreaming about this." Shelly nibbled at the skin under Claire's ear, pulled her hips back to help Claire's attempts at getting Shelly's panties off. She stepped out of them without taking her lips off Claire's neck and earlobe. Her hands continued to touch and massage along Claire's back, her ass, her hips.

"Me too." Claire let out a breath, her excitement building. Shelly stepped back and looked over her nakedness; she was curvier than Shelly, more hips, more ass. Her breasts appeared to be a little larger, but Shelly's hand covered them easily, tracing a jagged line from her collarbone to her nipple and toying with it a little. Shelly lightly pinched her nipple and Claire moaned, reaching out to grasp Shelly's hip and bring her closer again.

"Let's get a little wet, Claire." Shelly kissed her lips and took the hand Claire had resting on her hip in her own, leading her into the shower under the hot, streaming water.

Claire closed her eyes as the water rained down over her face. The temperature was perfect, not too hot, not too cold. The side jets caressed her back as the overhead shower soaked her. Shelly held her close, her hands brushing hair out of Claire's face, her lips on Claire's mouth, her leg stroking up along the back of Claire's. The sensations were unbelievable. Insistent and tender. She felt safe with Shelly here, naked and exposed, under this water, washing their day away. She was aware that this might have been Shelly's intention all along. A fresh start, literally.

"You feel so good," Shelly said against her lips, her hands cupping Claire's face, deepening the kiss. Shelly's tongue teased at her lips and she felt like she was drowning from the affection, the attention Shelly gave to her mouth overwhelming her.

"No one has ever kissed me like you do." Claire panted as Shelly sucked on her bottom lip. She reached between them and squeezed the flesh of Shelly's breasts, savoring the sounds and whimpers Shelly let out as she plucked and pulled at her nipples.

"Good." Shelly's right hand left her jaw and traced along her stomach before slipping lower, teasing at the skin on the inside of her thigh. "I want to touch you, Claire. Are you wet for me?"

Claire thought she might faint. Shelly seemed to know—she guided her against the slick wall of the shower, kissing her hard as she spread her legs and slid her fingers along the lips of her sex, pressing in lightly before pulling away. "Fuck."

"I plan to." Shelly positioned her leg between Claire's, holding her open as she pressed in again, this time sliding through Claire's wetness and entering her fully. "Yes." Shelly let out a pleased sigh as Claire felt herself adjust around Shelly's two fingers, her wetness accommodating Shelly easily.

"Oh my God, Shelly." Claire dropped her head back against the shower wall as Shelly slowly began sliding in and out of her, her thumb circling Claire's clit while a gentle hand kept their mouths close together, holding her in place. Shelly's mouth never left Claire's for very long, and Claire loved it.

Shelly moaned when Claire reached out to cup her pussy, her fingers exploring the soft, wet hairs above Shelly's opening before she pressed against Shelly's clit. She clawed at Shelly's ass, pulling her close, letting Shelly get deeper inside with every thrust.

Claire started to whimper. Shelly's mouth and her fingers and the wetness she felt over Shelly's clit were winding her up too fast, she was too close. The water rushed over them and she felt her insides start to tighten with every ministration Shelly continued against her. "Shelly," she warned.

"I know, I can feel how tight you are." Shelly's lips left hers only long enough to seduce her further. "Come for me now, so you can come for me again." Shelly shifted her leg a little more, bottoming out inside Claire, the knuckles of her hand stimulating Claire's opening while her fingers pressed and pulled Claire toward her climax.

Claire cried out when a well-timed swipe of Shelly's thumb on her clit pushed her over the edge, her body curling forward as her orgasm ripped through her. Shelly's lips were on hers again, the aftershocks of her pleasure intensified by the pressure of Shelly's body against hers, holding her against the shower wall, kissing her lips and caressing her thigh. Shelly seemed to be everywhere in that moment.

The water continued to blanket them as Claire recovered. Shelly never left her side or her mouth, kissing her sweetly and supporting her when Claire's legs protested, sated from her climax, her body warm and buzzing. Somewhere along the line her hands had left Shelly's sex and were clinging to her back and hip. She moved forward to touch Shelly again, but Shelly stopped her.

"Later." Shelly kissed the pout that Claire couldn't stop from forming. "I want to feel you over me. I want to be under you, Claire." She kissed her again before brushing Claire's hair out of her face, deflecting the water to look at her. "Okay?"

"I think I can handle that." Claire laughed at the mild look of concern on Shelly's face. She was adorable. An adorable soaking-wet sex goddess.

"Good." Shelly smiled the first genuine smile Claire had seen all night.

❖

Shelly watched Claire towel off after their shower. She was so gorgeous. Shelly had always thought that Claire had just the right amount of curve to fill those work skirts and pants, but underneath her clothes, Claire was stunning. Her skin was soft and creamy white. She had a few freckles on her shoulders that Shelly made sure to kiss under the water. Her breasts were perky and full, round and ample in Shelly's hands. She was looking forward to feeling the weight of them in her hands again.

When Claire looked up and gave her a smile, Shelly felt renewed. The heat of the shower had soothed the ache of her muscles from her time at the gym. Claire's hands massaged her shoulders after she lathered Shelly's hair with shampoo and conditioner, stroking her skin gently before the water washed away the difficulty of the day. Claire stood behind her and slid the loofa across her abdomen, between her breasts, along her neck...Shelly couldn't remember a more intimate experience with another person. And yet it felt completely normal to share that with Claire. She was careful to show Claire the same amount of attention, her feelings of closeness and connection healing the pain she had felt before. Claire made her feel safe—even when she was completely naked in front of her. In more ways than one.

"What are you thinking about?" Claire asked as she squeezed the moisture out of her hair, the lovely auburn color a shade darker while damp. Shelly wanted to run her fingers through it. She decided she would soon.

"You." She tied the towel around her chest, covering herself more to prepare for the cooler air outside of the bathroom than to shield her nudity. She looked in the mirror as Claire came up behind her.

"I see you gave me a gift." Claire pointed toward the faint bruise above her collarbone.

Shelly turned and leaned against the counter, pulling Claire to her front. She kissed her. "You should see the one I left on your shoulder."

Claire gave her a surprised look and spun to check her reflection. Shelly laughed as Hedy scratched at the door. "Someone is looking for you." Claire swatted at Shelly for making her look for nothing in particular.

"She's not used to being locked out of places." Shelly looked down in time to see the tip of Hedy's paw trying to sneak beneath the door.

Claire leaned against Shelly, placing her hands on either side of Shelly's hips, holding her in place at the counter. She kissed Shelly, smiling against her lips. "You spoil her."

Shelly melted into the kiss, her arousal still thrumming from earlier. "Sometimes it's nice to be spoiled."

"Mm-hmm," Claire hummed as she trailed a finger over the knot in Shelly's towel, separating the overlapping fabric to skim over Shelly's stomach.

Hedy scratched at the door again, this time letting out an annoyed meow.

Shelly was taking short panting breaths by the time Claire's hand was flat on her abdomen, fingers moving down with every breath she took in.

Claire increased the pressure of her palm only to pull it off Shelly with a teasing laugh. "We shouldn't keep her waiting, then."

"Oof. What a tease." Shelly's cheeks felt hot under Claire's gaze.

"I'll make it up to you later," Claire promised as she opened the door and Hedy came spilling in, a happy meow coming from her little face. "Hey, cutie pie. What's cookin'?"

Shelly watched as Claire wrapped the towel around herself and followed Hedy out of the room and onto the bed. Hedy bounced along the white comforter, weaving her way to Claire's hand and out of reach before doubling back again, purring loudly.

"She really does like you. I can say that with confidence because she's been fed." Shelly sat at the edge of the bed with Hedy between them prancing along without a care in the world.

"What's not to like?" Claire leaned back, rolling to her side. Hedy stopping flitting around long enough to take a piece of the comforter into her mouth and start kneading the blanket. Claire petted her and scratched behind her ears as Hedy's purring increased in volume. Shelly mirrored Claire's position, on the other side of Hedy, watching with amusement as Hedy shamelessly soaked up the affection. "Not much, honestly."

Claire gave her that easy smile that she loved. She reached beyond Hedy to take Shelly's hand. "You're very sweet."

Hedy looked up, annoyed that the petting had ceased, and let out a meow of complaint while still holding the blanket in her mouth.

"Shh, Hedy, Mama's flirting." Shelly spread her fingers so Claire could entwine them with hers.

Claire laughed and scooted a little closer, leaning forward to kiss Shelly. "Yeah, Hedy, shh."

The soft purring in the background became a distant memory as Shelly found herself being walked up the bed, away from Hedy, toward the pillow. Claire was over her in no time, tossing their towels to the ground and helping Shelly crawl beneath the comforter. Shelly let out a contented sigh when Claire's warm, naked body rested on top of hers, Claire's weight distributed through the elbow and knee. She slid off Shelly's side, draping herself across Shelly's hips and chest.

"I believe I have something to make up for." Claire's eyes were dark as she looked down at Shelly.

Shelly slid her hands up Claire's back and into her hair. She was pleasantly surprised at how thick and full it was, the damp strands slipping between her fingers as she played with it. She merely nodded, lifting her head to press their lips together. She whimpered when Claire slipped her knee between Shelly's legs, pressing her thigh against Shelly's center with a gentle rocking motion. One of Claire's hands massaged her breast as her mouth slanted from Shelly's lips to the soft skin under her jaw. The pleasant weight and friction of Claire moving against her brought Shelly's arousal from their shower play quickly back to its peak. Claire shifted lower, her lips and tongue moving over Shelly's collarbone, settling on Shelly's erect nipple and sucking it between her teeth. Shelly arched her back, bringing her chest closer to Claire's teasing lips as Claire replaced her thigh with her hand.

"Yes, just like that." Shelly tried to string coherent words together as Claire went from lightly teasing her clit to swirling her fingers in Shelly's wetness. Claire increased her suction on Shelly's nipples, switching from left to right as she continued to move over her. Shelly didn't last very long once Claire slipped inside her, all of their foreplay catching up with her, her climax rolling through her after a particularly firm nibble from Claire's mouth on her breast. She moaned and Claire abandoned her nipple to capture her mouth, sucking on her tongue while Shelly shuddered and twitched as Claire continued to tease and stroke her clit.

Shelly panted, trying to catch her breath as Claire nuzzled her nose, kissing her cheek and settling to her side, her leg and arm across Shelly still.

Claire propped herself on her elbow and looked down at Shelly. She pulled the comforter back and traced little patterns on Shelly's naked stomach, smiling as Shelly trembled and squirmed the closer she got to her waist. She applied more pressure and pressed her palm flat, gliding up Shelly's stomach to cup her breast, her thumb toying with a swollen nipple until Shelly closed her hand around it, seeking respite from the stimulation.

"You're no fun." Claire wiggled her fingers under Shelly's, her blue eyes shining.

"I'll remind you that you said that once I've had a chance to catch my breath." Shelly stretched and basked in the happy warmth radiating from her core up into her abdomen. Her body felt relaxed, at peace—it had been a long time since she'd shared her bed with someone else.

Claire kept her hand on Shelly's chest as she rested her head on Shelly's shoulder. Shelly smiled at the smell of her shampoo in Claire's hair. It made her wonder what Claire's own shampoo smelled like. She hadn't been this close before, and there was so much she wanted to know about her. She swirled her fingers in Claire's hair, appreciating the thickness again.

Hedy squeaked from behind Claire, making her presence known. Claire looked up at Shelly with a guilty expression. "Do you think she noticed?"

Shelly laughed, "I don't know how she could have missed it."

Claire hung her head. "Worst. Houseguest. Ever."

Hedy popped her head over Claire's hip and purred, climbing up onto her waist and walking along the comforter to settle on her shoulder, effectively pinning Claire to Shelly.

"Looks like you're stuck here, Claire-Bear." Shelly petted Hedy and praised her. "Good work, princess."

"This was all an elaborate ruse to get me in bed with you, wasn't it. Cute cat? Perfect green eyes?"

"Irresistible charm?" Shelly supplied casually.

Claire gave Shelly her favorite smile. "Precisely."

Shelly stage-whispered to Hedy, "She's on to us. Hide her keys." Claire's laughter vibrated against Shelly's chest and neck and she felt complete. This was not the ending she would have predicted earlier, but she was plenty fine with the outcome.

Claire lay on her for a few moments, her breath skating across the bare skin of Shelly's collarbone. Hedy had stopped purring and was stretched out along Claire's back, slumbering quietly.

"So, should we talk about earlier?" Claire didn't lift her head, her lips moving against Shelly's skin softly.

"Earlier when you were moaning in the shower? Or earlier when you were checking me out at the gym?" Shelly tried to sidestep the conversation that was looming.

Claire kissed Shelly's collarbone, sucking it for a moment before she asked again, "Toby wasn't talking about his girlfriend earlier, was he?"

"I find it disturbing that you bring up Toby when attempting to give me a postcoital hickey. Just putting that out there." Shelly closed her eyes and savored the sensation.

"Not attempting. Succeeded." Claire dragged her tongue over the area, soothing it a little.

"One might say all this marking is juvenile and immature." Shelly shifted as Claire's hand on her breast moved again.

"No more juvenile than dry-humping against a car at night like horny teenagers." Claire brushed Shelly's hand away from hers so she could freely toy with Shelly's breast, uninhibited.

Shelly laughed. "Who was dry-humping? I distinctly remember kissing and maybe groping, but I think I missed the dry-humping."

"Tell that to the orgasm I nearly had." Claire blushed and tucked her head under Shelly's chin.

Shelly looked down, lifting Claire's chin with her free hand. "Really?"

"Yup. Super embarrassing. Let's move on to other topics. Like Toby. What was Toby talking about?" Shelly decided the color on Claire's cheeks was endearing.

"Wait, I wanna talk about that a little more...So like, really?" Shelly was beyond amused.

"I should have rubbed one out in the shower like Jamie alluded to. Then I definitely wouldn't have nearly finished embarrassingly early."

"Or maybe you would have anyway. Maybe it's not all about you," Shelly teased.

"Well you certainly have a way about you, I'll give you that." Claire's eyes were bright. She shifted a bit and Hedy let out a low snore. "I'd kiss you, but I'm trapped here. Your cat is keeping things PG. I'm not a fan."

"Good things come to those who wait." It wasn't an empty promise—this was the best Friday night she had had in years. She had every intention of making this night last forever.

"As long as you keep using *come* in that sentence, I'm yours." Claire scooted up a little, careful not to dislodge Hedy, but close enough to kiss Shelly. She dragged her tongue along Shelly's bottom lip, requesting entrance. Shelly complied eagerly, happy to be dominated by Claire's mouth.

"Let's put Hedy out so we don't traumatize her any further, yeah?" Shelly bent her knee, shifting her hips toward Claire.

"Sure." Claire pulled back from Shelly's mouth long enough to give her a meaningful look. "As soon as you tell me about the Toby thing."

Shelly let her head fall back in frustration. Claire was not going to let this go. "Again with mentioning Toby in bed, *my* bed, mind you. With you all hot and naked and delicious."

"Shelly." Claire pursed her lips and waited.

"Fine. But know that I am against this type of interruption."

"Duly noted. Go on." Claire encouraged her with a small smile.

"Toby was probably talking about work. D'Andre came into the office today and basically told me he wasn't coming back. Maybe ever. Then he sent out an office memo saying that in not so many words and left. Cleaned out his office and left in the middle of a workday on a Friday." Shelly said it quickly for fear of getting emotional. Just summarizing it made her heart hurt and her stomach swirl with panic.

"What?" Claire propped herself up on her elbow, causing Hedy to slide off her back with an ungraceful thump. Hedy shook her head and stretched, walking toward the end of the bed in annoyance. "What do you mean he just walked out?"

"I mean he came in and told me he wasn't happy and that he hadn't been in a long time and said that he was taking some time to himself. But that the time was indefinite and he'd have his lawyer call me." Shelly felt that lump in her throat forming again. She hated this feeling.

Claire sat up in bed, covering her chest with a sheet while she seemed to contemplate what Shelly had said. After a moment or two she looked down at Shelly, her expression softening. "What are you going to do?"

"I have no idea." Shelly could feel herself about to cry again. She literally couldn't stop it. This was such a shock to her. "I am so lost."

Claire frowned and stroked Shelly's cheek, brushing a stray tear away. "Let me look into this. You're a client at Clear View—this is what we do, we fix problems and help smooth transitions. I can help you with the Expo and get you in touch with the right people to figure this all out. You don't have to do this alone. I'm here."

Shelly's heart felt like it doubled in size at Claire's words. That was exactly what she needed to hear in that moment. She didn't want to do this alone. She couldn't. And figuring it out with Claire was doubly appealing. "Okay."

"Okay." Claire smiled at her brightly as Hedy wandered back up the bed, this time along Shelly's side. "Sorry, cutie patootie. Your mama and I need to have a work conference right meow and Imma need you to guard the door."

Shelly laughed as Claire hopped out of bed and scooped up Hedy, kissing her head and depositing her outside the room with care. She slipped back in and closed the door with a mischievous grin. "Now, what was that you said before about good things and waiting?"

"Come here." Shelly pulled back the covers and beckoned Claire back to bed.

"Yeah, that's it." Claire crawled on top of her and Shelly forgot about everything else except the blue eyes and auburn hair enveloping her.

CHAPTER FOURTEEN

Claire woke up feeling like she had slept the best sleep of her whole life. The sun was peeking through the french doors leading out to what she assumed was a balcony, the long drapes fluttering gently in a slight breeze. The overhead fan blades were shaped like giant palm leaves and stirred up a cooling prickle against her shoulder. The sheets felt like they were warm butter against her skin, smooth and inviting. She decided this was the most comfortable bed ever.

"Good morning." Shelly was propped up against the cushioned headboard, her hands flying silently along a keyboard, the tablet propped on her bent knees as she worked on something. She wore glasses today—it occurred to Claire that she had never seen her in regular glasses. They fit her. She looked like a sexy librarian with her hair tousled and falling haphazardly over her T-shirt.

"Morning." Claire stretched and spread out—Shelly's bed was monstrous compared to the queen-size she had at home. Her foot nudged something firm at the bottom of the bed. She lifted her head to find Hedy's green eyes blinking with surprise. "Sorry, Hedy."

The cat stretched and repositioned, closer to Shelly's feet than Claire's probably to avoid further disruption.

"She needs her beauty sleep, you know." Shelly smiled as she continued to work next to Claire, glancing down when Claire yawned. "Evidently, so do you."

"Was that a roundabout way of you calling me beautiful or lazy?" Claire closed her eyes and snuggled into the mass of sheets and blankets.

Shelly's hand settled on Claire's shoulder, rubbing it once before sliding up to her cheek. "You are beautiful. I don't need to approach that in a roundabout way."

Claire opened her eyes to find Shelly facing her, the computer set aside, Shelly's glasses pushed up into her hair. Her eyes were so green today. Aside from a light smudge of mascara under her right eye, she looked refreshed, happy. Quite the contrast to how Claire had found her last night—Shelly's pain and insecurity had been palpable. It had surprised Claire that Shelly was able to accept being physically comforted so freely. She wondered if it was something she got often.

"So you're calling me lazy, then," Claire teased. She felt a little overwhelmed by the closeness, by Shelly's touch. Last night had been something else entirely—she wasn't ready for the feelings that threatened to pour out.

Shelly laughed and pulled her hand back from Claire's face, running her thumb along Claire's bottom lip before settling on her side, her head propped up by her elbow. "Lazy? Nah. But you are a heavy sleeper. I thought Hedy was going to wake up the neighbors howling at the bedroom door, but you didn't even stir."

"Probably because you wore me out." Claire shifted, rolling her shoulders and spreading out her fingers and toes.

"Do you regret that?" Shelly's question was soft, her expression unreadable.

"Falling asleep?" Claire knew what she was getting at, but she wasn't really ready for that line of questioning yet. Not without coffee. And some long, hard thinking.

Shelly raised her eyebrow at Claire but didn't say anything. Claire thought Shelly's eyes were calculating something, as they seemed to flicker and glow. Like a supercomputer analyzing data. She wondered what Shelly was thinking—if she was like those people she'd read about, the ones that could see numbers hopping off the page. She'd ask her about it sometime, maybe.

"I don't regret falling asleep. I needed a rest." Claire reached out to take Shelly's hand in her own. "And no, I don't regret anything else either." That was the truth, but she wasn't ready to think about the complications it may have caused.

"Good." Shelly gave her a small smile and squeezed her hand once, her thumb gliding over the three connected diamond bands Claire wore on her ring finger. "This is pretty. Have you had it long?"

Claire looked down at their joined hands. Shelly shifted their handhold and ran her fingertips along the jewelry, spinning the ring a little. It was about a half size too big for Claire, but she wore it all the same. "It was my mother's. The boys gave it to me when I graduated from college. My father got it for her after the twins were born—one row for each pregnancy: Craig, Austin, and then the twins."

"What about when you were born? No new row?" Shelly was giving her that same laser focus she had seen at the office the other night. But the intensity didn't bother her. She knew it came from a curious place, like Shelly was learning about her. It was flattering to know she was captivated by her.

Claire laughed. "My father always said the twins were more than they bargained for. He promised her he would get her something different to represent me. He gave her a tiny solitaire pendant when I turned three. She wore it all the time."

"Do you have it?" Shelly brought Claire's knuckles to her lips. She kissed them, one by one. It soothed Claire. This wasn't something she liked to talk about.

"No. They couldn't find it after the accident." It was something that had always haunted Claire.

Shelly stilled her lips and looked up at Claire. "I'm so sorry."

That was what everyone said. Claire merely nodded and shrugged. There wasn't anything anyone could do about it. Any of it. It was in the past.

"I'm a good listener if you want to talk about it." Shelly's expression was patient. She wasn't digging for information, and Claire appreciated that.

She sighed. "There isn't much to discuss. We went for a family photo. The boys were raucous as usual. We stopped to get ice cream and Craig drove the rest of us kids home so my parents could have a little date night. But they never came home."

Shelly shifted closer, their legs touching beneath the warm cocoon of covers. She held Claire's hand, but she said nothing.

Claire continued, "The boys found out that night, but they let me sleep. Craig and Austin took over the family responsibilities with some help from my aunts and uncles. We worked together—we grew up together. It all eventually worked out, but it felt impossible a lot, too." Sadness settled in her chest, but she didn't cry about it. She hadn't cried about that in a long time. She had her brothers still. They had made it work. There were definitely times she had felt sorry for herself, like when she didn't have a father for the father-daughter dance, or when she had started dating and wanted her mother's input on an outfit or hairstyle, but it had happened early enough in her life that she had found ways to adjust, to adapt. To persevere. The Moseleys never took handouts; you were to earn everything that you had. Hard work resulted in success. Those were sentiments that her brothers felt strongly about and it was one of the reasons she felt so compelled to succeed at Clear View. It was why she had warred with herself over Shelly. She was resilient. She could do anything. And yet, here she was in Shelly's bed, the soft weight of Shelly's thigh resting on her own, potentially endangering her chance at success. But there was something that felt so right about it at the same time. It was quite the conundrum.

After a few moments, Shelly spoke. "Thank you for telling me."

Claire smiled. Shelly's sincerity was touching. Claire could tell she was legitimately grateful to know about that part of Claire's life. Most people skirted away from it, but it was nice to have someone address it so directly. As much as it was in the past, she knew it had changed the entire course of her life. How could it not? "I'm glad you asked."

"I want to know all the things there are to know about you," Shelly replied, looking shy. She kissed Claire. When she pulled back, Claire could see a blush coloring her cheeks. She looked almost bashful. It was adorable. Shelly released her hand in favor of walking her fingers up Claire's arm. "Hungry?"

"Starving." Claire's stomach grumbled loudly in reply, causing them both to laugh, the heaviness of their previous conversation forgotten. Shelly's laugh was light and melodious, her smile so genuine Claire was tempted to ignore her hunger to satisfy another urge instead. She leaned forward and kissed Shelly, her actions greeted with a soft moan and warm tongue against her own. Kissing Shelly was easily the most exhilarating thing she had ever experienced. She seemed to know all the right ways to wind Claire up, applying just the right amount of pressure and teasing. The way she glided along Claire's lips and tongue was mesmerizing. Claire couldn't get enough of the way it felt to be equally worshiped and pursued. It was unbelievable.

Shelly pressed Claire onto her back, the fabric of Shelly's T-shirt rubbing against Claire's chest as the sheet slipped down toward her hips, exposing her to the cool breeze of the overhead fan and the contrasting warmth of Shelly's body. It didn't take long for Claire to melt into the bed, her movements timed to match Shelly's as Shelly's hand gripped her ass and guided her to meet each roll of her hips.

"Fuck." Claire gasped when Shelly's mouth left hers and licked at the skin on her neck, weaving lower with each panting breath that escaped Claire's lips. Shelly's hand closed over her breast as she trailed wet kisses along Claire's abdomen, moving the sheet away from Claire's waist and replacing it with her mouth. It was maddening. Until Claire's stomach growled again and Shelly halted her progress.

Shelly laughed as she kissed the skin under her mouth once before propping herself up on her elbow, hovering over Claire. "Sounds like we should continue this another time."

Claire didn't know whether to whine or laugh. Shelly's hand slid off her breast and a frustrated sound from Claire's lips followed. Evidently whining won out.

Shelly gave her an amused look. "C'mon. I'll make us some breakfast."

Claire pressed the heels of her hands against her eyes and tried to focus on which longing was more important: the desire for food or the desire for Shelly's mouth to be on her again. She felt Shelly place a kiss to the pout she couldn't stop if she tried, and she smiled against it.

"I pulled out some comfy clothes for you to slip into and left them on the counter in the bathroom. Come down to the kitchen when you're ready."

Claire opened her eyes to see Shelly's glasses back on the bridge of her nose, a sweet smile on her face. Shelly reached out and tickled Claire's naked side before leaving the room. Claire watched as Hedy followed close behind her, purring so loudly that Claire could hear it all the way from her side of the bed. Shelly's bed. *Her* side of Shelly's bed. Claire looked up at the fan blades overhead and tried not to overthink that too much.

She lay there for a few moments, taking in her surroundings in a way that she wouldn't have felt comfortable doing with Shelly still in the room. The room was large and airy, her attention drawn to the cream-colored drapes with sheer curtains billowing from the opened doors across from the foot of the bed. Claire slipped out from under the sheet and walked, naked, toward the doors, pausing just inside to preserve her modesty. Her assumption before had been correct—off the bedroom was a small balcony with two wrought-iron seats and a circular table facing a decent-sized backyard encased by large, vibrant trees and shrubs. A wooden fence surrounded the perimeter of the yard with unkempt woods beyond. Claire didn't step out on the balcony for fear that one of Shelly's neighbors to the left or right might get more than an eyeful, but she was tempted to feel the fresh air on her skin.

She looked back at the bed and took in the rest of the room she had neglected to notice last night. The king-size bed was all white: white sheets, white comforter, plush white cushioned headboard. It was clean and fresh looking, inviting, like a hotel bed after a long day of traveling. The furnishings in the room were clean and simple as well: light pine with accents of metal hardware, a few framed pictures, the surfaces free of clutter or knickknacks, a stark contrast to the dresser she had in her own bedroom littered with scented lotions and perfumes to match her mood on any particular day. She glided across the room toward a set of closed doors across from the bathroom. She pulled them open to reveal a spacious, walk-in closet lit from within. Shelly's clothes were neatly arranged on hangers in color order. She noticed a few drawers at the far end of the closet were askew. She glanced over her shoulder to make sure she was alone before venturing in to satisfy her curiosity as to the contents of drawers.

The opened drawer was filled with graphic T-shirts. They were folded, but with less precision than the clothing on the hangers. Some of them were faded, some worn nearly thin around the collars. Claire smiled as a heather gray shirt off to the right caught her eye—it was Ms. Pac-Man winking back at her. These clothes were clearly well-loved—she wondered if each one had a story. She bet they did.

Claire resisted the urge to search through Shelly's other drawers, instead giving in to the sudden urgency of her bladder. She closed the closet door with care and stepped onto the cool tile floor of the bathroom, her nakedness reflecting back at her in the mirror. She had always appreciated the soft feminine curves of her body, grateful for good genes. Years of softball and track in high school and college kept her lean and fit, with strong legs and a firm backside. She had been told by her aunts and uncles that she had inherited her mother's ample chest, but she couldn't remember that very well, only having pictures to reference as she got older. Not having her mother during the trying years of puberty was one of the things that had been the hardest on Claire. If she was being honest, though, it had all been difficult.

She plunked down on the toilet across from the shower and let her mind wander back to last night. She swore she could see the faint outline of a handprint on the glass. She wondered if it was hers or Shelly's. As she washed up, she noticed the neat little stack of clothes on the counter topped with a fresh toothbrush, still in the package. That was adorable.

She laughed as she lifted the T-shirt. Yoshi from Mario Kart smiled back at her, giving her a thumbs-up. It would fit, but it would be snug—she half wondered if that was intentional. A pair of oversized men's gym shorts with MIT on the leg awaited her, and she was grateful to find that Shelly had put out something for her to wear below the waist. She made a mental note to search for her panties after breakfast. She braided her unruly bedroom hair and freshened up before leaving the bedroom and heading toward the stairs.

As she approached the top step, she became aware of the faint sound of thumping music that grew louder as she got closer to the kitchen on the main level. She leaned on the frame of the doorway and smiled at the action unfolding before her: Shelly was humming along to some rock song Claire was unfamiliar with, whisking eggs in a bowl as she swayed side to side, moving with the beat. Her black T-shirt cut off at midthigh and the blue striped sleep boxers she had worn when she'd left Claire in the bedroom were in a heap in the corner, giving Shelly the appearance of being naked from the waist down. Claire let herself appreciate the lean lines of Shelly's legs as she drained the contents of the bowl into a warmed frying pan on the stove, the eggs popping and bubbling as they contacted the pan. Shelly bent over to pull something out of the oven and Claire got a glimpse of black and red boyshorts with—

"Are those Spider-Man Underoos?" Claire asked over the music, causing Shelly to jump back with surprise as she closed the oven.

"Jesus, Claire. You scared the crap out of me." Shelly held a spatula to her heart as she braced herself against the counter.

"So is that a yes?" Claire cocked her head to the side and decided Shelly was the cutest person ever.

Shelly walked toward the island and touched the tablet that was sitting there, shutting off the music with a quick swipe of her finger across the screen. "Sorry, I thought you were still upstairs."

"What did I tell you about saying sorry all the time?" Claire walked into the kitchen and leaned against the counter across from Shelly. She made a show of looking down at Shelly's legs as she asked again, "Spider-Man Underoos, Shel? Really?"

Shelly blushed and wiped her forehead with the back of her hand—the hand still clutching a spatula—nearly dislodging her glasses in the process. "They're not Underoos."

"But they are Spider-Man," Claire pointed out.

"Well, duh. He's clearly the best superhero ever." Shelly gave her a playful look but jumped when the oven timer went off behind her.

"You seem a little jumpy," Claire teased as Shelly reached over and shut off the oven, reaching in to pull out a fresh tray of cinnamon buns.

"I'm not jumpy," Shelly protested halfheartedly as she turned to the cabinet and pulled out two plates. "I'm just not used to having someone else here besides Hedy." She nodded toward the furry form stretched out on the window bench that served as seating at the kitchen table.

Claire's mind flitted back to the toothbrush from upstairs, wondering how often Shelly had the opportunity or the need to leave out dental supplies the morning after. Her face must have given her away.

"What?" Shelly adjusted her glasses and looked at Claire curiously. "What are you thinking?"

Claire considered lying to Shelly but something compelled her to be truthful. "I was wondering how many spare toothbrushes you keep on hand."

Shelly blushed again, this time averting her eyes. "Uh, none."

"Huh?"

"I use an electronic toothbrush ever since I got my retainer so I just happened to have a spare from the last time I—" Shelly sighed and shook her head. "And I just told you I wear a retainer. Great."

"And glasses. Don't forget the part where I get to see you in glasses." Claire couldn't suppress the grin on her face. This was too much fun.

"Oh right, those." Shelly's spatula hand went to the rim of her glasses and she groaned, tossing the offending utensil onto the plate. She wiped her hands on the hem of her *Buffy the Vampire Slayer* T-shirt and slid her glasses up into her hair. "I usually wear contacts at work because I have a bad habit of chewing on the ends of my glasses when I'm stumped. It's something that Samantha recommended."

"Samantha? Lucinda's Samantha?" Claire raised her eyebrow. Shelly and Samantha seemed pretty close. She wasn't sure why that was so curious to her.

"One and the same." Shelly reached into a drawer and pulled out a butter knife. She frosted the cinnamon buns and put one on each plate as she retrieved the spatula and scrambled the eggs in the pan. "She's a wealth of useful suggestions. It took me forever to get used to poking myself in the eye to get the contacts in, but it's much easier to see. I can't tell you how many times I scratched the lenses of my glasses before or dropped them and had to drive home blind." Shelly transferred the eggs to plates with the cinnamon buns and paused. "I didn't even ask you. Do you eat eggs?"

"I do." Claire giggled when Shelly breathed a sigh of relief.

Shelly motioned toward the kitchen table. "Shall we?"

"Can I help with anything?"

"You can grab the iced coffee out of the fridge, if you'd like." Shelly wiped the edge of the plate with a napkin Michelin-starred restaurant style with that same determined focus Claire had gotten used to her displaying when working on the Expo stuff.

Oh, right, they were colleagues.

It took Claire a moment to find the fridge—Shelly had one of those upscale kitchens where the cabinet panels matched the front of the Sub-Zero refrigerator. When Claire looked around, she could see Shelly's wealth in the materials and light fixtures. There were multiple electronic gadgets in the kitchen supplying music or television or internet access all at hand, but also slightly hidden. It seemed like Shelly had replicated a Williams-Sonoma catalog in her kitchen and married it with Amazon's latest and greatest electronic toys.

She pulled open the fridge and pulled the glass pitcher of what she assumed was iced coffee off the top shelf. The rest of Shelly's fridge was mostly empty—except for a few peppers, an avocado, some lettuce, and a handful of tomatoes.

"I know. It's a pretty pathetic existence. I'll have Ramon restock it later," Shelly supplied from behind her, reaching past her to retrieve the glass bottle of milk hidden behind a canister of whipped cream.

"She says, as she moves the whipped sugar to get the organic milk," Claire teased, elbowing Shelly playfully.

Shelly laughed and pointed toward the vegetable drawer with a shy smile. "In the interest of full disclosure, there are no vegetables in there, only Girl Scout Cookies. The drawer keeps them crisp."

Claire shook her head in mock despair and followed Shelly to the cutely decorated kitchen table with their plates and napkins set up and a single rose in a small flower vase.

She must have stared at it for a moment too long because Shelly cleared her throat and shrugged. "It's from the bush outside. I'd love to say I keep fresh flowers around all the time, but that's not true for two reasons—I'm not usually home enough to enjoy them, and Hedy love over there is a flower and plant monster. If left unsupervised, the little minx will chew them to death and strew their carcasses around like trophies. She's the absolute worst."

Claire reached out and patted Hedy's head, as she slept soundly in a little patch of sun on the L-shaped bench they shared. "Hedy, how dare she tell such abhorrent lies about you? You would never do such things."

"I see she's hypnotized you with those green eyes, works every time. Le sigh. I should have warned you." Shelly poured them each a glass of iced coffee and pushed the milk bottle toward Claire. "I don't have any hot coffee in the house. My French press finally quit on me and I haven't had the heart to get another one. Besides, I usually just grab coffee at work since I'm there most mornings."

Claire stopped petting Hedy long enough to fill her mug with some milk and tasted the coffee—it was a little sweet. Not that she should be surprised by that, considering Shelly's sweet tooth. "This is good."

"Thanks. Micah actually taught me how to brew it myself. Coffee is one of the major food groups in this family." Shelly referenced the owner of the café in her office building as though they were friends. Claire was reminded of how easily Shelly had conversed with Max from the racquetball gym last night. There was something about Shelly that was so unassumingly friendly and approachable. She lived a life in contrast to the privilege and superiority one would assume her obvious wealth would produce. It was one of the things Claire liked so much about Shelly—she was seemingly unaffected while being incredibly aware of the good she could do with her money and knowledge. Those were the qualities that had drawn her to work with Shelly after she had received that phone call a few months ago. She could never have predicted that she'd be sitting at Shelly's breakfast table next to her lounging cat having eggs and cinnamon buns after a night of mind-blowing sex...while wearing a Yoshi T-shirt.

Claire let this thought marinate a bit as she sipped her coffee. She watched with amusement as Shelly cut her cinnamon bun into small pieces, careful not to let them touch the eggs. "Do you always separate your food?"

"What?" Shelly gave her a confused look.

Claire used her fork to point toward Shelly's plate. "Sweet and savory. Divided."

"Oh." Shelly looked back at her plate. "Yeah. I've been doing it since I was a little kid. I had those plastic dividing plates when I was younger—it sort of became a habit until I started using real plates as an adult. It was just easier that way when I was making my own meals to put them into categories so I wouldn't forget to eat my vegetables."

"Did you make your own meals a lot? As a child, I mean?" Claire tasted the eggs on her plate and smiled. "These are good."

"Thanks." Shelly gave her a shy grin.

"So?" Claire waited for Shelly to answer her question.

"Right. Uh, yes. I made almost all of my meals as a child. Until a teacher caught on that I was having graham crackers and chocolate for lunch every day and convinced my father to get me a nanny. Then I had some help. But my father didn't like other people in his space, so once I was old enough to prepare food that was appropriate in nutritional content, he let her go."

"Shelly, I'm sorry, that sounds so—" Claire didn't want to say *sad*, but that's what she felt.

"I know." Shelly gave her a nod, her eyes piercing as she looked at Claire. "I know. But it was how things were. That was my normal. I realize now that it wasn't ideal. It's not the way I would want my children to experience life. It's probably where my breakfast sweet tooth originated. I always have something sickeningly sweet at breakfast. Lunch and dinner usually contain greens and are terribly adult. But breakfast always has a little something sweet for the little girl in me that had Entenmann's cake for breakfast, lunch, and dinner when my father forgot to go grocery shopping."

Claire bit the inside of her cheek to keep from saying anything. She was curious though. "What about your mother?"

"She left when I was eight." Shelly's response wasn't cold, but it lacked her previous warmth.

"Eight?" That was just a few years older than Claire had been when she'd lost her mother, although the circumstances were very different. She knew without a doubt in her mind that her mother and father wouldn't have left her and her brothers willingly. This was such a foreign concept to her. "Why?"

Shelly shrugged. "I've asked myself that question for most of my life. Why does any parent abandon their child? Maybe it's selfishness, maybe it's fear of not being a good enough parent. Who knows?"

Claire frowned and considered this. This must have been the painful understanding that Shelly expressed to her that night at her brother's house on the couch when they'd nearly kissed. Shelly just seemed to get it—the difficulty she had with being in the house she grew up in, the memories that haunted her there. And yet she couldn't stay away from it either.

After a moment or so, when she didn't reply, Shelly looked up at her and continued, "My father told me once in a fit of anger that my mother left because I was too smart. He told me that my genius intimidated her and scared her away. That she didn't want to be dumber than her child. He blamed me for it." Shelly wiped her mouth with her napkin and pushed her plate aside, abandoning the remaining bites. "I was too young to understand that he was just overwhelmed by being a single parent. And I struggled with kids at school and teachers over the same issue. I never really fit in. But my father was just like me—or that's what I had always told myself. So even though he later apologized in his own roundabout way, it sort of sat with me. For a long time, I believed that she didn't want me because I was too different." Shelly sipped her coffee, then smiled as she placed the glass down. "That was long before I turned out gay, too. Imagine the lifetime of disappointment she escaped."

"Shelly." She knew Shelly was making light of the situation, but Claire's heart hurt for her. She reached out and took the hand Shelly rested on the table.

Shelly entwined their fingers and rubbed Claire's thumb with hers. Her smile was missing when she spoke this time, her voice softer, more vulnerable. "I found her when I was thirteen. It took some real detective work because the internet wasn't quite as established as it is now, but I tracked her down. She lives in Scottsdale. Now she has two college-aged sons and breeds golden retrievers with her husband Alan. He works for some power plant out there doing administrative tech work. She was on the PTA."

"You keep an eye on her?" Shelly's hand was warm in hers. She remembered the look in Shelly's eyes last night, the desperation in them when Shelly asked her to come home with her. That same restlessness was in them now.

"That's probably too strong a statement. I check in every once and a while because I'm curious. I probably shouldn't, though. I should use my hacking skills for good, not evil." She gave Claire a nudge.

"With great power..." Claire nodded and leaned forward to kiss Shelly because she felt like it and because it looked like Shelly needed to be kissed.

Shelly leaned into her lips, kissing her for a moment before laughing and pulling back, a look of realization on her face as she asked, "Did you just toss out a Spider-Man reference while trying to soothe me about my broken family?"

"That all depends, did it work?" Claire wiggled her eyebrows and leaned in again, because Shelly's lips were her favorite part of her body.

Shelly scooted closer, the naked skin on her thigh pressing against Claire's, her free hand dropping to Claire's knee, making Claire rethink the favorite body part thing because Shelly's hands were pretty magical, too.

"So far, it's working. Let's see how long it lasts."

Shelly kissed her again, more deeply this time. Claire let her hand slip out of Shelly's grasp and she began to massage along Shelly's thigh when a thought occurred to her. "Why are your shorts across the room on the floor?"

"There was a small debacle at the first attempt at making breakfast. Eggs died in vain. The shorts didn't make it. They were left on the battlefield." Shelly's lips stayed on Claire's, kissing as she spoke. "Are you complaining?"

Claire shook her head, allowing Shelly to dominate her mouth and thoughts. She tasted sweet like the icing from the cinnamon bun with a little bit of coffee mixed in. She decided it was her new favorite breakfast flavor.

Claire felt Shelly push the table back and move along the bench, straddling her hips in a quick motion. She slid her hands up and down Shelly's bare thighs, feeling them flex and relax as she lowered her hips down to Claire's. Claire had a fleeting thought that maybe Shelly was distracting her from asking any more questions, but she had sort of started this. Sort of.

All other thoughts left her mind entirely when Shelly's lips made their way to her ear. When Shelly sucked Claire's earlobe into her hot mouth, Claire felt herself flush, everywhere. Shelly's hands found Claire's, stopping their rubbing motion up and down the front of her thighs and guiding them to the skin under her T-shirt. She pulled back from Claire's ear long enough to take the glasses out of her hair and pull off her shirt in a slow, teasing fashion. Here, in the soft morning sunlight coming through the windows behind them, Shelly White had never looked so beautiful, so naked, so open.

Claire let her body move instinctually, her hands gliding up Shelly's flat abdomen to cup her breasts, her fingers massaging and teasing the skin that shivered under her touch and in the coolness of the room. She kissed Shelly with a renewed vigor, the desire to make her feel wanted and desired reignited from last night, from their bedroom play early this morning. When Shelly's soft moans fueled her further, she abandoned Shelly's mouth in favor of taking a pert nipple between her lips instead. Shelly's chest was positioned directly in front of Claire's mouth and she did her best to show her appreciation for that.

Shelly's fingers clutched at the back of her head, holding Claire's mouth tightly to her breast as she rocked her hips against Claire's, causing Claire to fidget uncomfortably, both turned on by Shelly's legs trapping her own and frustrated by her inability to spread her legs wider to really feel the full potential of Shelly's pelvic rolls. As her mouth continued to lavish Shelly's chest with attention, she dropped one hand to Shelly's hip, encouraging her motion, while the other scratched up Shelly's back, holding her close, anchoring her to Claire's lips.

Shelly's head dropped back with another moan, louder this time, and Claire slid her hand up to grab a fistful of her hair, pulling it a little as Shelly arched her back and rolled her hips again. She hissed when Claire tugged more forcefully at her hair, biting at the nipple in her mouth with a playful tease. Shelly spread her legs wider and Claire followed suit as Shelly's free hand gripped Claire's on her hip and moved it between them to cup her sex over her boyshorts.

"Can you feel how wet I am for you, Claire?"

The heat from Shelly's core almost overwhelmed her. Shelly had positioned herself in such a way that the knuckles of Claire's hand stimulated her own clit as she pressed against the soaked fabric of Shelly's panties. It was a multitude of delicious sensations. She nodded against Shelly's breast, breaking contact only long enough to reply, "I bet I can make you wetter."

"Fuck." Shelly closed her eyes and whimpered as Claire slipped inside her boyshorts and rubbed against Shelly's swollen clit. She released Shelly's hair to slide down the now slick skin of Shelly's back and settle at her ass, pushing and pulling her forward and backward as much for her own selfish needs as Shelly's.

"You're so hot when you make those noises, Shelly." Claire left Shelly's kiss-bruised nipples to lick up along her sternum as Shelly started to make more erratic movements with her hips, her breathy pants the only sounds Claire needed to know she was getting close. She felt her own clit ache and throb with each bump of her knuckles against herself.

"Claire, I'm going to—" Shelly dropped her chin to catch Claire's lips with hers as she surged forward and twitched, her orgasm overcoming her and resulting in a sharp, aggressive thrust against Claire's hand that launched her across the precipice into her own orgasm, the buildup too much for her to resist. Not that she really wanted to.

"Ugh, yes." Claire sighed and let the tremors ride through her, the small, continued motions of Shelly's hips as she started to wind down sending little lightning bolts through Claire's clit and abdomen.

Shelly let out a pleased sigh and pressed her forehead against Claire's, her hands cupping Claire's face, kissing her slowly as Claire wrapped her arms around Shelly's waist and pulled her close. They stayed like that for a moment, Shelly sinking into Claire's embrace and seeming to get smaller on her lap as she tucked her head into Claire's neck. Claire felt her heart swell at the way Shelly went from sexually charged to cuddly in a flash. She hoped it was because Shelly felt comfortable with her. She knew she felt comfortable with Shelly. She always had—there was just something about her that snuck around Claire's defenses. Like, how suddenly she'd found herself calling or texting Shelly outside of work or about work stuff in a way that felt so second nature it was as if they had been best friends their whole lives. How did this happen without her realizing it? And here they were, embracing, coming down from something truly passionate and lovely and fucking hot, like a couple that had shared intimacies and pain for far longer than they actually had known each other. A *couple*. She wondered if they were a couple now. The thought made her fidget a little.

Shelly kissed her once and shifted, swinging her legs to the side to sit up, her body still draped across Claire's lap, the warmth a comforting distraction from the swirling thoughts inside Claire's head. Shelly reached for her discarded shirt and pulled it back on, slipping her glasses back into her hair. She looked shy again, but she didn't pull away. "I have no idea why being emotionally vulnerable with you makes me want to fuck you and be fucked by you so badly, but it's a new experience for me and I'm not quite sure how I feel about it."

Her honesty made Claire laugh out loud. "The feeling is mutual." She caressed Shelly's thigh with her hand before clarifying, "I mean, I feel the same way, and I'm not sure why."

"Listen." Shelly chewed the inside of her lip before she replied. "I'm not great at relationships. I probably have deep-seated abandonment issues from my mother, and my father is a hot mess all unto himself. And my business partner just quit, so my life is kind of a train wreck, but I really like you and I want you in my life. In whatever capacity you feel is possible. If you want that, too. You know, in case you feel the same, like, at all. Please stop me from rambling." She gave Claire a pleading smile.

Claire sighed, not sure what to say. She was both convinced and conflicted. She'd had every intention to break things off with Shelly last night at the gym, and yet she didn't, and here Shelly was being honest and vulnerable with her again, and it dawned on her that she wasn't even sure she could match that honesty. Claire knew she was living entirely in the moment right now, and that scared her more than she wanted to think about. "Okay. Let's make a deal."

Shelly leaned back a little and nodded. "I'm listening."

Those eyes were so serious again, that calculating look was back from last night. Shelly's eyes flickered and glowed, seeming to power up and thrum as she waited. It was hypnotizing to watch. "I'm not sure what this is between us, but I'm willing to admit that it's *something* worth investigating further."

"Like research. Data collection. Scientific experimentation for the betterment of womankind."

Shelly's expression was almost too serious. Claire laughed. "Sure. For science."

"For science." Shelly smiled and breathed out a sigh of relief. "Wait, so what does that mean?"

Claire shrugged. "I have no idea."

"So we are basically in total agreement."

"Totally." Claire nodded.

"Well, good. I feel like that's major progress. Look at us, being progressive." Shelly shook her head and laughed.

A little meow drew their attention to Hedy, who was sitting up on the cushioned bench next to them, watching them intently.

"Shit. We did it again." Claire looked at Hedy with a frown. "I want so badly to make a good impression on you, Princess Hedycakes, but I only seem to be able to scandalize you. It's like a compulsion. I'm compulsively groping your mama in front of you and I'm not sure how to stop that."

Hedy meowed in response and rubbed her head along Claire's elbow.

"We've created a voyeur." Shelly shifted off Claire fully. She yawned and stretched, briefly reaching out to squeeze Claire's hand to add, "I don't mind the compulsive groping at all. In case my opinion matters."

Claire squeezed her hand back before pretending to cover Hedy's ears with her hands. "Shh. That was a private conversation between me and Hedy." She stage-whispered for effect, "Your opinion does matter. Just FYI."

Shelly stood and stretched again. "Good to know."

A phone rang and the tablet on the counter lit up. Claire looked around but was unable to see an actual phone anywhere. "Where's your phone?"

Shelly walked to the tablet and touched the screen. "It's my cell phone. I network it when I'm home. My landline is only for faxes. I keep a tablet in most of the rooms of the house so I don't miss any important calls or emails."

"Wow, that's pretty high-tech." Claire was impressed.

"Nah, it's lazy. But thanks for the compliment." Shelly swiped across the screen and slipped an earbud into her ear, motioning for Claire to wait a moment. She spoke into the mic attached to the earbud. "Hey, Ramon, what's up?"

Claire watched her nod and touch the tablet screen, scrolling through something while she furrowed her brow in concentration. At some point Hedy had wandered onto Claire's lap and was purring contentedly. She scratched under her chin as she leaned forward to try and reach her coffee from the table Shelly had pushed aside. It was a hairsbreadth out of reach, but she didn't want to disturb Hedy. She felt like she needed to make something up to Hedy for all she had inflicted upon her over the past day.

"Sure, thanks, Ramon. I'll head right over." Shelly disconnected the line with a frown. "Sorry about that."

"No biggie." Claire leaned down and kissed Hedy's head as she flopped to her side in a very unladylike gesture. "I'm working on rebuilding my relationship with your cat."

"I can see that." Shelly walked to the table and passed Claire her drink. "I also saw your struggle to hydrate—don't let her win. She'll take advantage of your weaknesses."

Claire took the glass and gave Shelly a grateful smile. "Your wisdom is invaluable."

"I'm glad someone appreciates it." She rubbed Hedy's belly before sighing. "As much as I'd love to spend all day in and out of

clothes with you, the grocery delivery guy has informed me that my
father's groceries are rotting on his front porch. So I have to head over
there and check it out."

"Ah, this is the same Ramon you spoke of earlier when you tried
to look healthy with the organic milk next to the Girl Scout Cookies."

"It was whipped cream. The cookies are in the crisper," Shelly
replied. "But yes, he delivers my groceries from time to time, too."

Claire stretched and put Hedy to the side as she stood, her position
change stimulating her clit and causing her to pause briefly.

Shelly gave her a knowing smile and leaned against the counter,
her arms crossed as she looked down at the gym shorts Claire was
wearing. "You look good in my shorts."

Claire walked toward Shelly and stopped just short of touching
her. "Don't forget the Yoshi shirt. The subtlety of that choice was not
lost on me."

Shelly reached out and wrapped her hands around Claire's waist,
pulling her closer. "Champion of Rainbow Road, forevah."

Claire leaned forward to kiss Shelly but stopped short. "Wait,
shouldn't you be checking on your dad?"

Shelly sighed. "Please hold." She released Claire's waist with one
hand and pulled the tablet across the counter toward her, swiping the
screen quickly and pulling the earbud out of the jack. The sound of a
phone ringing filled the speakers in the kitchen. Shelly leaned forward
and pulled Claire back to her, kissing her as the phone rang seven,
eight, nine times.

On the tenth ring, a gruff voice answered, "Sheldyn. What? Why
do you feel the need to let the phone ring for so long?"

Claire tried to stifle her laugh as Shelly leaned back and pressed
a finger to her lips. She called over her shoulder toward the tablet in
response, "I hate when you call me that, Dad."

"Why? It's your name. You don't make any sense sometimes."
There was a shuffling noise in the background. "What do you want?"

"Ramon called and said you left the groceries out. I was just
calling to make sure you were okay."

Claire smiled against Shelly's finger and nibbled the tip a little.
Shelly rewarded her with a silent kiss.

"I'm fine. I'm working. Stop bothering me."

Shelly pulled away from the kiss long enough to end the call.
"Okay, fine. 'Bye, Dad."

Shelly leaned back in to kiss Claire, but this time Claire stopped her, leaning back. "Sheldyn? Your name is Sheldyn? How come I didn't find that when I researched you and Boston Pro App?"

"You researched me?" Shelly gave her a broad smile. "Probably because I make sure that it never makes it to print." She tickled her fingers up and down Claire's side in a keyboarding motion. "The benefits to being internet savvy."

"With great power…" Claire teased, snapping the waistband of Shelly's Spider-Man boyshorts.

Shelly adjusted the glasses on her head before sweeping a stray hair off Claire's forehead. "So, you're a Spider-Man fan, huh?"

"Jamie and Jerry went through a phase one can only describe as obsessive. It's a hazard of growing up with all brothers. Some of that stuff sneaks in by osmosis."

Shelly looked thrilled. Claire figured she'd earned some major brownie points. "I knew I liked those twins. Since my father is obviously still alive and doesn't need immediate medical intervention, are you free for a little bit longer?"

Claire looked over Shelly's shoulder at the tablet on the island to check the time. "I don't have softball practice until four today. I have a few hours before I need to take you back to your car."

"Great." Shelly laced her fingers with Claire's and pulled her in the direction of the bedroom.

CHAPTER FIFTEEN

"You're humming. Why are you humming?" Her father was looking at her like she had two heads.

"I'm not humming." Shelly was so used to arguing with her father that she hadn't even considered that maybe he was right. Had she been humming?

"Yes, you are. You're humming and you're smiling. Are you sick?" He squinted through his filthy glasses and poked her in the arm. "Maybe you should take some medicine."

"Dad"—Shelly shook her head with a laugh—"if I were humming and smiling, which I don't believe to be true, but I'll humor you, those aren't typically the actions of someone who is sick. Just for future reference if you ever decide to get a medical degree."

Her father bristled and pushed his glasses back up the bridge of his nose. "That's not true, Sheldyn. You read all the time about cats crawling under beds or trees and purring as they die. I read about it in *National Geographic*."

"Dad. Seriously? Did you just compare me to a dying cat?" She thought of Hedy and immediately wanted to drive home and check to see that she was safely snuggled on the blankets in the bedroom. "And what issue of *National Geographic* featured information about cats dying? I need to better monitor the magazines you subscribe to—"

"I read it on the internet, Sheldyn." He looked almost proud.

"Not everything you read on the internet is true, Dad." Shelly frowned at the heap of rotten fruits and vegetables in the case in front of her. "Why didn't you bring in the food on Friday?"

"I was busy." He looked like a scolded child. "Why didn't you come by and bring them in?"

Shelly raised her eyebrow at his challenge. "Because you are a grown man and can walk to your front door by yourself. Because I pay to have fresh food brought to you and prepared for you by me or Greta and you still leave containers of food untouched in the fridge. Because at some point you have to take responsibility for your own nutritional needs."

He crossed his arms over his chest and huffed. "I liked it when you were humming before. At least then you weren't so bossy."

Shelly ignored his response, choosing to trash the contents of the grocery bin and clean it with bleach and paper towels. She frowned and decided it might also need to be hosed and aired out a bit. She should have Ramon bring by a second one in case this kind of thing happened again.

"You always come by on Friday night." He was sitting at the island now, picking at his cuticles and avoiding eye contact. His voice was softer than usual.

Shelly looked up at him, surprised. That was true, typically. She often came by after work on Friday to see her father and make him some meals for the weekend with the fresh produce just dropped off. It hadn't even occurred to her to call him and tell him she wasn't going to make it. D'Andre's announcement on Friday had completely thrown her for a loop. Claire's appearance at the gym had put some things in motion that she hadn't wanted to stop. And Friday night, well, that was something she hoped she'd never forget and something she hoped to repeat again soon. But still, she hadn't called her father and it appeared as though he had been counting on her.

"I'm sorry." Shelly stood and faced him fully. "That must have been disappointing for you, I apologize. I should've at least called you and told you I was busy."

"What were you busy doing?" He gave her a curious look, obviously moving on in the way that only her father could.

Claire. That's what she wanted to say, but she chose a more tactful approach. "I spent some time with a friend."

Her father leaned forward a little. "A friend? A female friend?"

"Yes, Dad. A female friend." Shelly went back to cleaning the bin because they apparently had moved on to Twenty Questions.

"That's why you were humming. Because you like this female friend." He nodded to himself at his conclusion. "What's her name?"

"Claire." Shelly answered without thinking and immediately regretted it because her father had a tendency to be like a dog with a bone about these things. She braced herself and waited for the floodgates to open.

"That's a nice name, *Claire*. What does Claire do?"

Shelly decided to humor him. She had abandoned him on Friday, after all. "She's in marketing and public relations."

"How did you meet?"

"Uh, at that mixer a while ago." That was a particularly specific question.

"The one that Lucille hosted?"

"Lucinda," Shelly corrected. She stood up and leaned against the counter, giving him her full attention. "You remember that?"

"You wore makeup and no glasses," he said matter-of-factly. She wondered what else he catalogued to memory when he was appearing aloof, which was always.

"I did, you're right." She cocked her head to the side and decided to ask him a question. "Why do you refuse to bring in your groceries?"

He blinked, considering this a moment before answering. "Because if they sit out there and rot, then you'll come over and make me dinner."

Shelly felt like she had been punched in the stomach. There had always been a part of her that wondered if he intentionally made things difficult for her, if he intentionally let food go to waste and his appearance fall apart. She wondered if he was truly neglectful, so brilliantly consumed by his work that he didn't function, or if he purposefully avoided that part of his life out of spite. And yet here it was, a clear defiance of independence.

She wasn't sure what to say; part of her was enraged that he was so perpetually juvenile, and yet another part of her looked at him with pity. How sad it must be to admit that. How difficult it must be to ask for something when you needed it. She had warred with herself over whether to ask Claire over, to tell her that she needed her the other night. It had been a risk, but it had paid off. Maybe this was his attempt at a calculated risk.

"Okay."

He looked at her as if waiting for her to say something else. When she said nothing he replied, "So, you'll make dinner tonight?"

"I'll make dinner for you two nights a week. And Greta will make dinner for you two nights a week, maybe three times if she can accommodate it. But you are responsible for feeding yourself something—either premade or self-made meals—the other two nights in addition to all daytime meals. And take your Parkinson's meds on time, every time. Is that fair?"

"I suppose." He drummed his fingers on the countertop.

"And squeeze cheese on crackers does not count as a meal. I asked Greta to stop enabling you by picking that up. We have to follow the rules of your diet, Dad."

He huffed. "What will I put on my crackers?"

"I think what you mean to ask me is what will you put on the celery sticks I wash and cut for you each week, and the answer is hummus." She gave him an encouraging smile and patted his arm.

"That sounds awful."

"Cheese that comes from a can is not cheese. I bet even the internet would tell you that." She pulled out the fresh groceries she'd picked up on the way over here. "Now, pork chops or steak for dinner?"

"Steak."

She wondered if she had won the cheese and cracker conversation or if it was merely a parlay until another time. She decided to call it a victory and move on. "Potatoes or green beans?"

"Squeeze cheese."

She whipped her head around to find him giving her a shy, playful smile. Victory confirmed.

❖

Claire sat at her brother's café and stared out the window. Shelly would be there any minute and she was really excited. And terrified. But mostly excited. She and Shelly had spoken a few times since their impromptu weekend rendezvous, but Shelly had been slammed trying to iron out the details of the new app. There was some glitch that kept popping up with complex background feedback—if the background wasn't perfectly dark or still, it altered the image. Or something with bigger and more complex words, but that was the gist of it. She thought. She decided she'd just ask when Shelly got here. If she ever did. Where was she?

"You look like a virgin waiting for her prom date." Jamie plunked down next to her with a towel draped over his shoulder.

Claire shoved him and rolled her eyes. "Tell me this isn't a terrible idea."

"This isn't a terrible idea," Jamie parroted back. "Wait, what am I giving you encouragement for again?"

"Jamie," Claire whined. "You're letting me know that going on a date with Shelly is not professional suicide and that I'm not making a terrible mistake."

Jamie looked at her with a sly grin. "You're worried about dating her after you spent the entire weekend getting to know her horizontally?"

Claire almost regretted telling him about that, but it wasn't like she could have hidden it if she tried. He noticed the kiss bruise above her collarbone when she changed into her practice clothes at the softball field Saturday afternoon. She didn't have time between dropping Shelly off at her car and getting to practice to go home, so she'd changed into some of the spare gym clothes she kept in the car. But Jamie's eagle eye missed nothing. Ever. By the end of practice, Jamie had weaseled everything out of her. She hadn't stood a chance.

"I'll have you know that I also got to know her vertically and perpendicularly, too. In case you were wondering." Claire went for the easy tease to cover up the knot in her throat. He was right. She had already had sex with Shelly, multiple times. How could dating her be any worse?

Jamie gave her a disgusted face. "That's too much information."

"You started it." She checked the time on her phone. Not only was Shelly not late, but she wasn't even supposed to get here for another eight minutes.

"Claire-Bear, chill. You're stressing me out." Jamie nudged her as he scrolled through the night's menu on his phone.

"I can't help it." Claire bit her bottom lip for something to do. "We have a meeting with my boss tomorrow, to go over some business stuff. And Shelly is like really close friends with my boss and her fiancée—"

"Ooh, the hot matchmaker?" Jamie's full attention was on her now.

"Her name is Samantha. And yes, the hot matchmaker is my boss's fiancée. And Shelly's really good friend."

"So what does that mean exactly?"

"It means that tomorrow I'm meeting with my boss and my—" Claire wasn't sure what word she was looking for here. Client? Girlfriend? Were they at the title part of the relationship? Did they even have a relationship?

"Girlfriend. Go ahead, try it on. I think you'll find it rolls off the tongue rather easily."

"Did you just make a lesbian sex joke?" Claire didn't know whether to be impressed or offended.

Jamie laughed. "Seems like I did. Not entirely intentional, but I'll take the praise."

"Anyway," Claire said, attempting to regain control of the conversation, "Lucinda and the legal department are meeting with Shelly and me to go over the change in leadership structure of Shelly's business, and I'm freaked out because this is a *huge* strategy meeting about something I know Shelly is anxious about."

"Because you like her. You're freaked out because you don't want Shelly to know that you know that this meeting is a big deal and that you could potentially crash and burn in front of her." Jamie nodded to himself as he spoke.

"Jamie. You're not helping." Claire's shoulders drooped. "Yes, I'm worried about pleasing the client."

"Whom you happen to be sleeping with," Jamie supplied with a smile.

"Well, that's the other part. I'm a little worried that legal or worse, Lucinda, may find out we've been intimate and that our relationship has gone past the professional one and into the—"

"Shower, bedroom, kitchen." Jamie counted on his fingers. "Did I miss one?"

Claire dropped her chin to her chest and sighed. "Master bedroom balcony, walk-in closet, and front seat of my car."

Claire looked up to find Jamie gaping at her. "For real, Claire? Damn, you were busy."

"Okay, the front seat of my car happened a while ago and it was more of an intense make-out session, but I'm counting it." She was getting wound up just thinking about it.

Jamie held up his hands and nodded. "Count 'em all, sistah. Don't let me stop you."

Claire rested her head on her hands and stared out at the busy Cambridge street in front of them, unsure of how to feel or what to do. Her brain told her over and over again that getting involved with Shelly was not a wise idea. And yet her heart broke to see Shelly so upset. She hadn't realized until that night at the gym how much she truly cared for Shelly. In the time they had been apart since their weekend together, Claire went back through her texts and emails and realized that she'd talked to Shelly throughout the entire day, almost daily, ever since they had started working together. It had started so organically she hadn't noticed it, but everything changed that night in Shelly's office. The night of the fireworks. Nothing had been the same since, and she wasn't sure it could ever go back to the way it was. Not that she was sure she even wanted that.

"I can see you're struggling here, so let me give you some advice"—Jamie touched her arm and lifted her chin to look at him—"favorite brother to only sister."

Claire laughed, "Okay, *favorite* brother, lay it on me."

"You like Shelly. She's smart and funny, and a fucking kick-ass Mario Kart player, which I have to admit came entirely out of left field for me—"

"Jamie."

"Right." He cleared his throat. "You like her and she obviously likes you. And these kind of things happen in the workplace all the time. You aren't the first person to invent sliced bread, Claire. I know, because I'm a chef." He grinned. "The truth is you are very good at your job. You will do an awesome job tomorrow at the meeting and be the utmost professional because you're just that, a professional. Any relationship you have with Shelly outside of work is up to the two of you. I think you should get out of your own way on this one and see how it plays out."

"Really? You think so?" Claire felt an iota of hope that she could make this work and manage to keep her job.

"I do. And more importantly, Shelly pulled up like five minutes ago and has checked and rechecked her hair in the mirror of her car enough times that if it's not perfect by now, it's never gonna be. Go save her from herself. I'll get the snacks ready."

CHAPTER SIXTEEN

Shelly had been looking forward to seeing Claire since the minute they parted ways in the gym parking lot last Saturday. Although she would have liked nothing more than to spend every night this week with Claire, the fact was that they were in the final stretch before the Expo and there was still a lot of work to be done.

She looked into the mirror and checked her hair—it was fine, just like it had been fine the last ten times she looked at it. Really, though, she was more concerned about her eyes, which looked tired. She had been logging a lot of hours in front of the computer the last few days, and they'd ached when she tried to put in her contacts earlier, so she'd worn her glasses instead. But her eyes still looked a little tired, glasses or no glasses.

She reached into the center console of her car and dug around until she found some eye drops. She slid her glasses up into her hair and tilted her head back, moisturizing her eyes in hopes of chasing the redness away. She reclined with her eyes closed and decided to let them rest a bit before heading in to Claire's brother's café for the cooking class date night they had planned.

A soft knock at the glass drew her attention to Claire's smiling face. She looked great with the setting sun behind her, her hair glowing a vibrant shade of red. She was gorgeous.

"Hey." Claire leaned against the car as Shelly climbed out of the driver's seat.

"Hi." Shelly reached out and took Claire's hand, just because.

Claire rubbed her thumb along Shelly's knuckles. "You sure you want to do this? We can always reschedule."

"What? No. I mean, yes. I want to do this. I've been looking forward to seeing you like you wouldn't believe." Shelly hoped she didn't sound overzealous. Because she was totally feeling the right amount of zeal and she didn't want to seem over the appropriate level. If there was one.

Claire laughed and gave her that easy smile her heart skipped beats for. "You had your eyes closed in the car. I just want to make sure you're not burning the candle at both ends and overdoing anything."

"I probably am, but mostly my eyes were dry and I was waiting for the Visine to kick in." Shelly stepped a little closer. "Do my eyes still look red?"

Claire reached up and touched her face, stroking her cheek. "No, they're the same gorgeous green they always are."

"Good." Shelly leaned forward and pressed her lips to Claire's, the weight of the day slipping off her shoulders as Claire stepped closer, her hips touching Shelly's, her hands sliding into Shelly's hair. If they spent their entire night like this, it would be fine by her.

Claire opened her mouth and deepened the kiss, guiding Shelly backward so she was pressed against the car. Shelly smiled against Claire's lips. This position, though reversed, was pleasantly familiar. Claire's hands combed through Shelly's hair and settled at her neck, looping around loosely. Shelly loved the feel of Claire's arms resting on her shoulders, the warmth that radiated from Claire's body touching every part of Shelly's that would be socially acceptable in public. Shelly decided that any time spent in Claire's presence not kissing her was entirely a waste.

"We should probably stop kissing if we're ever going to make it to Jamie's cooking class." Claire pulled back from Shelly's mouth infinitesimally. Her breath skated across Shelly's lips as she reasoned, "Or we could tell Jamie we'll catch the next one because you're tired and you need to lie down."

Shelly moaned when Claire sucked on her bottom lip. She used all of her willpower to put a little space between them before things escalated too far, which, if the sensation she had right now that her pants were suddenly too tight was any indication, was already upon them. "I've gotta be honest—I've really missed you and there is nothing more in this world that I want right now than to take you home and do horrible things to you—"

"Yeah?" Claire leaned in again, her tongue halting Shelly from completing her thought.

"Mm-hmm." Shelly vaguely remembered she was trying to make a point.

"What kind of things, Shel?" Claire's right hand had found its way from Shelly's neck to the hem of her shirt. Claire's fingers slipped below the fabric and traced the waist of Shelly's skinny jeans, stopping at the button and pulling it away from Shelly's skin.

Shelly gasped, "But—"

Claire nodded, keeping their lips together as she spoke. "Button. Right, Shelly? You're trying to say *button*, right?"

Shelly's resolve was quickly fading as Claire pulled on the waistband of her jeans again, accentuating the word *button* by slipping two fingers underneath it and dragging her thumb along the seam of Shelly's crotch.

"I'm never going to forgive myself for this, but—" Shelly pressed one final kiss to Claire's lips before pushing Claire back enough to catch her breath.

Claire sighed, dropping her head so that their foreheads were touching. "But? Why is there a but?"

"*But* I've been looking forward to this class so I can spend some quality time with you outside of the bedroom at least once, so we can have a legitimate date." Shelly was already regretting this statement. Claire's pout was heartbreaking.

"Be honest, it's so you can hang out with my brothers, isn't it? Do you like them more than me?" Claire teased.

"I don't think there's anyone I've ever liked more than you." The words came out before Shelly could stop them. When Claire didn't reply, she was afraid she'd spilled all of her emotions and ruined everything.

Claire didn't flinch, though. Instead she stepped forward again and kissed Shelly very sweetly on the lips. No words, just a kiss. And that was fine by Shelly, too.

Claire reached out and took Shelly's hand. "C'mon, Jamie wants you to taste his new froyo recipe before the other people arrive for the class."

"Dessert *twice* before dinner? This is going to be the best date ever."

Claire looked over her shoulder and gave Shelly a smoldering look. "Oh, that stuff by the car wasn't dessert. It was just an appetizer."

Shelly swallowed hard and followed Claire through the doors, excited to see what happened next.

❖

"Shelly, you gotta hold it above your heart if you want it to stop bleeding." Jamie laughed and propped her arm up on a stack of cookbooks.

"This is why you should cater all of my meals for the rest of my life." Shelly looked at the bandage wrapped around her left index finger and frowned. "Which is probably going to be significantly shorter now that I've probably contracted a staph infection."

Jamie scoffed. "Are you implying my kitchen is anything less than pristine?"

Jerry walked over holding a rolling pin. "It's clean enough to eat off the floor, Shel. Well"—he used the rolling pin to point toward the floor by her table—"not over there where your blood contaminated everything. That spot is off-limits."

"Boys," Claire said, bearing a first-aid kit, "let's not pick on Shelly. She's been gravely wounded and needs immediate medical attention."

"This is some weird choreographed naughty-nurse fantasy, isn't it?" Jamie's accusation elicited a roaring laugh from Jerry and a sharply delivered elbow from Claire to Jerry's midsection.

"Oof, Claire-Bear. Watch those weapons, there's been enough blood spilled here tonight." Jerry rubbed his side and jumped out of the way as Claire launched some flour in his direction.

"Cleanup on aisle five!" Jamie tossed a wet cloth at Claire and jogged to the other side of the table to hide behind the couple across from them.

Claire laughed and shook her head. "You okay, Shelly?"

Shelly nodded and smiled. She loved being around the three of them. Even the near maiming didn't bother her because their interaction was so genuine and so real it made everything seem light and fun. "I'm totally fine. It's nothing. Really."

"I can honestly say I never would have guessed that making dessert would cause you bodily harm after you survived separating a rack of lamb and dicing potatoes." Claire took off Shelly's soiled bandage and dabbed the area with alcohol.

Shelly winced and gritted her teeth as the cut burned. "I think that's the answer. Let's just say dessert has been on my mind since I got here."

Claire looked up and gave her a shy smile. She put a clean bandage on Shelly's finger and gave her a quick kiss on the cheek. "Let's finish up here and head out."

"So, about that naughty nurse thing…" Shelly figured it was worth a try.

"We'll see if further medical intervention is necessary, after you feed Hedy." Claire wiped the excess flour off her hands and started to tidy up their workspace.

"Sounds like a solid plan." Shelly tried not to swoon at Claire's statement. What kind of perfect human thinks to check in on someone's cat before potential role-playing? This perfect human. Claire was absolutely perfect.

Claire deposited the used pans and dishes in the dishwasher as Shelly shrugged off her apron. Shelly glanced up at the clock on the wall and noticed the time. She had told her father that she wouldn't be able to swing by for dinner tonight but asked Greta to stop in instead. She hadn't heard back from Greta before she'd silenced her phone for her date with Claire, so she figured she'd call and check if she'd stopped by.

She patted her back pocket and frowned.

"Looking for something?" Claire gave her a curious look.

"My phone." Shelly looked around for her jacket. "Maybe it's in my jacket pocket."

"I'm going to help them clean up a bit while the class finishes up." Claire nodded toward her brothers who were wrapping up the leftovers for each couple to send home with them.

"I'll help. BRB." Shelly jogged toward her jacket and skidded to a stop, her feet still slippery from Claire's flour assault on Jerry. She shook her head and chastised herself, "Chillax, Shelly."

She found the phone in her right jacket pocket and pulled it out with a yawn. The long day was catching up with her. Her screen lit up with a dozen missed call notifications and texts from Greta, her father's housekeeper. The phone vibrated in her hand, the friction against her fresh cut shocking her—she almost dropped it. It was Greta.

"Everything okay?" Claire came up behind her, her hand on Shelly's shoulder.

"My father's housekeeper is calling." She frowned. This was unusual. "Greta, what's up? What's wrong?"

"Ms. Shelly. Your father fell. He won't go to the hospital. You need to come over and talk some sense into him." Greta spoke quickly into the phone, muffled by the sound of her father grumbling in the background.

"He what? Is he okay?" Shelly pulled on her jacket and began to pace. She felt like a switch went off inside her, and all the joy and lightness she'd felt from moments before was gone. She felt only panic now. "Did he take his meds? When was the last time he took his Parkinson's meds? What was his last blood sugar? Put him on the phone, Greta."

Shelly could hear a shuffling sound and her father voice came on. He sounded groggy. "Sheldyn, it's nothing."

"He's bleeding, Ms. Shelly," Greta called from the background.

"You're bleeding? How bad are you bleeding, Dad?"

"It's just a scratch, Sheldyn. Greta is overreacting." His voice was hoarse.

Shelly turned so quickly toward the door that she bumped straight into Claire. Shelly held the phone a little from her face, aware that her father was talking but not quite hearing the words. Claire was looking at her like she was going to shatter. It made her feel like she would.

"I'll be right there. Put a towel on it and I'll be right there." Shelly disconnected the line while holding Claire's gaze. "I'm sorry, I have to go."

"I'll take you." Claire looked worried. It made her more anxious.

"No, you have to help your brothers clean up. I can manage." Shelly tried to contain the feeling of panic that was washing over her. This was one of her greatest fears—her father's illness was getting worse. It had only been a matter of time until something like this happened. She could feel tears forming behind her eyes; it made her feel shameful and weak.

"Shelly, you're shaking. Let me drive you there. Please." Claire reached for her hand, pulling her closer. "Let me take care of you."

"We have to hurry." Shelly dropped her head in defeat, the tears flowing freely.

"C'mon." Claire quickly updated her brothers and shuttled Shelly into the passenger seat of Claire's car.

Shelly sat there, unmoving. Claire reached across her and buckled her seat belt in, looking at her for a moment before asking, "Where are we going, Shelly?"

"My father's." Shelly stared out the window, trying to take slow, steadying breaths. She gave Claire the address and returned to her silence. Claire didn't press her for any more information.

Claire maneuvered between cars and traffic with ease, accelerating and decelerating often to get them where they needed to go as quickly as possible. Shelly was grateful; she was grateful Claire was rushing to get her to her father's and grateful for the silence.

It struck Shelly as ironic that she'd had some of her most powerful emotions in this car, in this seat. The first time they kissed, she had felt such a connectedness in that moment. And then the ride from the gym to her house, how she had felt so desperate and alone. Claire had grounded her; she had offered to help her. Just like tonight, like right now. Claire didn't shy away from being strong for Shelly. She wondered how she had found someone like Claire—she was so different, so unlike Shelly herself. When Shelly had received that call she'd felt herself shut down, just like she had last week when D'Andre told her he was leaving. She felt small and childlike and weak. She felt alone. And yet, Claire was right there by her side, offering to help. It made her feel unworthy.

"My father has Parkinson's. I didn't mention it the other day when we were talking about the food delivery. That's why his food is delivered, because he has difficulty walking and getting around." Shelly's voice sounded flat to her own ears. "He's notorious for skipping his meds and meals. God, he's so difficult sometimes. You know, the other day he told me that he intentionally leaves his food out so I'll visit him more often. Tonight was my night to have dinner with him."

Claire didn't say anything, instead changing lanes and taking a hard right, leaving the GPS directions briefly to cut around traffic.

Shelly continued, "I should have been there tonight. I should have been home with him."

Claire looked left and changed lanes again, this time faster. She slipped between a truck and sedan with inches to spare. The car behind them honked. Claire didn't acknowledge it, her eyes focused ahead, her expression indecipherable.

"I didn't mean to keep you from a prior engagement." Claire's voice was soft, and it sounded a little hurt. Shelly immediately felt guilty.

"I'm sorry. I didn't mean that—I wasn't trying to say that being with you was a problem. That's not what I—" Shelly was struggling to make sense. She felt like she couldn't get out of her own way. Shelly thought back to the café with Jamie and Jerry laughing and being playful. She enjoyed being around Claire with them because they gave her a semblance of family. They supported each other. But she didn't have that, not really. She was alone. "It's just that, it's only the two of us. He and I. We're like this little disgruntled pair of misfits. We only have each other. He's a pain in the ass but he's my pain in the ass. I'm not sure you can understand."

"Why? Because my parents are dead?" The hurt was louder this time. It shocked Shelly.

"No. That's not what I meant." Shelly backtracked. She hadn't even considered how Claire must feel when she complained about her father like he was a burden. She felt guilty because there had been more than a few times that she had wondered whether her life would have been different if he'd been the one to leave instead of her mother. There was a good part of her that resented him for being sick and she was ashamed of it.

"I get it. You don't have to explain." Claire glanced over at Shelly before looking back at the road.

"Claire, I'm sorry. I didn't mean to—"

"It's okay." Claire looked over at her again, and this time, she looked tired. "You don't need to apologize."

Shelly stopped herself from doing just that. But she wanted to, and that made her feel bad all over again.

By the time they arrived at her father's house, there were emergency vehicles everywhere. Claire hadn't even pulled to a complete stop before Shelly bolted out of the passenger door and sprinted to the front door, waving off a police officer standing nearby.

"Greta? Dad?" Shelly called out as she got to the foot of the main stairs leading up to the bedrooms. "Where are you?"

"In the kitchen." Greta's voice sounded stressed.

Shelly turned the corner and nearly fainted at the sight. Her father was slouched in a kitchen chair, his face and neck covered in blood. Two firefighters stood off to the side while an EMT knelt before him taking his vitals. Greta rushed to Shelly's side to update her.

"I got your text about coming by, to bring in the food from under the bush. But the house was still dark. I found him at the bottom of the stairs. He doesn't remember falling." Greta looked anxious, and Shelly could see flecks of what she assumed was her father's blood on Greta's shirt and pants. "I tried to reach you but you weren't at the office. He wouldn't let me call 9-1-1 until after you called back."

Shelly just shook her head in disbelief. It was her night to be here to prep dinner and bring in the food, but she had gone out with Claire instead, so Greta had agreed to come after she finished her other work. "How long was he like that?"

Greta shrugged. "I don't know, Ms. Shelly. The house was dark, like always."

The EMT stood and cleared his throat. "Well, Mr. White, looks like you got a pretty good goose egg on your head there. We think you should go to the hospital for some tests."

"I'm not going," Louis grumbled and crossed his arms, looking off to the side.

"You are." Shelly felt an overwhelming mixture of anger and panic. Anger was winning the battle.

"You look like crap. Have you been crying?" Her father's glasses were crooked. He rubbed his hand under his nose and fresh blood started to drip out.

"Worry about your own face, Dad." Shelly sighed, directing her attention to the EMT. "Take him to the hospital. I'll meet you there."

"Like hell you will. I'm not going." Her dad grabbed a tissue and plugged his left nostril. A bruise was forming along the laceration on his forehead. He was a mess.

"Sir, you should listen to your housekeeper and daughters."

Louis adjusted his glasses and rolled his eyes at the EMT's comment. "What daughters? Sheldyn, he seems to think there's more than one of you. Do you really think he should be the one recommending I go to the hospital? He's seeing double. Someone should check him for drugs."

The EMT glared at him before looking back at Shelly. "Sorry, I assumed you two were related. My apologies, miss."

Shelly looked over her shoulder to find Claire standing by, Shelly's keys in her hand. She had been so frantic running in here that she had totally forgotten Claire had driven her. That her date with Claire had been interrupted.

Claire looked overwhelmed. The feeling was mutual. "Can I help?"

"What's her name?" her father barked in Claire's direction.

"Her name is Claire, Dad. Don't be so rude," Shelly huffed back as she rummaged through the kitchen drawer for the list of his medications she kept on hand in case of emergency. She handed them to the EMT and nodded toward the list. "This is all of his meds. I'll call his PCP on the way to the hospital."

"Oh, that's the girl you like." He squinted and leaned forward to get a better look. Shelly tried not to die from embarrassment. "She's pretty."

"I know, Dad." Shelly tried to redirect—her father didn't need any more distractions. "Let's go get you checked out."

"I'm not going to the hospital, Sheldyn." He shrugged off the EMT's attempt to help him stand.

"Dad, you need to have some tests done. You know, make sure you didn't scramble that egg with the fall." She pointed to his head and tried to appeal to him with humor.

He crossed his arms and shook his head. "No. I'm fine." He swayed a little and overcorrected, nearly falling out of his chair.

Try as she might to remain calm, Shelly had reached her boiling point. "For fuck's sake, Dad. Get on the goddamn gurney and stop arguing."

Greta, the EMT, and her father all looked at her in shock. Her father pouted for a moment but let the EMT guide him onto the stretcher nearby. He refused to look at Shelly as they strapped him down, choosing instead to squeeze his eyes shut like a child. Nothing new there, Shelly thought.

"We'll take him to Brigham and Women's," the EMT said as he maneuvered her father out of the room with the assistance of one of the firefighters.

"I'll meet you there. Let me clean up." Shelly looked over at the piles of towels and blood-soaked cloths on the kitchen floor. This place looked like a crime scene.

"I'll clean up the blood, Ms. Shelly." Greta appeared at her side with gloves on and a bottle of bleach spray. "The pasta is almost done anyway."

Shelly glanced at the stove and realized Greta had probably started making dinner while her father was refusing medical assistance. Because that's exactly something Greta would do. Shelly was grateful. "Thanks, Greta."

Shelly went to grab for her keys to follow the ambulance until she realized she hadn't driven there. "Shit."

"I can take you to the hospital, if you'd like." Claire was waiting in the hallway outside of the kitchen, her expression sincere.

"Shelly?" A familiar voice sounded from behind Claire—the other firefighter who had come on the call.

"Sasha? What are you doing here? I thought you were in

Washington on that training thing." Shelly's eyes jumped from Claire to Sasha, one of the matches Samantha had set her up with. Shelly felt like she was having an out-of-body experience.

"Change of plans, I never ended up leaving. Long story." Sasha smiled. "I didn't realize the patient was your father until I saw that picture of you on the wall by the stairs. I had no idea you wore braces."

"I like to pretend those years never happened." Shelly would have expected that seeing Sasha again would make her feel...something. They hadn't ended on bad terms. She liked Sasha, after all. Shelly hadn't had the opportunity to see her in her firefighting gear—she looked great. But seeing her so close to Claire was making her uncomfortable.

"You look good, Shel." Sasha never did resist an opportunity to flirt. Shelly glanced down to see that the zipper on her jacket had slid down a little, and she was showing more cleavage than she had intended. She adjusted it as Sasha glanced back to Claire and extended her hand. "Where are my manners? Sorry. I'm Sasha."

"Claire. Nice to meet you." Claire shook her hand and looked over at Shelly, her eyebrow raised.

No one spoke for a moment. Shelly just looked between Sasha and Claire, Claire and Sasha.

"How is it you know each other again?" Claire directed the question to Sasha.

"Oh, Shelly and I dated for a little while." Sasha gave Shelly a genuine smile. "But I don't think the timing was right."

Shelly's anxiety peaked. She felt a little naked by Sasha's disclosure. This wasn't how she wanted to introduce Claire to this part of her past. She had to say something; she couldn't just stand there. She nodded in reply, trying to focus doubly hard not to stutter. "Yeah, uh, Samantha introduced us."

Claire only blinked in response.

Shelly's head was swirling. Her father was on the way to the hospital, her ex-matchmaking-date was the firefighter on scene, and her current-ish girlfriend was looking at her like she'd just royally fucked up, but she had no idea why. She felt a little faint.

"Hey, you okay?" Sasha stepped forward and reached out for Shelly, stopping just short and looking back to Claire. "Maybe she shouldn't drive herself to the hospital."

"She doesn't have a car to drive." Claire held up Shelly's keys with a jingle. Her voice lacked its usual warmth. She handed the keys to Shelly. "I should go, let you sort all of this out. I'll see you tomorrow at the meeting."

"Well," said Sasha, "you can ride with me in the truck to the hospital if you want—it's the end of my shift, maybe we can catch up a bit." Sasha looked relieved Shelly wouldn't be driving herself.

"Sure. That sounds great." Shelly kept eye contact with Claire, unsure of what had just transpired. Claire's face remained impassive. It was like trying to read stone. Shelly sighed. "Thanks for the ride, Claire. I really appreciate it."

"Anytime." Claire's lips barely moved. "Good luck."

"Thanks."

Claire ducked out the front door without another word. Shelly watched her leave, a heaviness in the pit of her stomach making her feel uneasy. Today had not ended at all like she had expected.

"Ready?" Sasha held out her hand.

Shelly took it with an empty nod. She was certainly not ready. For any of this.

CHAPTER SEVENTEEN

L ucinda sipped the glass of white wine in front of her while eyeing the glass of red waiting for her attention. Samantha had stopped by a local winery to pick up a few bottles to taste test for the wedding. They had both been too busy to coordinate an evening after work to do an in-house tasting at the winery, but Samantha had somehow convinced them to send over a few bottles. Six bottles arrived in total, with some local cheese, honey, and a fruit assortment in a large wicker picnic basket wrapped with an equally large red bow.

"I'm still a little in awe that they sent over this entire spread." She sipped some water to cleanse her palate before picking up the bottle of red and reading the back. "We probably didn't need entire bottles either. I'm sure they have half bottles for this purpose."

"Don't be too impressed by my negotiation skills." Samantha walked into the room wearing an old loose dance shirt of Lucinda's and nothing else. "I booked them as a venue for next month's mixer. It's a combination thank-you and marketing basket."

Lucinda swirled the Malbec in the glass as she watched Samantha lean over to pick her purse up off the kitchen floor. Black panties made an appearance to the party. "You look comfy."

Samantha slid onto the stool next to her at the kitchen island with a big stretch and purr. "If we're having wine, cheese, and assorted cured meats for dinner, pants felt unnecessary. Are you complaining?" She sipped Lucinda's glass of chardonnay and wrinkled her nose with a subtle head shake. "Not this one."

"No complaints here." Lucinda reached below the counter to touch the side of Samantha's leg. "Agreed on the chardonnay, it's too—"

"Forgettable." Samantha supplied as she scooted forward, affording Lucinda better access to her thigh.

"Mm." Lucinda appreciated the soft skin under her fingers as she tried the Malbec. It was crisp, but full-bodied. It had a delicious aftertaste that lingered in the best way. "This is very, very good."

Samantha reached for the glass and motioned for Lucinda to start cutting into the cheese. "How was work, love?"

"Fine. I ducked out an hour early to swing by the studio and see Elijah's progress. They're doing their best to contain the dust, but I still had to sweep twice in the hour I was there." Lucinda begrudgingly removed her hand from Samantha's thigh to check the phone that blinked nearby on the counter.

"We knew this would be part of the difficulty of starting the new build and keeping the studio open. I can send over a cleaning crew a few nights a week if you think it would help." Samantha took a second sip from the wineglass. "This is delicious. Yes to the Malbec."

"I second that notion." Lucinda scanned through the emails on her phone briefly as she started moving cheeses onto the cutting board that Samantha had placed in front of her. She paused when she came across an email from Claire about their meeting with Shelly tomorrow.

"So I should send the cleaners? Or we agree on the Malbec?" Samantha unwrapped the cheeses Lucinda had abandoned as her focus shifted to the phone.

"I'll have the dance instructors do a sweep before and after each class, no cleaners necessary. And yes to the Malbec." Lucinda didn't look up from her phone. She felt her brow furrow as she read the brief two-line email a second time. Claire was confirming the appointment time and outlining the plan for the meeting. Still, something about the wording Claire chose struck her as off.

She put the phone down and looked up as Samantha held up a bottle of sauvignon blanc. "Shall we try this with the chèvre?"

"Sure." Lucinda began cutting the meats and cheeses as Samantha retrieved two fresh glasses from the cabinet. She organized the food on to the serving platter to her left and reached for the bread as she contemplated how she felt about Claire's email. Samantha placed warm olives on the tray in front of her and pushed a small glass of the new wine toward her and waited.

"What do you think?" Samantha asked as she popped an olive in her mouth and closed her eyes with a pleased sigh. "These are good."

Lucinda sampled the contents of the glass and nodded. "Better than the forgettable chardonnay. So, hey, Claire just emailed me about tomorrow's meeting with Shelly."

Samantha blinked her eyes open and her eyebrows raised ever so slightly. "That's great—she wants to be prepared. Why do you not look happy about that? Is that not great?" She put a sliver of goat cheese on the French bread Lucinda had cut and chewed it for a moment. "Let's just serve cheese at the wedding, this is orgasmic."

Lucinda opened her mouth to respond but Samantha slipped some bread and cheese in there, kissing her briefly as she picked up Lucinda's phone and looked at the screen. "What's the big deal?"

"That note seems a little short, right? Or am I just imagining things?" Lucinda swallowed her bite and waited for Samantha to comment further.

"You're imagining things." Samantha avoided eye contact.

Uh-oh, Lucinda recognized that behavior. Samantha knew something she wasn't telling her. "Samantha. Spill."

"You're imaging a shortness to an email." Samantha looked her straight in the eye only for a moment before she smiled broadly. "And maybe I didn't mention it before but Shelly and Claire sort of went on a date."

"A date? Why am I just hearing about this now? When did they go out?" Lucinda's chest felt tight. She'd had reservations about this when Samantha had first mentioned it, but she had been so caught up in the renovations and the wedding planning that it had slipped her mind. She had a hard enough time talking herself down when she'd received Claire's initial email letting her know about Shelly's interest in the company. And she had been extra careful to check in with Claire sparingly so as not to let her personal involvement with Shelly mix with work. But dating? That was not something she was prepared for.

"A while ago, after the mixer."

"After they started working together? She's a client of Clear View, Samantha. A client now. Not just our good friend Shelly." Lucinda reached for her wine, hoping it would lessen the tightening in her chest.

"Don't go all doomsday on me yet, Luce. I assure you, I didn't imagine their chemistry," Samantha soothed, her hand caressing Lucinda's arm. "I told you I thought they would be a good match. I know what I saw at the mixer. This is going to work."

"I have complete and utter faith in your intuition and am a *huge* fan of your imagination." Lucinda wiggled her eyebrows suggestively before pulling Samantha onto her lap and kissing her sweetly in part to calm her own anxieties about this revelation. "Mostly, I want to know what goes on in that beautiful mind of yours."

Samantha reclined in Lucinda's arms and fed her a grape from the platter. "It's simple. Claire likes girls. Shelly is a girl who happens to like Claire. Claire does PR work. Shelly had a new project she needed PR help with. Claire danced with Shelly at the mixer for the entire duration of the dance portion of the evening, not switching partners even once. They had great eye contact, nice physicality, lots of intimate touches exchanged, and afterward Claire gave Shelly her business card for future use. The future happened. Shelly put the business card to use. Personally, I think it may be my best work to date."

Lucinda laughed and accepted a second grape. "I always thought our relationship was your best work."

Samantha sighed. "As much as I'd like to take credit for this, you swept me off my feet long before I had plans of getting you to fall in love with me. This"—she pointed between them—"this is what makes me want to find Shelly that perfect match. It's something people search their whole lives for, and I'm right about this. I can feel it in my bones."

"Beautiful and wise? You must be too good to be true." Lucinda tried to quiet the nagging concern lingering in the back of her mind. "Promise me this won't backfire and result in me losing my best PR executive or Shelly as a friend if it doesn't work out?"

"I can promise you that if it doesn't work out, it won't be because of you or me. I've done as much as I can at this point. The rest is up to Shelly and Claire. If it's meant to be, it will be."

Lucinda held Samantha close and let the simplicity of that statement wash over her. If it was meant to be, it would be. It was as easy as that.

❖

Calling it a fitful night of sleep was generous. Claire looked at her reflection and frowned—the bags under her eyes were so dark it looked like she had gone swimming with yesterday's mascara on. She sighed and opened the medicine cabinet in search of Advil for the throbbing in her head. She contemplated the recommended dose and added one for good measure. She needed her wits about her at this meeting today. Who was she kidding? She needed her wits about her to face Shelly today.

She padded to the kitchen and looked at the clock—it was barely after six in the morning but she was wide awake. Or rather, she'd never really fallen asleep. The few moments of peace she thought she might get were filled with images of Shelly with the handsome firefighter. Her dark hair and equally dark eyes were a striking contrast to her uniform. Sasha was very, very attractive. And it made Claire furious.

She leaned against the counter and had a banana, dragging her toe along the cool tile floor while she tried to settle her emotions. Last night had been...a lot. Everything had been going fine with Shelly, better than fine, actually. Shelly had made a comment about not knowing if she had ever liked someone as much as Claire and the sincerity of it made her stomach flutter. She wasn't sure what to say in return so she had done what felt natural: she kissed her. It reminded her of the conversation they had had in the kitchen, when Shelly straddled her hips and looked into her eyes; she had told her that she felt comfortable being vulnerable and affectionate with her. It was something Claire mirrored—kissing Shelly, being intimate with her felt very natural. That's what had frightened her at first; she could see herself happy with Shelly and it terrified her.

Claire discarded the banana peel and undressed on her way to the shower, hoping it would help her clear the fog in her head. She turned on the water and waited for it to heat up before stepping in, letting the almost too hot water cleanse and massage her skin. She willed it to calm the beating sensation in her temples. She needed some respite. But the shower offered her no relief; instead she was inundated with visions of Shelly clutching at her hip, her lips inches from Claire's mouth. She could hear the soft, panting moans as she relived their first time together. If she closed her eyes, she could almost feel Shelly's palm splayed across her abdomen, moving lower with every breath she took. It was maddening.

She let out a frustrated whine and hung her head. She wanted the rage from last night back. She wanted to hide behind the anger. Anything was better than the insecurity and anxiety she felt right now. But why was she insecure? Shelly clearly liked her. It wasn't as though she was intimidated by Shelly's history with Sasha. No, it was the *history* itself.

Claire thought about the mix of emotions she had felt last night—the vividness was intense. It took a moment for the realization to settle in, but Sasha had opened the door and Shelly had confirmed it: Samantha had introduced them.

Shelly knew Samantha and Lucinda because she was a *client* of Samantha's.

Initially she was shocked by the matchmaker revelation, but that quickly gave way to anger. All along she had been worried about her job, her first real promotion and a huge opportunity for her. She was worried about disappointing Lucinda, who'd gone out on a limb for her, promoting her on the fast track because she had faith in her, pushing her ahead of people that she'd worked with who had much greater experience in the field. It was important for Claire to be successful, to prove that Lucinda had taken a worthy risk. But to find out that she might not have gotten this project with Boston Pro App on her merit alone? That was devastating. How much had Shelly's matchmaker influenced her becoming the lead on Shelly's case?

Claire was definitely mad, but she was mostly mad at herself. The fact was that she had jeopardized her job by engaging in a sexual relationship with her client while they were still in the midst of working together. It wasn't a bright move, and yet, it was as if she couldn't stop herself. She'd blurred the lines, and now everything was a mess.

Claire didn't dawdle in the shower too long. She had made up her mind—she wouldn't come out of this looking like a fool or a victim. She chose her outfit carefully, picking something that she knew accentuated her curves, intending to make a lasting impression. She slipped on her tallest heels and her mother's ring. She would need all the luck and strength she could get from it.

❖

Lucinda tapped her fingers along the smooth wood of her desk in thought. She had come into the office a little early to review Boston Pro App's holdings and ownership information. It had surprised her to see Claire busy at work at her desk, the door to her office slightly ajar.

That type of dogged motivation was one of the qualities she valued in Claire. It was one of the things that had turned her on to Claire's true potential. She was a talented and creative marketer. But more than that, she was a levelheaded and cool crisis management force. She was reminded of the way she had seen Claire interact with her predecessor, how he had issued her a thinly veiled threat when he thought he was out of earshot and she'd volleyed back a response so appropriate and cunning that he was dumbfounded. Firing Richard Thomas and giving Claire his job was one of the easiest decisions Lucinda had ever made. Claire was deserving of the position of senior executive. She worked hard and turned out work product that exemplified her ability to work closely with the client and get the job done. And her work with Shelly was no different. In fact, it was inspired. That's why Samantha's admission last night unnerved her.

Lucinda had reviewed the work Claire had done for Boston Pro App's upcoming exhibition at the tech expo. It was just a few days away now, but she could tell that Claire had logged long hours working on the pitch and marketing. She could see the pages and pages of research Claire had done about Boston Pro App's competitors, even seeking out the floor plan for the event and highlighting key access points and high traffic zones. She was obviously committed to making Shelly's product debut a major success. It was some of her best work.

Lucinda shifted in her chair. When Claire had emailed her last week to tell her about Shelly's business partner's unexpected departure, she had been a little surprised. This type of ownership shake-up in a company rarely came on quietly. She wanted to ask Shelly about it in person, but outside of the meeting. Today was a strategy meeting, not a friendship meeting. She needed to made sure she kept *business* Lucinda and *friend* Lucinda at different corners of the ring today. It made her wonder about the plan Samantha had implemented—this would be the first time she saw Shelly and Claire together in the same room since the lauded Miss Match had set things in motion. She was curious to see what had come of it, if anything. Samantha had been rather hush about the whole thing until last night. She couldn't tell if that was to spare her any concern or because nothing had developed. Lucinda had made it clear she wasn't willing to damage her friendship with Shelly or negatively impact her professional working relationship with Claire. *Business* and *friend* Lucinda were two parts of a whole, but they could not exist at the same time.

Her phone alarm chimed on the desk. It was time for the meeting.

❖

Lucinda tried to stifle the wince that was threatening to break the masklike face she was trying to project, but it was near impossible. The meeting had been going fine. That wasn't it. It was what was happening silently in front of her that made her want to cringe.

Claire had gathered a very competent team of legal and PR people to weigh in on Shelly's options regarding the D'Andre situation. The plan they presented was smart, well thought out, and creative. It gave Shelly the chance to save face while respecting her long-standing friendship with D'Andre, and at the same time protect the future of Boston Pro App. There would need to be concessions made on each side, but the plan was fair and reasonable. What was extremely unreasonable was the amount of tension between Shelly and Claire. They sat at opposite sides of the table and made little to no eye contact. Or rather, Claire made no eye contact with Shelly. Shelly, on the other hand, looked a little wounded. Lucinda wasn't sure if anyone else noticed, but from her vantage point at the front of the room, she saw everything. Every ignored, longing glance from Shelly and every suffocated emotion from Claire. All of it. And it pained her because this was when business trumped friendship.

"Great, that sounds like a good plan. I think there's plenty to consider here. Shelly, do you have any questions?"

Shelly looked surprised to be directly called upon, "N-no. I'm all set. Lots to c-consider. Thanks."

Lucinda frowned. Shelly was stuttering again. This was way worse than she'd thought. "Okay. Let's break for now and plan to finalize things by Monday."

The meeting started to break apart and Claire packed up her presentation materials in preparation to leave.

"Not you, you two stay." Lucinda stood and pointed to Claire and Shelly.

Claire looked at her blankly, then sat without saying a word. Shelly was still in her seat, her fingers nervously tapping the table.

"Shelly." Lucinda softened her voice and the tapping stopped.

Lucinda walked to the conference room door and closed it, the three of them contained in a bubble of silence. She walked back to the head of the table and sat, the other two women looking at her.

"I'm not going to ask anything because I don't want to know anything outside of what I do know, which is this: I know you two have done exceptional work on the Boston Pro App Expo launch that is coming up this weekend, and I know Shelly's company is in need of crisis management regarding D'Andre's position change in the company." She paused to let that sink in before continuing. "I also know that, Claire, you are more than qualified to handle that crisis management now that your work on the Expo is behind you and the actual event and launch are up to Shelly."

Claire nodded. She crossed her legs and shifted in her seat.

"With that being said, I'm removing you from lead on this new case." Lucinda sighed and watched Claire's brow furrow.

"What? Why? That was my plan the group just presented. It's perfect. I mean, it's a good starting point. Once all parties agree, we can move forward immediately. This whole thing can be tied up in a nice little bow before the end of next week. Long before Boston Pro App's next quarter review is due. It will save them any delays in production from the ownership change. If we move forward now, we can cut back on the losses." Claire leaned forward in her seat, defending her position as lead.

Lucinda frowned again. "I'm well aware of the depth of your work on this. I'm not removing you from it, I'm just moving you back from lead to a more supporting role—"

"But why?"

"Look at Shelly." Lucinda leaned back in her chair and watched as Claire hesitated. "That's why. We fix problems, Claire. We don't cause them. You not willing to look at your client is a problem."

"That's not...We're fine." Claire huffed.

"Enough. I'm not asking because I don't want to know." She looked at Shelly, who was pale. "You two need to fix whatever it is that is brewing here if you have any intention of working together, or otherwise. And to be clear, I don't want to know what that *otherwise* is in this office or at this table. Boston Pro App needs Clear View's help with D'Andre's potential departure. It's time sensitive and of the utmost importance. It needs to be handled the right way. And this"— she pointed between them—"is not working. Fix it."

She stood and gathered her belongings, stepping out of the conference room and closing the door behind her. She pulled her phone out of her vest pocket and texted Samantha, *We have a problem.*

❖

Claire cursed under her breath as Lucinda walked out of the room.

Shelly had been staring at Lucinda's empty seat, counting. Counting helped her calm her nerves. Counting was something reliable and familiar. It soothed her, so she counted. Until Claire finally spoke. She looked over at her and to her surprise, for the first time in two hours, Claire stared right back at her.

"I need you to review the plan I laid out and get back to the team as soon as you can. The faster we move on this the better. I'll have... whoever Lucinda puts in charge contact you with the details." Claire blinked and started to stand.

"Wait." Shelly had to bite the inside of her cheek to stop the stutter. Claire looked at her but didn't say anything. She made a move to stand again.

"Claire." Shelly tried again, this time her voice sounding more sure of itself.

"What?" She was met with resigned frustration.

"What happened? Why didn't you return my texts? Or my calls? Or anything? Why won't you look at me?" Shelly tried not to whine. But the desire to whine was in full force. Well, that and cry.

Claire stared back at Shelly like her questions were redundant. "Shelly, Lucinda's right. We should keep things professional. It may not matter to you, but it matters to me."

Shelly watched in disbelief as Claire again stood to leave. "What are you talking about? Am I the only one who was on that date last night? Did I imagine you kissing me against the car and talking about after-dinner plans? What changed?"

"What changed is the truth about you and Sasha meeting. That's what changed, Shelly."

Shelly had never seen Claire look so angry. "What does Sasha have to do with any of this? She's just a friend. Moreover, she's a firefighter who happened to be called to my father's house last night. That's all. Is that why you're upset? Do you think I'm interested in her, because I'm not—"

Claire held up her hand and closed her eyes. "I'm not worried about Sasha."

"Then what are you so upset about? She just drove me to the hospital, that's all—"

"Shelly." Claire opened her eyes and frowned. "I know you aren't interested in Sasha."

"Then why are we in a fight right now? Clearly, I'm head over heels for you and really want a chance to redo last night. I'm sorry it got interrupted, I—"

"You don't even know what you should be apologizing for, so stop." Claire's nostrils flared.

Shelly wasn't sure if she was supposed to say something or wait for Claire to speak. So she waited.

Claire huffed with frustration. "I'm upset because you neglected to mention to me that you know Samantha because she was your *matchmaker*."

"What does that have to do with anything? Of course I didn't tell you that's how I knew her. The first night you and I met, you went out of your way to tell me that you thought matchmaking was a crutch for people who were unlucky in love." Shelly hadn't even considered that Claire would care about her history with Samantha.

"Why did you ask me to dance?"

"What?" Shelly was lost again. She thought they were talking about Samantha.

"The dance at the fundraiser. Why did you ask me to dance? Is it because you thought I was attractive?"

"Well, yes and no." Shelly got the distinct impression she was being walked into a corner.

Claire scoffed. "Tell me, Shelly, why did you call me to work with you to begin with? Truthfully."

Shelly thought for a moment. "I called you because I needed help with a project and you came highly recommended. Plus, I'd met you and I thought we got along pretty well—I figured it was worth a shot."

"Really? Because it seems to me like you met me at a fundraiser hosted by your, quote, *matchmaker* and reached out to me afterward because you were attracted to me." Claire's air quotes amped up the hostility of the conversation. Shelly felt herself start to retreat. She was definitely cornered.

When she didn't reply, Claire continued, "You wanted to work with me because of how appealing I looked to you, not because of my merit or skill alone. God, this whole fucking time I've been warring with myself about whether or not acknowledging my attraction to you would be to the detriment of my career when all along you only reached out to me because you thought I was attractive. Do you have any idea how hurtful that is? I worked my ass off for you. I put in more hours and more time than anything I have ever done because I wanted to prove to you and everyone else I was capable of handling a client of your caliber."

"Claire, I didn't mean to—I'm sorry. It's not like that." Shelly tried to reason with her.

"What's it like then, Shelly? Tell me. Because that's what it looks like. Tell me I'm wrong." Claire crossed her arms, her face red with anger.

"I started talking to you at the fundraiser because that's what you do at those things. You talk to people and mingle. I asked you to dance because you were so easy to talk to, and yes, I thought you were attractive, because you are. It's not a crime to want to get to know someone because you're attracted to them."

"Did any of this happen organically, Shelly?" Claire pointed between the two of them. "Because I can't help but feel this, like everything else, is just some choreographed chess game."

"Of course this is r-real." Shelly took a breath to calm down.

Claire shook her head. "I can't believe anything you say."

"Claire, I've never lied to you. Maybe I omitted the Samantha thing, but only because it didn't matter. My feelings for you are real. I want this to work." Shelly hated the pleading in her voice. It made her feel weak. She was struggling to hold back tears; this was going all wrong.

"What else have you omitted, Shelly?" Claire challenged her. "How about, oh, I don't know, the tech company you purchased in Scottsdale? Care to discuss that?"

Shelly bit her tongue. Shit. "How did you—"

"How did I find out?" Claire pulled the stack of papers out of her bag and spread them out in front of her, facing Shelly. "I'm good at my job, Shelly. I researched Boston Pro App and all of its holdings to protect you and the business from D'Andre's departure. And you neglected to tell me, when you were pouring your heart out to me while you straddled my lap in your kitchen, that you owned the company your mother's husband worked for. I checked the dates, Shelly. You acquired it after he started working there. It's the only purchase you've made through the company's name without D'Andre's involvement. That's a little more than keeping an eye on things."

She pointed to the highlighted text in front of her. "One more chess piece in the puzzle. How many pieces did you have to move to make me fall for you? Was that night at the gym all fake, too? Did you know I was going there to break things off with you? Is that why you asked me to come home with you? To keep the pieces in motion? I can't believe I let myself think these two things, this work and our relationship, were completely separate. They never have been, have they?"

Shelly blinked, unsure of what to say.

"You never had anything to lose in this, Shelly. Not one thing. At the end of the day you are still a successful multimillionaire with the world at your fingertips. I had everything to lose, and against my better judgment, I took a risk on you, on us. I developed feelings for you and didn't keep it professional, and where did that get me? Taken off the case, embarrassed in front of the one person who went to bat for me all along. You played me, and now I lost an opportunity of a lifetime because you couldn't be honest with me from the beginning." Claire scooped up the papers and stood, marching for the door.

"Nothing between us has been orchestrated, Claire, I promise you that. I should have been more open with you—I was wrong. But I've never lied to you about my feelings for you." Shelly stood and raced to meet her, catching her as she reached for the door handle. "Please, wait."

Claire stopped and looked her straight in the eyes. "I was wrong, too. I should've been honest with you that night at the gym. I should've told you this wouldn't work. I knew that going into that weekend, and I regret that. Good luck at the Expo, Shelly."

And just like that, Claire walked out of the conference room and out of her life.

Chapter Eighteen

Claire struck out for the second time at bat this game. Her teammates screamed encouragement from the sidelines, but it didn't help. She wasn't focused, and she hadn't been in days.

"You need to get it together. It's the finals. This is the only thing standing between us and the championship." Jamie put his arm around her and walked her to the back of the dugout. He handed her a water and patted her on the shoulder. "We need to keep people on base, even if you have to bunt. It's all tied up, Claire-Bear. We need to win this."

Jamie gave her a quick hug and jogged to home plate for his next at bat.

She wanted nothing more than to make her brother proud. Jamie had managed to hit at least one home run in every game this season and they were favored to sweep the playoffs, but this last game was a lot harder than they had expected. It didn't help that she kept checking her phone to see what time it was. The Expo would be ending any minute now. She couldn't help but wonder how Shelly did. She tried not to think about it, but it felt hopeless.

Jamie swung the bat and sent the ball flying toward the outfield. It bounced once, then twice, before it was scooped up—a solid hit, but not a home run. As one of their runners crossed home plate with a dramatic slide, the crowd gasped. They scored the run, but their pitcher had been injured in the process. Jamie was stuck on third, holding his head in disbelief as the pitcher limped into the dugout. Their next player walked up to bat, but no one bothered watching. He was notorious for striking out—that's why he batted after Jamie. Jamie's home run streak made him a near shoo-in for runs. It didn't matter if this guy struck out or not. And tonight was no different, strike three. Out.

Jamie jogged into the dugout and grabbed Claire by the shoulders. "Listen, all those times I made fun of you for being the backup pitcher, I take back. We are up by one and you need to close out this game, Claire. You can do this. Mope later, it's time to get your head in the game."

"Jamie." Claire wasn't ready for this, she hadn't practiced pitching all season. "I can't."

Jamie shook his head. "You can. You have to. I believe in you. Now go out there and win this damn game for us. Three outs, that's all you need."

Claire was aware of the eyes of her teammates on her as she gave Jamie a halfhearted nod. "Okay."

"That doesn't sound like the *okay* of a winner, Claire. Try it again." Jamie nudged her in the side.

"Okay, I can do this." Claire didn't believe a word she was saying, but he was looking at her so earnestly that she felt compelled to lie.

"Good. Go get 'em."

❖

Shelly sighed and dropped her head. That was the fifth person to walk by with auburn hair that was not Claire. No matter how many times Shelly reminded herself that Claire had made it abundantly clear that she wouldn't be at the Expo, she still couldn't stop feeling let down, over and over. They had worked tirelessly on this project; Claire had even advised Shelly on the colors and spacing of the words on her marketing materials with consideration to the distance from the lights and the path of foot traffic. This entire event was organized and planned by Claire and she was nowhere in sight.

The launch had been flawless. There were multiple local and national news agencies that came by to witness a demonstration of the new products. She had given half a dozen interviews already, doing her best to stay focused, not stutter, and not think about the person who was missing. Shelly's torture continued when it became very clear that she wouldn't be able to change the subject of her hologram app in time for the Expo. Shelly had been working herself to the bone to adapt a daytime video for the Expo. She had gotten enough live-action feed from Claire's softball game to rework the app with both still and moving background images. It had taken a miracle and a prayer, but she had finally finished it the day of her cooking class date with Claire.

She had intended to show Claire that she would be the star of the Expo footage: a hologram of her playing softball, hitting a winning run and sliding across home. It would have been a perfect end to their night and their project together. But things didn't turn out that way.

"Shelly." Toby gave her a broad smile, his Expo staff lanyard hanging crookedly on his neck. "They want to shoot some pictures and a little video for the Boston Pro App website. Is that cool?"

The idea of being filmed made Shelly wince. It was hard enough for her to openly engage with strangers about her product without Claire here to give her that added bit of support she had grown accustomed to getting from her mere presence. Asking her to do a tutorial on video was crossing a line.

"I don't know, Toby." She bit the inside of her cheek when he looked back at her expectantly. She sighed. She was the captain now. This was something she just had to do, like it or not. "Okay. Sure."

"Great." Toby forced her into a high five and flagged over the videographer and photographer that Claire had encouraged her to hire for the event. "Shelly is going to answer some questions and do a little demo. It's gonna be so awesome." His enthusiasm should have been infectious, but she couldn't seem to rise to the occasion.

He looked at her and glanced over his shoulder, lowering his voice to add, "Claire's team is all tied up. They're still in it."

She looked at him with wide eyes. He gave her a subtle nod and held up his cell phone. The game was being broadcast live on local television.

"How did you—?" Shelly took his phone to get a better look. Jamie was up at bat.

Toby shrugged. "She told me about it the last time she was by the office. I made a softball shape with the rocks of the Zen garden for the occasion. She seemed bummed that the finals were the same day as the Expo. That's why she's not here, right?"

Shelly didn't have the heart to tell him Claire wasn't here because she'd royally fucked everything up. She handed him back his phone and tried not to think about it. "Yeah. Hey, keep me posted on the outcome, okay?"

"Sure thing, Boss." He handed her a cold water and stepped out toward the gathering crowd to get them in some semblance of a line before the filming began. She was grateful he had volunteered to be her assistant today—it was nice to have a friendly and supportive face around.

"Ready, Ms. White?" The photographer smiled at her brightly and she did her best to mirror his expression.

"Shelly, please. And yeah, I guess. Ready as I'll ever be." She took a sip of her water and decided it didn't really matter either way.

❖

Jamie and the team cheered as the third round of beers slid across the bar. Jamie raised his glass in a toast. "To Claire, for closing out the game in style—only two opposing players injured by wild pitches before the fourth struck out due to fear alone!"

Claire cringed and shook her head as everyone cheered and drained their glasses. The first batter hit a pop-up that was easily caught by her outfield teammate. It had not been her intention to hit the second girl—she'd limped onto first base and was tagged out when she tried to run for second when Claire's second pitch narrowly missed the third batter as he attempted to bunt. Two outs. The fourth at bat looked panicked. Claire barely missed her head on the first throw, and Jamie was right—she'd shied away from the other two pitches. Third out. Game over. They'd won. But Claire found no enjoyment in the win.

As the team started to break up into smaller groups and pair off, Claire found herself at the bar next to Jamie, who was snapping selfies with the championship trophy.

"C'mon, Claire. Smile for the camera." He held up his phone and scooted closer. She smiled and posed, the flash blinding her a little.

He pulled up the picture and frowned. "Claire, you look pained. For the love…We just won the championship. Can you please try to enjoy yourself? You had the winning play."

This was the only game of the season at which Jamie didn't hit a home run—but they'd won anyway. And greatly in part to Claire's unexpected pitching stint. She smiled, unbelieving that was how the night unfolded.

"That's what I'm talking about." Jamie gave her a cheesy grin and held the trophy between them, snapping a photo before she could pull away. He spun his phone around and showed her the picture. "See that? That's the face of a winner."

"The unstoppable Moseleys." Claire laughed as a few of her teammates cheered from the dartboard in the corner.

"Hey, rumor has it you've got a hell of a wild pitch." A velvety voice in her ear drew her attention away from her brother.

Barfly Nikki gave her a flirty smile and leaned against the bar, her customary outfit of leather and dark fabric appearing tighter than usual today. She looked as hot as always, maybe hotter. "Can I buy you a drink? You know, to help celebrate."

Jamie answered for her. "She'd love that."

Nikki nodded and waved down the bartender as Claire grabbed Jamie by the shirt collar and pulled him closer. "What are you doing?"

"Trying to get you laid. You've been in a funk since the middle of last week. Maybe you just need a distraction or two." Jamie nudged her toward Nikki, her back toward them as she called out the order to the bartender. "Or maybe you should just call Shelly and patch things up."

"Jamie, I told you, I'm not—"

"I know, I know. You're not interested in forgiving her even though you are clearly in love with her. Fine, suit yourself. But know, I am completely against that excuse." Jamie finished his beer and grabbed the trophy, carrying it toward the players chanting his name.

"So, how've you been?" Nikki slid a reddish looking cocktail toward Claire with a smile. "You look good."

"Thanks." Claire accepted the drink because it felt rude not to. It was sweet with the distinct taste of raspberry.

"I heard you had the play of the game." Nikki stood closer to Claire, leaning in to speak. The volume in the bar was increasing with every new round Claire's team ordered. They were chanting the team name over and over while doing the wave. It was hilarious.

Claire laughed as she watched her brother complete a mock home run swing and point toward the ceiling. "Yeah, maybe. I don't know about that. I think I was lucky."

Nikki winked at her. "Lucky is good. Maybe you and I can use some of that luck over there." She pointed behind them toward the darkened back corner of the bar by the stained velvet couch that was a notorious spot for drunken make-out sessions. Not unlike the one they'd shared this time last year when Claire's team lost.

Claire swallowed her drink awkwardly, coughing and gasping. "The couch?"

Nikki laughed. "At the dartboard, in the corner. Care to play?"

Claire felt herself blush. Of course she wanted to play darts. "Sure."

"Good. C'mon, champ." Nikki slid her hand into Claire's and pulled her toward the dartboard.

❖

Claire seemed to be batting a thousand—not once in her entire life had she won a game of darts, and tonight, she'd won twice. Granted, Nikki had also won twice, so they were tied, but Nikki was clearly a dart-winning seduction master, so she was feeling pretty proud of herself for winning at all.

Nikki's hands were on her hips, holding her from behind. Her fingers squeezed and massaged as she spoke into Claire's ear. "One more game, to break the tie? Winner takes all?"

Claire had had enough to drink to feel warm and tingly all over, those tingles intensifying as Nikki's lips ghosted near her ear, her hands staying firmly at Claire's waist. "One more game, and then I have to go home."

"Game on." Nikki chuckled and slid one of her hands down the front of Claire's thigh, while the other grabbed Claire's ass possessively. "You go first."

Claire's head felt a little foggy and she had to squint to focus on the board in front of them. There was no way she was going to be able to play a whole game. "On second thought, let's spice things up. First person to hit a bull's-eye wins."

Nikki leaned back and gave her a sly smile. "Full bull's-eye or whoever is closest? And how many throws do we let these shenanigans continue for?"

"Full bull's-eye. Five throws. If no one wins, we schedule a rematch."

"Oh, someone will be winning tonight." Nikki mulled this over. "Okay, deal."

"Good." Claire grabbed the nearest dart and stepped up to the line. Her first throw was way off, nearly missing the board. The crowd that had gathered around them booed.

"This is going to be a piece of cake." Nikki wound back and hit somewhere near the center, but Claire couldn't quite tell exactly where. She was having a hard time focusing.

"Hey, I'm on a lucky streak, remember? Don't be so cocky." She squared her shoulders and closed one eye in hopes of improving her aim. Round two went much better. She nearly matched Nikki's dart.

"Hmm." Nikki gave her another playful wink. "Let's raise the stakes. If I hit a bull's-eye on this next throw, you have to kiss me in front of all these people." A few people cheered behind her.

Claire glanced around to see Jamie at the edge of the crowd, watching. He was drinking what looked like a water. She felt suddenly thirsty. She licked her lips at the thought.

"So, deal?" Nikki was close to her again, her eyes on Claire's lips.

Not one to back down from a challenge, Claire nodded. "Deal."

Nikki stepped to the line and gave her one last brief glance before staring down the board and sinking a perfect score. Bull's-eye. The crowd hooted and hollered as Nikki threw her hands up in victory. She took one long stride toward Claire and placed both of her hands on Claire's jaw, pressing a firm, wet kiss to Claire's lips. Even though she had been expecting it, Claire still gasped, her open mouth interpreted as an invitation by Nikki, who deepened the kiss and walked Claire back to the high-top table behind them. As Claire's back pressed against the table, she paused, pressing her hands to Nikki's shoulders and easing her back.

Nikki gave her a lazy smile. "Just because your luck's run out doesn't mean you can't still get lucky. Why don't we get out of here and see what trouble we can get into together?"

Nikki's hands were on Claire's hips. Her thumb traced the pocket of Claire's jeans and her dark blue eyes looked hungry. As the alcohol swirled in Claire's system, making her feel warm all over, she thought about the proposition before her. The idea of getting fucked right now was more than appealing, and if this had been two months ago, she would have jumped at the chance to know what it was like to have Nikki's hands all over her, not unlike this very moment. But it wasn't two months ago. It was right now, and right now she was thinking about a different set of eyes altogether, a vibrant green pair.

She leaned forward and pressed a quick, short kiss to Nikki's lips with a frown. "I think I've had enough excitement tonight, but thanks for the offer."

Nikki ran a hand through her hair and nodded. "Another time, perhaps. Thanks for the game."

Claire stepped away from Nikki's embrace and tried to steady herself as she turned toward the door. She looked around for her keys and found Jamie standing nearby with a bottle of water for her. She took it and sighed.

"Ready to head out, Claire-Bear?" Jamie hefted the championship trophy in one hand and held out his other elbow for her.

"Yeah." Claire nodded and sipped her water, trying to ignore the sad pang that came with the term of endearment. Shelly had been calling her that lately. "I just have to find my keys."

"I have 'em. I'm driving home tonight." Jamie jingled her keys in his pocket.

"Sounds good." The room was spinning a little. She had a feeling she would agree to just about anything right now.

As she slipped into the passenger seat of her car, she looked out the window toward the bar's front door. Nikki was leaning against the building, talking on the phone. She waved at Claire and gave her another wink. Claire gave her a small wave in return.

"She winks a lot," Jamie commented as he put the car in reverse and headed toward their family home.

"Maybe she has a tic." Claire shrugged and kept looking out the window. She thought about complaining that Jamie was taking her back to the house instead of to her own apartment, but she didn't feel like talking much.

"So, how was the kiss?"

She turned to find him watching her as they idled at the stoplight. "It was fine." Claire shrugged. She had no desire to think about it anymore.

"Really? Because from where I was sitting it looked like it was lacking—"

"Fireworks." Claire sighed.

"Right." Jamie nodded and accelerated as the light changed. He reached out and took Claire's hand in his as they turned down the familiar streets of her past. "Tomorrow is a new day, Claire."

She nodded and hoped he was right.

Chapter Nineteen

Samantha laughed as Lucinda twirled her along the floor. Even after all this time she never bored of the sensation of flying that Lucinda so effortlessly granted her. Dancing with Lucinda was as important as kissing her. It was home. And that was exactly the type of respite they needed as of late.

"You're thinking too much. Let me lead you." Lucinda's lips at her ear reminded her to relax and be in the moment. She obliged because anytime Lucinda's mouth gave her a command that close to her ear, she was immediately going to benefit from complying. Often *benefiting* more than once.

Samantha nodded and focused, gripping Lucinda's hand harder and turning her hip in time with Lucinda's, planting her feet with more authority, her heels clicking on the floor in a well-practiced routine. This was their first dance, after all—she'd better represent.

The song ended and Lucinda dipped her, holding her in that delicate extension with full control, her hands and arms in all the key places to make Samantha feel weightless and supported at the same time. And just like every time Lucinda dipped her, they ended in a kiss and all those butterflies from the first time they'd ever danced so intimately came fluttering back, warming her stomach and her heart and usually some other places as well.

"Beautiful, Samantha." Lucinda praised her as she pulled her up and into a hug. "That was very, very good."

Samantha allowed herself to be snuggled close, taking the opportunity to breathe Lucinda in, the light sweat of her dance classes coating the faint smell of her perfume from her workday earlier. It was one of Samantha's favorite scents: corporate badass and sensual dance instructor.

"Very, very good is not perfect. You're not fooling anyone with that, Luce." Samantha kissed her fiancée because she was delicious and she could.

"No one is perfect, love." Lucinda spun Samantha in her arms, sliding up behind her and moving to the imaginary beat. "Not even me."

After a moment, Samantha turned in her arms again, then took Lucinda's face in her hands. "I beg to differ. You are the picture of perfection: tall, blond hair, blue eyes, great legs, perfect teeth. What else could one ask for?"

"Well, as long as you think I'm perfect for you, then that's all that matters."

"See? And you think I'm always right. Good thing I convinced you to marry me before you realized the error of your ways," Samantha teased and walked toward the bench for the stereo's remote to start the song again.

Lucinda waited for her with open arms when she returned, getting them into position as the music began. "You know, we have to talk about the wedding. And your apartment. And the seating chart. Don't think I forgot."

Samantha glided to the right and mentally applauded herself for not missing the step. "This is one of those distraction methods you use with Shelly, isn't it? Challenge my mind and emotion to get my body to do what we've been practicing. You're positively diabolical."

Lucinda turned them and led to the left. "Samantha."

"Fine." Samantha matched Lucinda's steps and adjusted her hand on Lucinda's back preparing for the first spin. "I agree that having life-sized ice replicas of us dancing is impractical and begrudgingly have canceled them because you feel it's over the top."

Lucinda smiled. "Because it is."

"Agree to disagree." Samantha twirled perfectly to the left. She was totally winning this dancing thing.

"Now the apartment." Lucinda glided them to the right and turned them toward the door, taking more dramatic steps, challenging Samantha's focus.

"I want to move in with you full time, Lucy. I do. See? I'm getting so good at that. *I do.*" Lucinda rewarded her with a hearty laugh and turned them again. Samantha readied herself for the upcoming spin. "I know you told me I can keep the apartment in the city and we can split time between both places, but it's a complete waste of money, and I love your place. I really do."

"You know that's what I want to hear, right?" Lucinda pressed against her hand and led her into a spin, this time to the left. "I just want to make sure you're comfortable with that."

"I am. As long as you hire someone to shovel and promise to walk the dog." Samantha nodded, stepping to the right more forcefully to cause her heel to echo on the floor.

"We're getting a dog?" Lucinda's question came with a smile. She was as agreeable as usual.

"Eventually, yes. Probably two."

"Two?" Lucinda's eyes were big but her lips remained curved upward.

"Lucy. Of course. We don't want one to get lonely. You know, when we're busy with the kids." Samantha loved saying that. It was common knowledge that they both had a desire to have a family. That's what had gotten her to agree to move out to Lucinda's house to begin with. It was plenty big enough for a family, it had a private yard, it was close to the Arboretum, there was green space everywhere, and the access to the schools and after-school programs was unbeatable. She would have moments when she missed the luxury of living in a high-rise city condo. But she was willing to trade all of those moments for a chance to have a family with Lucinda. It was a no-brainer.

"Okay. Two dogs. Kids. Snow removal service. Consider it done." She was beaming. Samantha knew Lucinda would do just about anything when she brought up having a family. Which was precisely why she'd just done it. She needed all the ammunition she could get for the inevitable next question—

"Now the seating chart." Lucinda was consistent as consistent was consistent.

Samantha narrowed her eyes at Lucinda and took a deep breath. They were entering the final sprint of this dance and there were a few really fast, tricky steps before the final twirl and dip. She needed all her wits about her if she was going to negotiate a seating change with Lucinda and manage to nail the steps.

"Okay, so, I'm fine with putting Connie and Nathan at the head table with Andrew and Ben, but I really think we should separate the Andiamos and my parents. It's a bad idea, Lucy—the Andiamos deserve better than my mother." Samantha knew Lucinda was in agreement with her, but Tessa and Antonino Andiamo had balked when they'd found out they would not be at the same table as Samantha's parents. Lucinda had tried to explain to them that she saw *them* as her true family with Connie, and was even having Antonino walk her down the aisle, but had begged them to sit at a table with their friends and family. The conversation quickly escalated into angry Italian with Antonino refusing to be placed anywhere else and Tessa telling Lucinda that family was family whether you liked them or not. And although both she and Lucinda knew that wasn't true, they knew better than to argue with the Andiamos. So they had conceded.

"Samantha." Lucinda looked pained. "You know I want nothing more than to banish your mother to the dishwasher's stand in the kitchen next to your brother and his intolerable wife, but Mama was very clear. She wants to be at the table with them—they want to try to bridge the gap. You know how she is, Samantha, once her mind is made up—"

"I know, I know. It's done." Samantha sighed and squared her shoulders in preparation for the final moves.

Lucinda twirled Samantha and held her in a dip, sealing their dance with a kiss before she pulled her back up with an ecstatic look on her face. "Samantha! That was perfect."

Samantha had been so busy trying to figure out a way to secretly change the seating chart to look like the wedding planner's error that she hadn't noticed they had finished the dance without a single mistake. Lucinda kissed her and spun her with a laugh, the sound music to her ears.

"You totally used the Shelly distraction technique on me, didn't you? Admit it." Samantha pretended to pout, but Lucinda's lips easily kissed it away.

"I would never do such an underhanded thing as talk about something that was very important to you only to use those brownie points to get a desired response about something else entirely." Lucinda held her in a hug even as she tried to wriggle away. "Because who would do something like that?"

Samantha laughed. "You got me. How'd you know?"

Lucinda kissed her forehead and pulled Samantha against her chest. "At this point, I can smell the mischief on you a mile away. Don't think I didn't notice that you asked to squeeze in a first-dance lesson immediately before Shelly's usually scheduled time."

Samantha turned and leaned back, batting her eyelashes at Lucinda in a flirtatious manner. "Lucy, you said yourself that we have a problem, and what better way for me to evaluate said problem than to get Shelly wrapped up in your arms, too distracted to be evasive. The way I look at it, if Claire and Shelly are at odds, it's because they both have something invested they are afraid to lose. Simple human nature—run from something that scares you. What's scarier than love? We'll get to the bottom of this. I know it."

Lucinda smiled and walked toward the remote, hitting play again. She stepped back up to Samantha and returned them to their starting position. "All right, Miss Match, we shall see. In the meantime, let's try it again, once more."

❖

Shelly anxiously tapped her hands on the steering wheel of her car as she sat outside Lucinda's dance studio. She usually loved these lessons—they'd been the highlight of her week for the better part of a year—but she had to admit she was a little nervous. She was nervous about seeing Lucinda again since Shelly had canceled their last session. She was afraid Lucinda would notice that things were different now— she had this sort of uncanny ability to sense things. Shelly felt like she might be able to fake it, as long as Samantha wasn't here to see her. Samantha knew her better than she knew herself, and she could spot Shelly trying to fake any and every emotion. The two of them were like psychics in that way. Lucinda could read a subtle physical tremor like a textbook and Samantha was the queen of breaking down any nervous, unconscious emotional reaction. Shelly often assumed this was why she had become so close with the women; they were able to tell her things about herself that she didn't realize herself. They could interpret her stress and anxieties without her having to voice them. It was refreshing to be around people who were so in tune with the little details of life that were so often ignored. She was guilty of ignoring a lot of things before she met Lucinda and Samantha. That was also why she was a little nervous to see Lucinda today. She was worried about disappointing her, because lately, feeling like a disappointment was as easy as breathing.

She opened the dance studio door and frowned. Samantha was there, too. There was no avoiding anything now.

The song ended and Lucinda smiled in Shelly's direction. "I'm glad you made it, Shelly."

Shelly didn't feel so glad, but she didn't say anything. She walked to the coat rack and shrugged off her oversized jacket—she hadn't been feeling much like her usual self, so she had reverted to a few older articles of clothing she had hoarded in the wardrobe overhaul Samantha had encouraged. She found security in the old quilted jacket. She needed that security today when she'd agreed to see Lucinda again after that meeting with Claire over two weeks ago. Things had been rough.

"Samantha, I didn't expect to see you tonight." Shelly tried to ease into casual conversation. Samantha was having none of that.

"Of course you didn't. You've been avoiding my calls." Samantha walked to her and held out her arms. "Come here and give me some love, I've missed you."

Shelly stepped into Samantha's arms and dropped her head. "I'm sorry."

"Don't be sorry. You don't need to apologize for how you feel." Samantha held her tightly and rocked them a little side to side. "Tell me what's going on."

Shelly let herself be enveloped in her friend's arms. It was the first time she'd had any real affection in weeks, outside of Hedy's concerned head-butts and meows. Things had been falling apart all around her. Her father was held for a few nights at the hospital following his fall and had been resistant to talking to her since his discharge, she and Claire fought at the meeting and then Claire never showed up at the Expo, and two days ago she started the restructuring of her company with D'Andre's lawyer—D'Andre had made no direct communication to her at all. In the span of two short weeks she had damaged her relationship with her father, lost her girlfriend, and was losing her business partner and one of her oldest friends at the same time. The weight of it all overwhelmed her and she sagged in Samantha's arms, grateful for the support.

"It's okay, Shel," Samantha cooed and rubbed her back. "Let it out."

That did it. Shelly started crying and didn't stop until she had run out of tears. Samantha held her close and waited it out with her, rubbing her back and combing her hands through Shelly's hair. At some point Lucinda had joined them, taking Shelly's hand in hers. She really did love these women, and she felt entirely loved back. It was exactly what she needed in that moment.

"Thank you." Shelly sniffled and Lucinda let go of her hand long enough to hand her some tissues.

Samantha loosened her arms to allow Shelly to blow her nose and wipe her eyes, but she stayed close. They both did.

After a few minutes, Shelly exhaled, ready to talk. "Okay."

"Okay," Samantha parroted and released her, stepping back. Lucinda's hand settled between Samantha's shoulder blades and they both looked at her with patient attention. Not pity. And Shelly appreciated that.

"I'm not sure where to begin." Shelly dragged her toe along the floor.

Samantha nodded. "Let's start backward a bit—what happened after your softball non-date?"

"Well." She glanced at Lucinda, unsure of what to say considering the meeting she'd had with Claire and Lucinda two weeks ago. "Um, some work stuff happened. D'Andre left."

Samantha nodded and Lucinda spoke for the first time. "I let Samantha know a little bit about the structural change at work. Nothing detailed, but she's aware."

"Oh." That didn't really answer Shelly's unasked question. "Does she know about the meeting?"

Lucinda considered this before nodding in acknowledgment. "A little, yes."

"Lucy told me that you and Claire had some hostility at the meeting, but that's all I know. Feel like filling me in?" Samantha gave her that patient smile again, and she felt better.

Shelly looked at Lucinda again. "Am I supposed to tell you or just Samantha? Because I'm not sure…you said you didn't want to know."

"Ah, right." Lucinda looked between her and Samantha. "You finished your end of the negotiations with D'Andre, right? You're just waiting on his final approval?"

"Right."

"And Claire's involvement has all but ceased, correct? Legal is handling everything now, is that true?"

"Yes." Shelly hated that her interactions with Clear View of late didn't include Claire. But at the same time she assumed that was for the best. They hadn't spoken since that day in the office. She wasn't sure she could even face her if she had to.

"Well, then it's up to you whether you want me to know anything. As far as I'm concerned you and Claire worked together in the past and had success with the Expo and the restructuring, but she is no longer the primary on your case and any future involvement from her is unlikely. So"—Lucinda tossed an imaginary hat from her head and put on a new one—"business hat is gone, friend hat is on. This is a safe friend space, Shelly."

Shelly exhaled. She wanted them both to know what happened because she valued their input. "So, D'Andre told me he was leaving and I kind of freaked out. I just left work and locked myself in a room at the gym and beat balls until I was too exhausted to function. Claire came by to talk to me about something, but D'Andre had just walked out and I was super upset, so I asked her to take me home, and maybe she spent the better part of the weekend in bed with me."

Samantha blinked, her previous expression overtaken by a sly grin. "Well, that's a new development."

"Mm-hmm." Shelly wasn't sure what to say. Samantha had this look on her face, like a mixture of triumph and contemplation. Shelly was a little frightened.

"So you had sex." Samantha's tone was light, playful. "And?"

"And it was incredible." Shelly didn't care if she sounded like a lovestruck fool. She was just so happy to talk about it with someone. Besides Hedy, who, though mostly attentive, didn't give her much constructive feedback.

Samantha gave her a broad smile, reaching out to squeeze Shelly's hand once before clapping her hands together. "Yes! I knew it. You two are perfect for each other."

"But then I fucked it up." Shelly frowned, her shoulders sagging again.

Samantha pouted. "Does this have to do with the meeting?"

"No, not exactly. Well, yes. Sort of." Shelly looked between Samantha and Lucinda. "It's complicated."

"Start at the beginning," Lucinda encouraged her.

"We had a great weekend—really, it was mind-blowing. She's so perfectly relaxed in her own skin. Like, she's confident and sexy and cool. She's a total opposite to how I feel at all times. She just came into my space and it was like she'd been there my whole life. She played with my cat and was eating breakfast at my table and it was just like a normal routine. Except with more sex and lots of kissing."

Samantha laughed. "Okay, sounds good. So what happened?"

"I'm not really sure. We formally scheduled a date and then at the end of it I got a call that my father had fallen and I was totally freaked out so Claire drove me to his house. And Sasha was there and she introduced herself to Claire and told her we used to date and I panicked and got beyond awkward and may have mentioned that Sasha was introduced to me by you." She motioned between her and Samantha.

"Your father fell?" Lucinda looked concerned.

"Sasha's back in town?" Samantha looked perplexed.

"Yes and yes." Shelly wasn't sure who to answer first. "My dad's fine, he's just mad that I had him sent to the hospital. Sasha was the firefighter on call. Turns out she never went to that training out west. And she was her usual charming self, and Claire asked how we knew each other and then you came up and shit hit the fan."

"Why?" Lucinda asked.

"Because Claire thinks matchmaking is a joke and a crutch," Samantha supplied with a sigh.

"Right." Shelly nodded. "And she thinks I lied to her from the start and that you choreographed the whole meet-and-greet business connection."

"Which I did," Samantha said.

"So what's wrong exactly?" Lucinda looked between them.

"Claire wasn't necessarily supposed to know that the mixer was a setup. It was supposed to happen organically, which it did, with some guidance." Samantha chewed her bottom lip. "She probably feels duped."

Lucinda gave Samantha a face. "Shit."

"Yeah." Shelly felt hopeless.

Samantha thought for a moment, one hand resting on her hip as she tapped her bottom lip in contemplation. "What did she say to you exactly?"

"Something along the lines that she felt like I used her like a chess piece and manipulated her into falling for me from the start." Shelly didn't think she could forget those words if she tried.

"Ouch." Lucinda winced.

"She said that?" Samantha looked oddly excited. Nothing about this seemed exciting to Shelly.

"Yes." Shelly started to wring her hands in anxiety.

"What else did she say?" Samantha asked again.

Shelly felt the desire to pull at her shirt collar. She wasn't looking forward to repeating this next part.

"Shelly," Samantha prompted.

"Uh, she also told me she had intended to break things off with me before I told her the D'Andre news and that maybe spending the weekend with me had been a bad idea." Shelly couldn't look at them when she said it, so she focused on the floor.

"She said what?" Lucinda's voice rose infinitesimally. Shelly looked up. She had never heard Lucinda's volume increase, ever.

"Shh." Samantha placed a hand on Lucinda's forearm and turned back toward Shelly. "She was hurt. Don't put much weight on that."

"How does someone not put weight on that?" Shelly felt nauseous as she relived the conversation. Claire's response had crippled her. She wasn't sure she would ever recover. Forget about seeing Claire again, she was pretty sure she would be celibate for the rest of her days. Alone and with her cat. The thought depressed her.

Samantha shook her head and continued, "She told you she felt like you manipulated her into falling for you. *Falling for you*, Shel. She likes you a lot. You hurt her feelings. She lashed out. It happens." Samantha shrugged like it was no big deal.

Lucinda was looking at Samantha like she had five heads. "The things that go on in that mind of yours truly mystify me."

"Ditto." Shelly wondered if Samantha had missed the part where Claire essentially told her to fuck off for eternity. "You do realize she basically told me she never wanted to see me again, right?"

"Did she say that?" Samantha crossed her arms and cocked her head.

"Not in so many words."

Samantha reached out and took Lucinda's hand, holding it up in front of Shelly. "Someone once told me if I couldn't live with the thought of Lucinda not in my life, then I had to get my shit together and tell her that, before the best thing to ever enter my life walked right out of it. Is Claire someone you want in your life, Shelly?"

"Yes." That was the easiest question they had asked her all night.

"Then you need to figure that shit out. Go get your girl, Shelly." Samantha brought Lucinda's hand to her lips and kissed it. Lucinda smiled at her and Shelly hated them a little.

"You make it sound so easy."

"Did you do anything intentionally wrong?" Samantha reasoned.

"You mean, besides neglect to mention you put us both in the same place at the same time?" Shelly rolled her eyes.

"That doesn't mean you two would hit it off. That was all you. I just made sure you'd intersect," Samantha pointed out with a raised eyebrow. "These sound like excuses."

Lucinda cleared her throat and looked at Shelly, her usual calm confidence on display again. "Claire's tenacious. When Samantha first mentioned pairing you two, I had my doubts. But I noticed a change in her immediately—the work she did with you was absolutely inspired, Shelly. I was worried she was too outgoing, too extroverted for you. I thought you were an unlikely match, but I have to say, without knowing why there was a change, I noticed a change. And now with a little backstory? It's pretty clear you two started something special. Now you have to finish it."

"What is it that makes Claire so special?" Samantha pushed a little harder.

"I don't know. I feel like I can talk to her without any pretense. It feels so natural and so normal. And when the conversation gets serious or deep, instead of backpedaling or changing the topic, I find myself being really, really honest with her. It's like—"

"She's your person." Samantha nodded confidently.

"Yes, she's a person. Is that a new development?" Shelly was lost but Lucinda nodded as well. Obviously she was missing something here.

"No, she's *your person*. She gets you. You feel comfortable with her. Like you can share things and be yourself and be honest without fear of rejection or judgment. That's why you were drawn to her at the mixer, why you shared a moment over the fireworks at the office, why you physically connected after meeting her family, and why you sought her out for comfort when you felt the most insecure and overwhelmed about D'Andre. She's your person." Samantha shrugged as if it were as clear as day.

"This is a whole new thing for me—give me a second to process this." Shelly scratched her head and let that sink in. "I think I love her."

Samantha smiled. "Then tell her."

CHAPTER TWENTY

Claire stared up at the poster-covered ceiling of her childhood bedroom and wondered if she could just change her name and start a new life somewhere else. Somewhere remote. Maybe with a lot of snow. She'd always liked snow. It was quiet and peaceful. Maybe quiet wasn't what she needed, though—she was trying to run away from her endless thoughts, so maybe she needed something bustling and full of life. Like New York City or Chicago.

Jamie knocked at her door and opened it without waiting for her to reply. "Claire, you have to leave."

"I'm moving to Chicago." She looked back up at the ceiling and wondered what inspired her to put up so many pictures of colorful cartoon ponies.

"You're not moving to Chicago." Jamie pushed the door open and looked down at the floor. "This place is a mess. Let's go. This is an intervention."

Claire looked over at him. "What are we intervening about? I was thinking maybe it's time to take down the ponies."

Jamie looked up at the ceiling and nodded. "Yeah, the ponies have to go. As soon as you do. Let's go. Move it."

"Do you think the ponies will miss me when I move to Chicago? I suppose I could take them with me. A few of them. I could be a single girl with a collection of rainbow ponies in Chicago—that'd totally get me laid, right?"

Jamie leaned against the door frame and laughed. "If getting laid was your number one priority, you would have done that the night of the championship when barfly Nikki practically put her hands down your pants. Methinks that is not the reason you are contemplating the Windy City."

Claire looked over at her brother and sighed. She had been living here since that night. She'd gone back to her apartment a total of three times to collect some clothes and mail, but she had come back here every night since. The desire to be home and with her brothers was too great to ignore. She didn't want to be alone. She didn't want to think about her relationship with Shelly, and she definitely, absolutely, didn't want to face her.

"Claire-Bear. For reals. It's time." Jamie pointed to his watch and tapped it. "I love you and I love you being here, but you've overstayed your welcome and you have to leave now."

"Jamie, this is my house, too." Claire pouted and pulled the covers over her head.

She felt the edge of the bed sag under his weight. "I'm going to count to three, and then Jerry and I are going to throw you in the shower and pack up your things and you are going to go over to Shelly's to make up with her because you can't spend the rest of your life talking to cartoon horses in your childhood twin bed. It's pathetic and you are making us all look bad."

Claire pulled back the blanket and scoffed at him. "I'm allowed to mourn the death of my relationship in any way I please, Jamie. Begone. Leave me to my loyal subjects—we have much to discuss." She pointed to the pony pictures and pulled the covers back over her head.

"Jerry!" Jamie called and Claire heard pounding footsteps on the stairs. Before she knew it, she was wrapped up in the blanket and carried out of the room. She strained against the blanket burrito encasing her when she heard the bathtub water turn on.

"Let me out of here." She tried to kick free but one of the twins held her feet.

"It's for your own good, Claire-Bear," Jamie called over the sound of rushing water that was getting closer by the second.

"You can't do this." She tried to flail her arms to no avail. She was definitely going to drown in her *My Little Pony* blanket, there was no way around it. She wondered if that detail would make it into her obituary.

All of a sudden the sound of the water stopped and she was dropped, rather unceremoniously, to the floor in a heap. She clawed her way out of the blanket and found the twins looking down at her.

"What the fuck?" She brushed stray hairs out of her face and straightened out her shirt that had gotten twisted during the abduction.

Jerry spoke first. "You're lovesick and it's depressing."

"We miss Shelly." Jamie nodded and crossed his arms.

"I knew you liked her more than me." Claire sat up and leaned against the tub. She glanced over her shoulder and could see it partially filled with water. "You really were going to dunk me, weren't you?"

Jerry shrugged. "Desperate times, desperate measures."

"Baptism by pony blanket drowning." Jamie nodded solemnly.

"That is seriously fucked up." Claire tried not to laugh but couldn't hold it in. The laughter spilled out of her slowly at first, but quickly became uncontrollable sobbing. Jamie sank to the floor and took her hand.

"Finally." Jerry exhaled. "I'll order pizza."

"Extra cheese," Claire croaked out in between hiccups, "and mozzarella sticks."

"Consider it done." Jerry nodded and walked out, leaving Claire to her heartbreak and Jamie there to help her sort out the pieces.

"I love her." Claire cried and hung her head.

"I know." Jamie rubbed her shoulder.

"I hate her, too." Claire hiccupped and wiped her eyes.

Jamie sighed. "For the moment you do. But you'll get over it."

"Never. I will never get over it." Claire pulled her knees up to her chest.

"Just like you'd never get over your rainbow pony obsession?" Jamie poked her in the side and she swatted him away.

"That's different."

"It's not." Jamie leaned against the tub with her. "You were happy when you were together."

"Are we talking about ponies now or not?"

"Nope, we're talking about Shelly."

Claire frowned. "I miss her."

"Yeah." Jamie nodded. "But we were serious about you leaving. And bathing. We noticed you kinda stopped trying. Jerry's right, it's depressing."

Claire glared at him but he smiled in return.

"The water's warm. Take a hot bath and come down for dinner. We'll help you figure it out."

"Promise?"

"Promise." Jamie ruffled her hair and walked toward the door, pausing to add, "We love you, little nugget."

"I know. I love you, too." Claire sighed as Jamie closed the door and left her to her thoughts.

❖

Claire drove down the street slowly, trying to figure out what she was doing. After forever, she'd gotten out of the shower and sat down with the twins for dinner where they talked about what she should do and say when she was ready, if she was ever ready. But they hadn't pushed her—well, they sort of shamed her and mocked her a bit, but she had decided to do this on her own. Although now, she was seriously second-guessing that decision.

She pulled into the driveway and put the car in park, tapping her fingers on the steering wheel as she tried to build up the courage to walk up to the front door, but she couldn't quite do it. What if things didn't go as planned? What if too much time had passed? What if Shelly had gone on a date with that hot firefighter because Claire had pushed her away?

"You say the dumbest things." She let her head thump back against the headrest. Shelly had looked so devastated when she'd said that completely false and untrue thing the last time they saw each other. Shelly had told her that she was head over heels for her and her only reply was that she regretted not ending things with her that night at the racquetball gym.

The truth was, that weekend had entirely changed things for her. It wasn't a mistake like she let Shelly believe. It was one of the most genuine, emotionally connecting experiences of her entire life. And it had terrified her. She had been looking for any reason to run, and Shelly handed her one on a platter. Like a coward, she took it.

But she couldn't just move on like it had meant nothing to her all along. She thought of Shelly constantly. She reached for her phone to text her a hundred times a day. She watched the marketing video Boston Pro App filmed of the Expo nearly a dozen times just to catch the five-minute product explanation that Shelly gave—she had been brilliant. Focused and adorable, she slowed down her speech when one of the people that visited her booth looked lost; she made a joke about the space-time continuum and started over, referencing the *Star Trek* emblem on his shirt to help him connect to the type of technology she had invented. God, she had *invented* something, because she was so smart. And gorgeous. She couldn't even think about the fact that Shelly had used a video of Claire playing softball as the focal point for her demonstration. When she realized it was her swinging the bat and sliding around the bases, she had cried for nearly an hour. Her stomach lurched at the memory.

"Get it together." Claire squeezed her eyes shut and took a deep breath. "You can do this."

She unlocked the car and stepped out into the cool night air. She pulled her jacket closed to ward off the shiver that was threatening. She started walking toward the front door, her stride nowhere near determined, but still her feet carried her to their destination. She paced in front of the door, going over the speech in her head again and again.

"I can't do this." Claire felt like she might vomit. Or faint. The verdict was still out. A soft rustling noise on the other side of the door got her attention. She smiled. "Hedy."

A muffled meow replied and her heart melted. She sat on the top step, turning her body toward the door and spoke to her soft, gray friend. "Hedy. I really screwed this whole thing up. I'm a complete moron. Your mama probably hates me and she has every right to and I'm sorry."

Hedy's reply was louder this time. A little paw pushed open the mail slot in the door and she cried again.

"Hey there, cutie patootie." Claire slipped her finger through the mail slot and Hedy rubbed against her.

"Hedy LaMeow? What's with all the whining?" Shelly's voice carried through the opening in the door and Claire pulled her hand back, nearly falling off the step. The curtain next to the door pulled back and Shelly looked out onto the dimly lit step, making direct eye contact with—

"Claire?" Shelly opened the door and Hedy shot out.

Shelly called out after her cat as Claire lunged forward and grabbed Hedy, pulling her to her chest as she balanced precariously on the top step on her knees.

"Jesus Christ, Hedy, get in the house." Shelly threw the door open and ran her hand into her hair, her glasses askew in an adorable way. Claire tried not to stare as the brisk night air caused Shelly's nipples to press against her tight gray shirt. It was the softball shirt she had worn to Claire's game, the night they shared their first kiss.

Claire looked down at the purring furball in her arms to give her something else to focus on. "You're in big trouble, missy."

Hedy burrowed deeper into her elbow and purred louder, clearly unaffected by the goings-on.

"Claire, why are you kneeling on my doorstep?" Shelly adjusted her glasses and leaned against the door frame.

"I, uh, well, I guess I'm catching your cat." Claire could only imagine what this looked like to Shelly. She was kneeling on her front step, holding her purring cat, at ten o'clock at night on a Tuesday. Totally normal. Nothing to see here.

A corner of Shelly's lips curled up as she added, "Well, if you're done playing with my pussy, would you like to come in? The neighbors might get the wrong idea if you stay on your knees outside my house." Claire's jaw dropped. Did Shelly just make a sex joke? Two sex jokes? "Uh, yeah. That'd be great, thanks."

Shelly stepped back and Claire stood, walking past Shelly as she cradled Hedy. She scratched Hedy behind the ear and patted her on the butt once she lowered her to the floor after Shelly closed the door.

"So." Shelly locked the dead bolt and glanced through the curtain onto her front lawn. "How are you?"

Claire wasn't sure what to say. She had expected Shelly to do one of two things: slam the door in her face, or greet her with open arms. Well, that last part was more of a dream than an expectation. But this was neither of those options and she wasn't sure what to do. "I'm good."

"Good." Shelly was facing her now, and Hedy was weaving around her ankles and purring. Claire could hear her from where she was standing about ten feet away; it made her want to smile.

She swallowed and nodded. "I was hoping we could talk."

"Sure." Shelly started walking toward the kitchen. Claire followed her, watching as she sat at the kitchen island in front of a tablet. "Give me a second to close this program."

Shelly ran her fingers along the screen before placing it aside and picking up a glass of amber colored liquid. She swirled its contents and took a sip before holding it toward Claire. "Bourbon?"

Claire took the glass, letting her fingers caress Shelly's in the process. It was completely deliberate and she hoped Shelly knew. She sipped the contents and smiled. "I shouldn't be surprised at the sweetness, should I?"

"Honey bourbon on the rocks, with a touch of simple syrup on the rim. That's the secret ingredient. True connoisseurs would scoff, but I like it that way." Shelly shrugged and tapped her fingers along the top of the island.

Claire noticed a scrambled Rubik's Cube on the bar stool next to Shelly. She nodded toward it. "Any new records tonight?"

Shelly frowned and picked it up, spinning it in her hands in a seemingly random way before placing it back on the counter, completed, right before Claire's eyes. "No, I've been a little distracted lately."

"I just watched you do that and I can't believe it. Every time. It's amazing." Claire leaned against the counter and sipped Shelly's glass again. The liquid warmed her throat and belly. She hoped it gave her courage to engage in more than small talk.

Shelly gave her a weak smile. She looked a little tired. And sad. Claire felt terrible and wondered if it was because of her or something else. Part of her wanted Shelly to be sad about her, just so she could know Shelly felt the same way she did, not that she ever wanted to make Shelly sad, but—"I'm sorry."

Shelly blinked at her but said nothing.

"I'm sorry I pushed you away and that I accused you of being manipulative and that I said things to you that weren't true and I'm sorry." Claire had replayed that meeting in her office over and over again. She had been more than harsh, and she knew it.

She watched as Shelly looked down at the counter and worried her lip between her teeth. Claire was too anxious about what it meant to be turned on by it. All her nightmares became a reality when Shelly finally replied.

"I don't forgive you."

CHAPTER TWENTY-ONE

W hat?" Claire looked stunned. And a little pale. But Shelly meant what she said. She didn't forgive the things that Claire had said to her, mainly because they were true.

"I don't forgive you," Shelly repeated before adding, "I don't forgive you because what you said was probably true."

Claire's surprised expression shifted to one of confusion. "I have no idea what you're talking about."

"Yeah, right, sorry." Shelly shifted in her seat, her heart rate doubling. She took off her glasses and pointed toward the bourbon in Claire's hand. "Can I have a sip of that?"

Claire looked from her hand back to Shelly and stepped forward. "Sure."

Shelly took the glass and sighed. She noticed that Claire's fingers made no contact with hers this time. She assumed that was intentional. She took a hearty sip and placed the glass on the counter, pushing it toward Claire. Claire made no attempt to take it.

Shelly closed her eyes and focused on the lingering sweetness in her mouth. She let her brain perseverate on the sensations of the liquid sliding down her throat, coating her insides like warm honey. She took the moment to collect her thoughts, trying to slow her heart rate in the process. Finding Claire on her front step tonight had been a surprise, but not a bad one. She had been doing a lot of thinking since she had left Lucinda's studio a few hours before—she had decided she would reach out to Claire tomorrow once she'd formulated her thoughts. But Claire had beaten her to it, and here she was, standing in front of Shelly and apologizing when Shelly probably should be the one saying that. She opened her eyes and found Claire watching her, looking anxious. She wondered if her own face mirrored the same emotion.

"I started working with Samantha's agency a little over a year ago. I was hopelessly lost and was desperate to find someone who could help me not feel so incomplete. Samantha was like a breath of fresh air. She helped me sort out a lot of the parts of myself that weren't open to change. From head to foot, she helped me find my best me. And once that process was started, I realized I never wanted to go back to the old me. But after a few solid matches, I still hadn't found the right person—at least, I thought I hadn't, so I went back to Samantha and asked her to help me once more. So she threw one last mixer, a fundraiser this time, but she invited someone she thought might be just the person I had been looking for all along." Shelly thought back to that first time she had set eyes on Claire and smiled. "She introduced me to you."

Claire briefly matched her smile and she felt a little more confident, so she pressed on. "I found it so easy to talk to you and had every intention of asking you out that first night, but you said that thing about—"

"Matchmaking being for losers? Yeah, I suck." Claire frowned and her shoulders drooped.

"Well, yeah, it kind of threw a kink in my plan." Shelly reached for the Rubik's Cube because she was feeling a little restless. She twirled the rows, jumbling it as she spoke. "Anyway, in addition to giving me a new outlook on my dating life and my vision of self-worth, Samantha encouraged me to take some risks at work that I had been fearful of, and thus, the Expo products were born. A new venture to breathe life into a job I was feeling lost in. And to be honest, I was attracted to you that first night and I did call you to work with me because of that, but I really did research your work history and thought you were the right candidate and not just the hottest candidate. Although you were that, too, but not only that. Okay, I'm going to shut up now." She placed the Rubik's Cube on the table, all the colors matching once again.

Claire picked up the cube, twisting the rows and sides into disarray. She handed it back to Shelly and stepped closer. "Fix it again."

Shelly watched her carefully before taking it back. Claire's expression was softer now—she didn't look mad, but she wasn't smiling either. Shelly reached for the cube, pausing before she took it. "I never meant to hurt you." She took the cube and began lining up the rows and sides as she spoke. "I asked you to work with me because of something Samantha had mentioned to me once. She told me to look for the qualities in a person that made me feel like I could be myself around them. Even that first night, dancing at the fundraiser, I felt that way about you. And it only increased the more time I spent with you. She may have put us in the same room, but I fell for you over late nights at the office tasting coffee and watching fireworks. And I'm not sorry about that."

Shelly looked up from the completed cube in her hands and found Claire a few steps closer. "But I probably should have told you some of that, so I'm so—"

"You apologize too much." Claire took the cube from her hands and placed it on the island, stepping closer still, this time cupping Shelly's jaw with her hands and leaning in to kiss her.

Shelly exhaled as Claire's lips pressed against her own; they were warm and soft, inviting. Shelly hesitated, not pulling back, but not fully committing to the kiss. Claire's words swirled in her head. She didn't want this to be another regret. She pulled back from Claire's kiss and looked in the eyes. "Did you mean what you said to me at the meeting?"

"At the time? Yes." Shelly moved to step back, but Claire still held her face in her hands, her thumbs soothing along Shelly's cheeks. It was the most tender and heartbreaking sensation she had ever felt. Claire was holding her like she was as fragile as glass, while at the same time confirming that Shelly wasn't worth her time. "Wait. Don't go, wait."

Shelly closed her eyes and tried to slow her breaths. The warmth of Claire's hands felt like fire on her cheeks. She started to cry, because this felt like torture, to be held and broken up with, all over again. She couldn't find the words to express herself but she didn't dare open her eyes.

Claire spoke again before she had the chance.

"I was wrong though, when I said that. I did go to the gym that night to call things off with you, that was true. But I don't regret what happened that night, or the nights following. I don't regret the feeling of waking up with you or holding you. I only regret that I let you think you didn't matter to me, because that's not true. That was a lie. I shouldn't have said that." Claire's lips pressed against Shelly's cheek, the left, then the right. They pressed against her tears, her eyelids, her lips. Claire's hands never left her face, holding her gently as she spoke against Shelly's lips. "I shouldn't have made you think I didn't love you. Because I do. I love you and I'm sorry I hurt you."

Shelly sobbed, overwhelmed by Claire's words and her touch. Claire's hands left her face to pull her against her chest, her arms holding them together. She kissed Shelly's head and her cheek as she repeated, "I love you and that scared me, and I'm sorry."

An ocean of emotions crashed through her, making her feel like she was drowning, but Claire's arms never left her. She was steady and gentle—and she loved her. Shelly found solace in that revelation. She found peace there because she felt the same way.

"I love you, too." She spoke into the skin below Claire's jaw, her head still nestled against her neck. But when Claire looked down to catch her gaze, she said it again. "I love you and it scares me, too." Shelly was surprised to see a few tears on Claire's cheeks as well. She laughed and shook her head. "God, we're a mess."

Claire gave her that genuine, easy smile she loved and kissed her, pressing a lingering, smiling kiss to her lips. "Yep, but you love me, so it's okay to be a little messy."

"I really do." Shelly kissed Claire back, savoring the salty taste of tears mixing with the taste of Claire's mouth, a taste she missed, a taste that was complemented by the slight sweetness of the bourbon. "You taste great."

Claire pulled back and reached for the forgotten glass on the counter, bringing it to her lips before holding it to Shelly's to drink. "You know, I could get used to this. It's not too sweet, but at the same time just boozy enough to make me feel all warm and tingly inside."

Shelly took the glass from Claire and placed it back on the island, sliding closer and pressing Claire's hands to her ass. "So that warm and tingly feeling isn't from me, then? Just the bourbon?"

Claire squeezed her ass and pretended to contemplate the question. "Nope, I'm wrong again. It's definitely from you. Let's just double-check to see."

Shelly laughed as Claire kissed her again, deeper this time, her tongue slipping easily between Shelly's lips and drawing a moan from the back of her throat. She had missed this. She had missed Claire's touch; she'd ached for it. Claire turned them so Shelly was pressed against the countertop. Her hands slid up Shelly's back and into her hair as they kissed, scrambling Shelly's brain.

"Let me show you all the things I've been missing from you these past two weeks." Claire's lips at her ear made her weak in the knees.

"Wait." Shelly pulled back, sighing once before speaking. "I want to clear something up first."

Claire nodded and leaned back. "Sure, yes, what's up?"

"About that company in Scottsdale…"

"You don't have to—I shouldn't have, I'm sorry." Claire shook her head and bit her lip. "It's none of my business."

"I want to talk about it, okay?" Shelly ran her hand along Claire's face, brushing a hair behind her ear. This was something she had thought a lot about these past two weeks.

"Okay." Claire's eyes were so blue right now, patient and clear. Shelly decided she would stare into them as often as possible.

"I got wind that the company was going under and knew my mother's new husband worked there and I was worried that if he lost his job and things got too hard, she would just leave them like she'd left me. Another family left behind. Her sons were just kids at the time. I felt like they deserved to have their mother. I figured if I could help make that happen, then I should. I know it doesn't make much sense, and I realize it's probably a little creepy. But"—Shelly shrugged—"being left behind and cast aside is the worst feeling in the world. To be unwanted. No one should experience that."

Claire frowned and as her arms tightened around her, Shelly felt some of her sadness leave her.

"It wasn't entirely selfless. We use them to manufacture some of the products and packaging we use—they operate as a sort of third-party vendor without actually being a third party. I wasn't trying to be duplicitous about it, but I have a little shame associated with it and I don't want to be considered meddlesome. I don't have any involvement in the inner workings of the company, not really anyway. They operate on their own. We just provided financial backing and contractual support for a while." Shelly sighed. "I never told D'Andre about it, the truth behind my interest in the company. I didn't want to admit that a piece of me felt lost and incomplete. I honestly never thought it would come up, so I didn't mention it."

"You're kind of amazing, you know that?" Claire looked at her adoringly and Shelly felt herself blush.

"I'm not."

"You are." Claire kissed her again. "And I promise to remind you every day that you are very much wanted."

Shelly liked the sound of that. She leaned into Claire's kiss and let herself get lost in the feeling of being so completely loved by another person. A familiar squeak broke them apart.

"Hedy," Claire purred, "are you supposed to be on the counter?"

Hedy wiggle-walked along the island behind Shelly, head-butting her as she traipsed by.

"No, she's definitely not, but maybe let's leave her there while we slip upstairs so you can show me how much you've missed me.

You know, so we don't have any interruptions." Shelly sucked Claire's bottom lip between her own and nibbled once before nodding toward the kitchen doorway.

Claire moaned with a nod. "Absolutely. One second, though." She reached into her pocket and dug out her phone.

"You're placing a call right now?" Shelly teased, sliding her hand under Claire's shirt and caressing her stomach.

"Just making a note to send Samantha Monteiro all the flowers. I hear she's in the business of perfect matches, any thoughts on that?" Claire typed onto the phone screen before abandoning it on the island next to Hedy.

"I have a lot of thoughts about that. But none are safe for listening ears." Shelly glanced at Hedy as she pulled Claire's shirt off and over her head. "Let's double-check that compatibility in private."

"Science and data collection, I love it." Claire helped Shelly take off her bra as she was guided out of the room.

"And I love you." Shelly kissed her before waving good-bye to Hedy and heading upstairs to do a little research, grateful she'd taken a chance on Perfect Match, Inc. and Claire Moseley.

EPILOGUE

"Claire," Shelly called over her shoulder toward the bedroom, "have you seen my—never mind."

"It's on the hanger next to your jacket." Claire's voice was slightly muffled from the sound of the shower water.

Shelly laughed. There was a bright pink Post-it on her silk braces, a note in Claire's handwriting that read *Wear these, please*. A meow at her feet interrupted her swooning.

"Hedy, you know you're not supposed to be in here." Hedy blinked up at Shelly from the floor of the closet. "I saw what you did to my racquetball shoelaces. Naughty girl."

"Who's a naughty girl?" Claire stood in the doorway of the closet, wrapped in a robe, drying her hair with a towel.

Shelly smiled. She never got tired of seeing Claire in her bathrobe, in her shower, in her bed. She had been toying with the idea of asking her to move in with her. She didn't want to rush things, but Claire practically lived here anyway. Not long after they'd started dating, Claire gave up her old apartment and moved back into her brothers' house, but she spent just about every night with Shelly.

Hedy walked over to Claire and rubbed against the bare skin of her legs, purring and squeaking.

"I can think of a few girls who need to be disciplined." Shelly held up the Post-it for Claire to see.

Claire gave her a flirty grin. "I see you saw my subtle suggestion."

"I'll have you know I was already planning on wearing those to the wedding, without your neon sticker note, thank you very much." Shelly put the note back on the hanger to save for later. She kept most of the notes Claire left around her house—they made her smile.

"Please tell me you aren't planning on hoarding that Post-it like you do everything else I write for you." Claire put her hand on her hip and the robe opened slightly.

"She's got so much to say, doesn't she, Hedy?" Shelly ignored Claire's tease in favor of looking at her little fur princess, which then drew her attention to Claire's naked leg and the robe that was almost completely open now that Claire was bent over, drying her hair. "How much time do we have?"

Claire's face was hidden by the towel she was using to dry her hair, but her movements stopped at Shelly's words. She flipped her hair back and looked at her, shaking her head. "Oh no. We don't have time for that. No way. We're supposed to stop by your dad's before we head to the wedding."

Shelly licked her lips and looked at Claire's exposed chest. "I'll be quick."

"You won't." Claire pulled her robe shut and stepped back, putting space between them.

"I will. I bet you're still charged up from this morning." Claire had done some naughty things to wake Shelly up this morning, but had jumped into the shower before Shelly had the chance to reciprocate. She'd been thinking about it the whole time Claire was all sudsy and wet. She took a step toward her, silently rejoicing when Claire didn't move. She was totally winning.

Claire's eyes settled on Shelly's lips and she let out a quiet moan. "This morning was rather titillating."

"See? All the more reason to revisit the bed for a few minutes. Just a few. I promise." Shelly slid her glasses up into her hair and strode up to Claire, pushing the robe from her shoulders into a heap on the floor and tossing aside the wet towel. She kissed the skin under Claire's ear. "Just let me taste you."

Claire moaned again, this time louder, as her arms looped around Shelly's neck and pulled her mouth closer.

Shelly smiled and guided Claire back to the bed, easing her onto it and walking her up toward the headboard. She leaned in to kiss Claire, taking time to tease and caress with her mouth until Claire began to grind against her. This was still one of her favorite things—being above Claire, feeling Claire's hands pulling her closer.

She kissed away from Claire's lips, along her jaw, down her sternum, pausing at her navel to suck the skin into her mouth. She massaged and squeezed Claire's breast as she kissed along the crease of Claire's left hip, moving inward.

Claire squirmed and clutched the comforter beneath them. She wondered if anyone had spontaneously combusted from teasing. She thought about asking Shelly afterward—

"Claire?" Shelly's voice interrupted her thought process. The sound was muffled against the skin on the inside of her thigh, her breath stimulating Claire a little more.

"Yeah?" Claire couldn't fathom what Shelly could possibly need to be talking about right now. Shelly's free hand gripped Claire's hip as the one on her breast focused on Claire's nipple, making Claire see stars.

Shelly moved again, her mouth leaving Claire's thigh to trace her tongue along the lips of Claire's sex in an agonizingly slow taunt. Claire quivered and twitched—she could feel the wetness from their grinding when Shelly placed a soft kiss just above her slit. She thought she might die.

"Claire." She could barely process the sound of her name when Shelly's nose bumped her clit.

"Mm-hmm?" The feeling of something cool and hard in her fingers drew her attention to her hand. She must have reached out, because her fingers where woven into Shelly's mass of dark hair, her thumb brushing along the glasses still resting on Shelly's head.

"Can I taste you, Claire?" Shelly was teasing her. She was too out of breath to be mad about it, choosing instead to pull Shelly's head closer, forgoing niceties.

When Shelly paused just before connecting her lips to Claire, Claire looked down to find Shelly looking up at her, waiting. Shelly pinched Claire's nipple and looked down at the lips in front of her before looking back up at Claire, her eyebrow raised. Claire's head was swimming. Was she supposed to say something? She vaguely remembered Shelly asking her a question. "Yes, please. Now."

Shelly laughed and lowered her head, running the flat of her tongue along Claire's lips, pausing at her clit to suck and tease before moving lower and thrusting into Claire.

"Fuck." Claire felt like Shelly was everywhere. She could feel her hand on her chest, her fingers on her clit, her mouth on her sex, pushing and pulling, the suction and release occurring at a maddening pace. She sucked in a breath when Shelly thrust into her again and felt her inner walls squeeze around her.

Shelly hummed in response, the vibration stimulating Claire past the point of holding back, her body flexing forward as her orgasm snapped through her.

She dropped her head back onto the bed with a laugh and tried to steady her breathing as Shelly continued to kiss along her lips and thigh until she swatted her away, pulling her up to kiss her and taste herself on Shelly's tongue. "Mmm."

Shelly nuzzled her and lay flat on top of her, the comfortable weight enhancing the tremors that continued to roll through her. "This is my favorite part."

Claire combed her hands through Shelly's hair, breathing in her smell as her heart rate slowed. "The cuddling part?"

Shelly nodded, lifting her head to kiss Claire again. "I was referring to all the parts—the orgasm part, the soft naked you part, but yeah, the cuddling part, too."

Claire nodded in agreement. "Yeah. You're right."

Hedy squeaked next to them on the bed and Claire groaned.

Shelly looked down at her with a grimace and asked, "You think she saw any of that?"

Claire grabbed the pillow under her head and playfully hit Shelly with it. "Of course she did. Go shower, we're going to be late."

Shelly hopped out of bed and threw the pillow back at Claire, calling over her shoulder as she jogged into the bathroom, "You started it."

Claire shook her head and laughed. She sort of had.

❖

"Louis," Claire called out as they walked through Shelly's father's front door. The fresh coat of paint on the outside of the house looked great now that the gutter had been repaired and the windowpanes updated. The house didn't look nearly as haunted as it had the first night Claire had come here. That had been a rough night for her and Shelly. They had come a long way in the last three months.

"Hi, Claire." Louis met them at the opening to the kitchen with his cane in hand. He was clean shaven and his hair combed. His pressed dress shirt fit him nicely in the shoulders but was a little tight around the waist. He held his arms out to embrace her and she stepped into them willingly. "How are you?"

"Good. Running a little late, unfortunately." She gave Shelly a playful glare but Shelly merely stuck her tongue out in response.

"Is Greta here?" Shelly carried in the food bin from the front porch and started unloading it onto the kitchen counter. Long gone were the piles of papers and debris scattering the countertops. This place looked like a completely new home. It had been that way since Louis's fall—Greta had moved in to do some live-in housework and aide work for Louis. Shelly was convinced that she and her father were secretly in love but couldn't admit it. Claire jokingly made the suggestion that Shelly introduce them to Samantha to see if it could be a possibility, but had to stop Shelly when she actually reached for her phone. She could be so literal sometimes. It was adorable.

"She's out with her girlfriends. She'll be back later." Louis adjusted his glasses and looked over at Shelly. "Sheldyn, you look nice. I like your suspenders."

Shelly looked up at him like he had insulted her. "Braces, Dad. They're braces. Not suspenders."

"Braces were those horrible metal things you demanded I get you for that gap-toothed smile you had as a kid." He bristled and sat at the kitchen island, pointing to her outfit. "Those are suspenders."

"Stop fighting, you two. We have a wedding to get to." Claire stepped between them and kissed Shelly on the cheek, patting her on the butt as she walked by.

"You're lucky you found this one, Sheldyn. She's smart." Louis's resting pout face returned as he examined his cuticles. Claire never bored of their unique but loving exchanges. Louis had completely embraced Claire in Shelly's life, often making Shelly whine that he liked Claire more than he liked her. But she could see how much he adored Shelly. He just had a funny way of showing it.

Shelly finished unloading the bin. "Yes, Dad."

"This is Lucille's wedding to Shenandoah?" Claire nearly spit out the water she was drinking when Shelly whipped her head toward him.

"Lucinda and Samantha, Dad."

"That's what I said." Louis looked to Claire for support. She merely shrugged.

"Sounded like that to me." Claire sidestepped the rubber band ball that Shelly launched in her direction before scooping it up and tossing it back to her. "Ready?"

"All set. Okay, Dad, we'll be by tomorrow night for dinner with

Greta. You need anything?" Shelly grabbed her keys from the table and looked up at him.

"Nope. Greta's making pasta for dinner. Say hi to Lucille for me." Claire could see the mischievous smile he was trying to cover under his hand. She winked at him in encouragement.

"'Bye, Dad." Shelly was halfway around the corner, shaking her head.

❖

Shelly couldn't remember the last time she had been to the New England Aquarium. It had to be almost a decade ago. The inside was entirely different from what she remembered. A part of her had been thrilled to find out that Lucinda and Samantha were having their reception here—she loved the idea that she could sneak away from the party to hang with the sea creatures if she got overwhelmed by everyone coming up to her.

Since the tech expo and the restructuring of her company with D'Andre's exit, Shelly had been thrust into the public eye in multiple media formats. Her demonstration at the Expo had over twenty million views on YouTube as of last week, and tech companies from all over the world were calling Boston Pro App to try to schedule a meeting to discuss the hologram technology she'd developed. Everyone had an idea and a plan—she didn't have nearly enough time to field all the calls. She had been working with Clear View's PR department to help narrow a list of potential assistants in hopes of tackling some of her backlogged emails. Things got further complicated when a major national news magazine had a cover story about her and the company in which they called her app a "Billion Dollar Game Changer." She was grateful Lucinda had assembled a strong team to help manage the marketing and PR boom. Suddenly that small risk had turned into a giant reward, and Shelly was still trying to wrap her head around it.

"You're doing that eyebrow furrow thinking-too-hard thing." Claire handed her a glass of bourbon from the bar set up to their right.

"Sorry." Shelly took the glass and sipped it. "Ooh, this is good."

Claire laughed and ran her thumb under Shelly's bottom lip, catching a drop of liquor. She slipped her thumb into her own mouth and smiled. "That's because I paid him extra to put simple syrup in it."

"You're too good to me." Shelly leaned forward to kiss her.

"Cocktail shrimp?" Shelly turned toward the voice and blinked in surprise.

"Sasha?"

"Oh, hey, Shel." Sasha held up a tray of hors d'oeuvres and a handful of napkins. "Shrimp?"

"These are huge." Claire took one and reached out to squeeze Sasha's elbow. "How are you?"

"Good." Sasha kissed Claire on the cheek, careful not to drop her tray. They had had dinner a few times with Sasha over the past few months once things had settled down between them. Shelly was happy to have Sasha in her life as a friend, something she had never thought of as possible before Claire made her life feel so complete.

"What are you doing here?" Shelly declined Claire's offer of shellfish, choosing instead to sip her sugary treat.

Sasha shrugged. "Picking up a few catering shifts here and there for some extra money. I jumped at the chance to be a part of Samantha's big day. She's the best."

Claire nodded. "She is." Claire had sent Samantha half a dozen Edible Arrangements over the past few months. Shelly secretly loved it.

Sasha excused herself and slipped away as the lights flickered overhead and the emcee announced the brides' arrival. Everyone clapped and cheered as Samantha and Lucinda floated through the doors and seamlessly began their first dance. It was Claire's first time seeing Lucinda outside of her role as boss, and her jaw was slack in awe.

"Yeah, Lucinda is something else," Shelly supplied as she leaned against Claire, Claire's hands wrapping around her waist in that comfortable familiarity that being a couple can bring. Shelly relished it. "It's not just her, they're just…it's like they're the same person. Samantha's not a professional dancer, too?"

Claire's expression was priceless. Shelly took the opportunity to kiss her because she could.

"No, but if you hear Lucinda tell it, she's always said Samantha had a natural sway and grace to her. Like she could have been a professional dancer with the right training, because she's got an innate talent for it. They really are a perfect match."

As the song came to a close, Lucinda dipped Samantha, both women visibly moved by their first dance as a married couple. The wedding guests cheered and flooded the dance floor, embracing the brides as the music kicked off the start of the evening.

"God, they are perfect." Claire's voice was dreamy in Shelly's ear. She wrapped Shelly tighter in her arms. "Do you ever think of this? Getting married and having that first dance?"

Shelly turned in her arms, feeling a little bashful. "These days, I think about it all the time."

Claire gave her that easy smile that she loved and leaned forward, kissing her sweetly on the lips. "Best. Wedding. Date. Ever."

Shelly let herself get wrapped up in Claire's arms and lips, savoring the moment. She couldn't agree more.

About the Author

Fiona Riley was born and raised in New England, where she is a medical professional and part-time professor when she isn't bonding with her laptop over words. She went to college in Boston and never left, starting a small business that takes up all of her free time, much to the dismay of her ever-patient and lovely wife. When she pulls herself away from her work, she likes to catch up on the contents of her ever-growing DVR or spend time by the ocean with her favorite people.

Fiona's love for writing started at a young age and blossomed after she was published in a poetry competition at the ripe old age of twelve. She wrote lots of short stories and poetry for many years until it was time for college and a "real job." Fiona found herself with a bachelor's, a doctorate, and a day job but felt like she had stopped nurturing the one relationship that had always made her feel the most complete: artist, dreamer, writer.

A series of bizarre events afforded her with some unexpected extra time, and she found herself reaching for her favorite blue notebook to write, never looking back.

Contact Fiona and check for updates on all her new adventures at:

Twitter: @fionarileyfic
Facebook: Fiona Riley Fiction
Website: http://www.fionarileyfiction.com/
Email: fionarileyfiction@gmail.com

Books Available From Bold Strokes Books

Complications by MJ Williamz. Two women battle for the heart of one. (978-1-62639-769-9)

Crossing the Wide Forever by Missouri Vaun. As Cody Walsh and Lillie Ellis face the perils of the untamed West, they discover that love's uncharted frontier isn't for the weak in spirit or the faint of heart. (978-1-62639-851-1)

Fake It till You Make It by M. Ullrich. Lies will lead to trouble, but can they lead to love? (978-1-62639-923-5)

Girls Next Door, edited by Sandy Lowe and Stacia Seaman. Bestselling romance authors tell it from the heart—sexy, romantic stories of falling for the girls next door. (978-1-62639-916-7)

Pursuit by Jackie D. The pursuit of the most dangerous terrorist in America will crack the lines of friendship and love, and not everyone will make it out from under the weight of duty and service. (978-1-62639-903-7)

The Practitioner by Ronica Black. Sometimes love comes calling whether you're ready for it or not. (978-1-62639-948-8)

Unlikely Match by Fiona Riley. When an ambitious PR exec and her super-rich coding geek-girl client fall in love, they learn that giving something up may be the only way to have everything. (978-1-62639-891-7)

Where Love Leads by Erin McKenzie. A high school counselor and the mom of her new student bond in support of the troubled girl, never expecting deeper feelings to emerge, testing the boundaries of their relationship. (978-1-62639-991-4)

Forsaken Trust by Meredith Doench. When four women are murdered, Agent Luce Hansen must regain trust in her most valuable investigative tool—herself—to catch the killer. (978-1-62639-737-8)

Letter of the Law by Carsen Taite. Will federal prosecutor Bianca Cruz take a chance at love with horse breeder Jade Vargas, whose dark family ties threaten everything Bianca has worked to protect—including her child? (978-1-62639-750-7)

New Life by Jan Gayle. Trigena and Karrie are having a baby, but the stress of becoming a mother and the impact on their relationship might be too much for Trigena. (978-1-62639-878-8)

Royal Rebel by Jenny Frame. Charity director Lennox King sees through the party-girl image Princess Roza has cultivated, but will Lennox's past indiscretions and Roza's responsibilities make their love impossible? (978-1-62639-893-1)

Unbroken by Donna K. Ford. When Kayla and Jackie, two women with every reason to reject Happily Ever After, fall in love, will they have the courage to overcome their pasts and rewrite their stories? (978-1-62639-921-1)

Where the Light Glows by Dena Blake. Mel Thomas doesn't realize just how unhappy she is in her marriage until she meets Izzy Calabrese. Will she have the courage to overcome her insecurities and follow her heart? (978-1-62639-958-7)

Her Best Friend's Sister by Meghan O'Brien. For fifteen years, Claire Barker has nursed a massive crush on her best friend's older sister. What happens when all her wildest fantasies come true? (978-1-62639-861-0)

Escape in Time by Robyn Nyx. Working in the past is hell on your future. (978-1-62639-855-9)

Forget-Me-Not by Kris Bryant. Is love worth walking away from the only life you've ever dreamed of? (978-1-62639-865-8)

Highland Fling by Anna Larner. On vacation in the Scottish Highlands, Eve Eddison falls for the enigmatic forestry officer Moira Burns despite Eve's best friend's campaign to convince her that Moira will break her heart. (978-1-62639-853-5)

Phoenix Rising by Rebecca Harwell. As Storm's Quarry faces invasion from a powerful neighbor, a mysterious newcomer with powers equal to Nadya's challenges everything she believes about herself and her future. (978-1-62639-913-6)

Soul Survivor by I. Beacham. Sam and Joey have given up on hope, but when fate brings them together it gives them a chance to change each other's life and make dreams come true. (978-1-62639-882-5)

Strawberry Summer by Melissa Brayden. When Margaret Beringer's first love Courtney Carrington returns to their small town, she must grapple with their troubled past and fight the temptation for a very delicious future. (978-1-62639-867-2)

The Girl on the Edge of Summer by J.M. Redmann. Micky Knight accepts two cases, but neither is the easy investigation it appears. The past is never past—and young girls lead complicated, even dangerous lives. (978-1-62639-687-6)

Unknown Horizons by CJ Birch. The moment Lieutenant Alison Ash steps aboard the *Persephone*, she knows her life will never be the same. (978-1-62639-938-9)

The Sniper's Kiss by Justine Saracen. The power of a kiss: it can swell your heart with splendor, declare abject submission, and sometimes blow your brains out. (978-1-62639-839-9)

Divided Nation, United Hearts by Yolanda Wallace. In a nation torn in two by a most uncivil war, can love conquer the divide? (978-1-62639-847-4)

Fury's Bridge by Brey Willows. What if your life depended on someone who didn't believe in your existence? (978-1-62639-841-2)

Lightning Strikes by Cass Sellars. When Parker Duncan and Sydney Hyatt's one-night stand turns to more, both women must fight demons past and present to cling to the relationship neither of them thought she wanted. (978-1-62639-956-3)

Love in Disaster by Charlotte Greene. A professor and a celebrity chef are drawn together by chance, but can their attraction survive a natural disaster? (978-1-62639-885-6)

Secret Hearts by Radclyffe. Can two women from different worlds find common ground while fighting their secret desires? (978-1-62639-932-7)

Sins of Our Fathers by A. Rose Mathieu. Solving gruesome murder cases is only one of Elizabeth Campbell's challenges; another is her growing attraction to the female detective who is hell-bent on keeping her client in prison. (978-1-62639-873-3)

Troop 18 by Jessica L. Webb. Charged with uncovering the destructive secret that a troop of RCMP cadets has been hiding, Andy must put aside her worries about Kate and uncover the conspiracy before it's too late. (978-1-62639-934-1)

Worthy of Trust and Confidence by Kara A. McLeod. Special Agent Ryan O'Connor is about to discover the hard way that when you can only handle one type of answer to a question, it really is better not to ask. (978-1-62639-889-4)

Amounting to Nothing by Karis Walsh. When mounted police officer Billie Mitchell steps in to save beautiful murder witness Merissa Karr, worlds collide on the rough city streets of Tacoma, Washington. (978-1-62639-728-6)

Crescent City Confidential by Aurora Rey. When romance and danger are in the air, writer Sam Torres learns the Big Easy is anything but. (978-1-62639-764-4)

Becoming You by Michelle Grubb. Airlie Porter has a secret. A deep, dark, destructive secret that threatens to engulf her if she can't find the courage to face who she really is and who she really wants to be with. (978-1-62639-811-5)

Birthright by Missouri Vaun. When spies bring news that a swordswoman imprisoned in a neighboring kingdom bears the

Royal mark, Princess Kathryn sets out to rescue Aiden, true heir to the Belstaff throne. (978-1-62639-485-8)

Love Down Under by MJ Williamz. Wylie loves Amarina, but if Amarina isn't out, can their relationship last? (978-1-62639-726-2)

Privacy Glass by Missouri Vaun. Things heat up when Nash Wiley commandeers a limo and her best friend for a late drive out to the beach: Champagne on ice, seat belts optional, and privacy glass a must. (978-1-62639-705-7)

The Impasse by Franci McMahon. A horse-packing excursion into the Montana Wilderness becomes an adventure of terrifying proportions for Miles and ten women on an outfitter-led trip. (978-1-62639-781-1)

The Right Kind of Wrong by PJ Trebelhorn. Bartender Quinn Burke is happy with her life as a playgirl until she realizes she can't fight her feelings any longer for her best friend, bookstore owner Grace Everett. (978-1-62639-771-2)

Wishing on a Dream by Julie Cannon. Can two women change everything for the chance at love? (978-1-62639-762-0)

A Quiet Death by Cari Hunter. When the body of a young Pakistani girl is found out on the moors, the investigation leaves Detective Sanne Jensen facing an ordeal she may not survive. (978-1-62639-815-3)

Buried Heart by Laydin Michaels. When Drew Chambliss meets Cicely Jones, her buried past finds its way to the surface. Will they survive its discovery or will their chance at love turn to dust? (978-1-62639-801-6)